A FAERIE'S SECRET

Also by Rachel Morgan

A FAERIE'S SECRET

SECRET

CREEPY HOLLOW, BOOK FOUR

RACHEL MORGAN

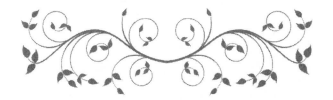

ISBN 978-0-9946679-5-3

RACHEL
MORGAN

PART I

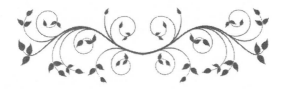

CHAPTER ONE

IT'S A PERFECT NIGHT FOR A PARTY. IF ONLY SOMEONE wasn't about to drown.

I rise to my feet, balancing carefully on the hood of the car, and pull my right arm back until my hand is in line with my ear. I grip the throwing star between my thumb and forefinger and point my left hand at my target: the kelpie gliding through the black water toward the four girls dangling their feet off the pier.

"Not yet," my friend Zed murmurs from somewhere behind me. "Not unless he attacks the girls. It's illegal for you to make a move against him otherwise."

I resist the urge to roll my eyes. "As if we haven't broken the law a hundred times already."

"Hey, the only time we're breaking the law is when we send

3

ourselves on pretend assignments like this one. I'm sure we haven't done a hundred of these yet."

"True," I say, closing one eye to better line up my hand with my target. "But you forgot about Mom's Law."

"Oh. Right. We've definitely broken your mother's law more than a hundred times."

My laugh is louder than I intended, but the sound is quickly lost amidst the shouting, chatting and giggling of the dozens of teens enjoying tonight's lakeside party.

"Concentrate, Calla," Zed says.

"Sorry." I ignore the firelight dancing at the edge of my vision and focus on the kelpie. He was in horse form earlier when we noticed him on the other side of the lake, but he's in human form now. Well, almost human. If I were closer, I'd be able to see the water reeds in his hair. He moves slowly, keeping close to the bank. Only his head and neck are visible above the water. As he nears the pier, he slides beneath the water and disappears. I watch the space beneath the girls' dangling legs, waiting for the moment the kelpie explodes from the water.

I wait.

And wait.

And wait some more.

The sound of boisterous laughter and breaking glass threatens to tear my attention away from the water, but I breathe slowly and keep my eyes trained on the girls' legs. And then, so slowly that at first I think I'm imagining it, the kelpie's head rises from the water beneath the girl closest to the bank. When his neck and shoulders are above the water's surface, she notices him. I expect her to jerk away in surprise or start screaming, but instead she leans toward him. Is he speaking to her? Casting a spell over her? Inviting her to join him in the water? The girl nods. The kelpie extends his hand toward her. She reaches down and takes it.

I should throw my weapon now. That's why I'm here. To stop this kelpie from dragging someone to a watery grave at the bottom of the lake. But what if that isn't his intention? What if he isn't tonight's 'bad guy' after all? His hands are around the girl's waist now as he helps her gently into the water. Her friends don't seem to have a problem with it. Maybe this has happened before. Maybe he and the girl are actually friends.

"Now, Calla," Zed says.

"But he hasn't done anything wrong yet," I say, my gaze still locked on the kelpie and the girl. He pulls her into an embrace, and she wraps her arms around him.

"He's made contact. He's revealed himself."

"But he hasn't hurt her or—"

"He could be seconds away from—"

"What if he loves her—"

Without warning, the kelpie plunges beneath the water, taking the girl with him. Flailing arms and kicking legs churn the water's surface. I can't tell human from kelpie, and the girls are screaming, and people are running onto the pier, and the kelpie is rising up—

"Now, Calla!"

This time I don't hesitate. I snap my arm forward and release the throwing star. It spins through the air and embeds itself in the kelpie's shoulder. He rears back, crying out in pain, and vanishes into the foaming water. The girl, now hysterical, swims with desperate, clumsy strokes toward the two boys waiting to pull her to safety. She scrambles onto the pier, and her friends crowd around her. The boys yell across the lake, challenging the prankster to show himself. But the ripples are already settling into an eery calm, and I'm sure the kelpie is far below the surface by now.

I do a front flip off the car's hood and bend my knees as I land. I straighten and turn back to Zed to find out how I did. Sitting on the roof of the car, he blinks at me in disbelief. "What if he *loves* her? Are you kidding me?"

I cross my arms. "It could have been possible."

"No." Zed jumps down. "I keep telling you, Cal. When you're on assignment, you have to assume the worst. You have to assume something is going to go wrong."

I look away. "Maybe it would be easier if the assignments were genuine. That way I'd know for sure something bad was going to happen."

"Maybe." Zed swings an arm around my shoulders and pulls me casually against his side. "But we don't exactly have access to genuine assignments."

"I know," I murmur, my mind focused more on his body pressed against mine than the words he's saying. My imagination skips ahead and fills in what I wish would happen next. A more intimate embrace, his hands caressing my face, my fingers sliding through his turquoise-streaked blond hair, his lips touching—

Stop. As always, my thoughts slam up against the imaginary wall encircling my mind. The solid, impenetrable mental barrier holding in every image my dangerous imagination conjures up. I used to have to make a conscious effort to hold the wall in place at all times, but now it's almost automatic.

"Come on," Zed says, his arm sliding away from my shoulders. "Let's get out of here." He heads between the cars, pulling a short stylus from his back pocket. Arriving at the nearest tree, he raises the stylus and writes a doorway spell onto the bark. As I reach his side, the bark ripples and melts away, revealing darkness beyond. He holds his hand out to me, and I smile as I take it. I find myself wondering, not for the first time, if he ever thinks of me the way I think of him.

I focus on my mental wall and nothing else as Zed leads us through the infinite blackness of the faerie paths. After several steps, a doorway materializes up ahead. We walk out to find early evening light bathing Woodsinger Grove in a lilac glow. I'm not sure what human time zone we were just in, but it was obviously several hours ahead of my home here in the fae realm. There, the stars were blinking in an ink blue sky beside a pale slice of the moon. Here, the clusters of pink butterfly blossoms are slowly closing their petals as the sun's light diminishes, and glow-bugs have only just begun to appear on the trees.

I reach down, pluck a blossom from the ground, and twirl it between my fingers. "So," I say as we walk between the trees toward the one that conceals my house, "since I've got all this vacation time now, could we start doing more assignments?"

"We could, if it wasn't so difficult to find them." Zed pushes his hands into his front pockets. "It's not as though we're linked to a Guild with Seers to inform us of anyone who needs rescuing. We're basically just visiting all the areas of the human realm where I know there's been fae activity and waiting for something bad to happen."

"I know. I just thought maybe ... don't you have any Seer friends who could slip you an assignment here and there?"

"No. You know I don't have any ties to the Guild anymore. And even if I did, there's always the risk of a genuine trainee showing up. We wouldn't want to get caught in the middle of that."

"I guess."

"There is another option, though." Zed glances at me with a playful smile curling his lips. "You could mention to your mom that you've done all this private training and would love to join a real Guild."

"Right. And you could mention to the Guild that you're still alive instead of letting them think you died in the Destruction."

He shakes his head, but the smile remains. "Private training it is, then."

"Exactly."

"Oh, I almost forgot." Zed stops a few paces away from my tree and removes something from his back pocket. "Your birthday present. It's a few weeks late, but at least I didn't completely forget like last year." He hands me a small box. "Happy seventeenth birthday."

I drop the butterfly blossom and smile as I take the box from him. "You didn't need to get me anything."

"Yeah, well, I'm making up for last year."

With nervous anticipation fluttering like sprites in my

stomach, I carefully lift the lid and push it back. Sitting on the cushioned interior, attached to a gold chain, is a delicate metal lily with a pearl at its center.

"It's a calla lily," Zed says. "Since, you know, that's where your name comes from. And I picked the gold one because it matches your look. The gold hair and eyes, you know."

"It's beautiful," I breathe.

"So you like it? I'm usually pretty terrible with girl gifts, but I had help with this one."

I beam at him. "I love it."

He grins back at me with a smile I know better than my own. A smile that has the power to turn my insides to liquid. His blue-green eyes move across my face, and I wonder, yet again, if he ever feels the way I feel. With his eyes staring into mine, I can almost imagine he does. And this gift is the most thoughtful gift he's ever given me. It must mean something.

I take a step closer to him as blood pumps faster through my veins. I've never been brave enough to do this before. I've always respected the distance our student-instructor relationship required. But I'm seventeen now. I'm basically an adult. What reason is there for me to hold back?

The nerves in my stomach give one final lurch as I rise onto my toes and press my lips against his. My eyelids slide closed. His hands grip my shoulders—

But instead of pulling me closer, he pushes me a step back. "Whoa, Calla, hang on." He shakes his head slowly, giving me a wary look.

Oh shoot. My eyes fall to the ground as embarrassment heats my face. "Um … I …"

"Look, it's not that you aren't … I mean, you're beautiful. You're an amazing girl. You're just … so much younger than I am."

I look up, managing to meet his gaze despite my humiliation. "There are only thirteen years between us."

"Exactly. That's a huge difference when—"

"My mother is thirty-eight years older than my father. It makes no difference to them or anyone else."

He hesitates, then says, "Faeries live for centuries. Decades mean nothing to us. We both know that. But when you're still growing up, thirteen years *is* a significant difference."

My gaze returns to the ground. "So you still see me as a child."

"Well … you *are* still a child."

I snap the small jewelry box shut and clench my hand around it. "I'm not a—"

"I have a girlfriend," he blurts out.

My breath catches. "What?" I whisper.

"She helped me choose your birthday present. She thought you'd really like—"

"Oh my goodness." I stride past him with my eyes still fixed on the ground. This is utterly mortifying. Of *course* Zed has a girlfriend. What on earth possessed me to think kissing him was a good idea? In what realm could that *possibly* have ended well?

"Calla, I'm really sorry," he calls after me. "I don't want to hurt you, I just—"

"Good night, Zed," I shout without looking back. I stop in front of my tree and bend to retrieve my stylus from my sock.

Before Zed can say anything else, I scribble a doorway onto the bark and hurry inside.

I run upstairs and fall onto my bed. Throwing stars attached to the inside of my jacket poke into my chest. I sit up, pull them all out, toss them into my bedside drawer, and flop back onto the bed.

I'll never be a real guardian.

I'll never have their sparkling magical weapons.

I'll never have their defining marks on my wrists.

And I'll never have Zed.

Despite the fact that he just rejected me, my stupid brain imagines Zed finding a way into my house, coming into my room, and confessing that he doesn't actually have a girlfriend. He loves me desperately, but there's some other reason he thinks we can't be together, so he made that story up.

My mental wall cracks, and, for a moment, I actually see him walking through the door into my bedroom.

"Ugh!" I squeeze my eyes shut and smack my fists against my forehead. I imagine the wall. I see the hole my crumbling emotional state has created. I push a brick into the hole. Another brick. And another. I fill up the tiny gaps with magical, imaginary cement.

When I open my eyes, Zed isn't there.

A noise downstairs signals my mother's return from work. Surprised, I adjust my position and pull my amber from my back pocket so I can check the time. The shiny, rectangular device is so thin I'm surprised I haven't snapped it in half by sitting on it. It's the latest of its kind; a birthday present from my parents. It's compatible with all the latest social spells, but that isn't why I wanted it. I wanted it for the art spell that allows me to draw and paint with my stylus or fingers and then transfer the image to canvas later on. It means I can create art whenever inspiration strikes, even if I don't have a sketchbook with me.

I touch my thumb to the amber's surface. Gold numbers swim into view. Just as I suspected, it's too early for Mom to be home. Tuesdays are 6 pm days, so technically she's still got twenty-three minutes of work left. And technicalities are something Mom pays great attention to.

I swing my legs over the side of the bed and stand. *Forget about Zed. Forget about secret training. Forget about how unfair it is that your brother gets to be a guardian and you don't.* I head out of my room toward the stairs, twisting a lock of golden hair around my finger. Whatever the reason for Mom's early return from work, I'm glad it happened after I got home. She would have freaked if—

I stop.

At the foot of the stairs is a man I don't recognize. A man in a dark, hooded coat that reaches his knees. A man with a long scar marring his left cheek. A man raising a knife.

And looking directly at me.

CHAPTER TWO

THE KNIFE FLIES STRAIGHT AT ME. I JERK TO THE SIDE instinctively, and it zings past my ear. The man raises an eyebrow. "Nice reflexes," he says. "But can you dodge this?" Red sparks sizzle through the air and strike my chest, throwing me back against the wall outside my bedroom. Momentarily stunned, I crumple onto the floor. Blinking, I look down at the singed hole in my T-shirt. If it weren't for the protective vest I wear beneath my clothes whenever I go out with Zed, my skin would be as burned as the T-shirt.

Footsteps sound on the stairs. My heart thunders in my chest. My lungs struggle to find breath. I close my eyes, playing dead while I gather power. "You know, it's a shame I have to get rid of you," the man calls as he climbs the staircase. "You are exceptionally pretty. Have you been told that before?"

His footsteps stop.

I crack my eyelids open and see him standing by my feet. I pull my leg back and kick his shin as hard as I can, grunting out, "Many times. Mostly by jerks like you." I spring to my feet, throw a conjured-up splatter of paint in his face, and dash down the stairs.

His cry of pain is short and followed by a string of curse words. I reach the living room and run to the other side, hoping to make it out before the man gets downstairs. But a loud thump makes me swing around before I can open a doorway. He must have jumped from the top to the bottom in a single leap, because there he stands, his hood fallen back to reveal his smirking face.

I can't get away, I realize suddenly. The thought is followed almost instantly by another: *Why do I* want *to get away?* I want to fight bad guys and now there's one standing in my living room. When am I going to get another opportunity like this?

"Remember when I said I have to get rid of you?" the man says. "Unfortunately, I meant that."

I don't think so. Magic glitters above my palms. The sparks transform into angry, winged insects, which zoom toward the man and swarm around his head while I gather more power in my hands. I've only stunned someone once before, and it's about time I tried again.

A strong gale sweeps the insects aside before I'm ready. They vanish as I duck behind a couch, a ball of magic swirling above my hands.

"You're not what I was expecting," the man says, sounding almost amused.

"Were you expecting to get your ass kicked?" I ask, hoping I sound more confident than I feel. "Because that's what's about to happen."

He laughs. "Definitely not what I was expecting."

I jump up and throw my hands out toward the man. But instead of stunning him, my magic hits the invisible shield I now realize is hanging in the air in front of him. Magic rebounds in all directions, sizzling one of my framed artworks, knocking an umbrella off the coat stand behind me, and smashing a glass lampshade. I drop down behind the couch again. "Shoot," I murmur. Mom is going to flip her lid.

Footsteps approach the couch. I clench my fists as I think of how useful guardian weapons would be right now. Even a simple throwing star would help. If only I hadn't removed every single one from my jacket less than five minutes ago. "Tired yet?" the man asks as he appears beside the couch.

I grab the fallen umbrella, hook it around his ankle, and yank. He goes down with a grunt. I jump up and bring the umbrella down fast toward his head. His hand snaps up, catches the umbrella before it strikes him, and twists it out of my grip. He throws it at me, but I duck down and it sails over my head. He rolls onto his side and pushes himself up, then kicks at me. I dodge backward and sweep my hand out toward the broken lampshade. Glass shards rise into the air and whizz toward the man. A flick of his hand turns the glass to dust. He pulls a piece of rope from the inside of his coat. Another flick, and the rope is a vine-like whip, curling toward me. I pull my arm out of the way just in time, feeling the sting of the whip's end as it snaps against my skin.

"Missed me," I say as I dance further out of reach.

The man lets out a breathless laugh. "Tamaria clearly didn't know what she was talking about when she said this would be easy." He snaps the whip once more, and flames blaze into existence along its length. "And *you* didn't know what you were talking about when you said you'd kick my ass, because I'm about to wipe the floor with yours."

Before the flames can reach me, I leap onto the back of the couch, jump into the air, somersault over the coffee table, and land on the other side. I spin around, drop down to use the coffee table as a shield—and see my mother standing in a doorway behind the man. Her features are frozen in a mask of shock.

Realizing there's someone behind him, the man swings around. He hesitates a moment, then runs at Mom.

"No!" I jump back over the table, onto the puffy couch cushions, and launch myself at the man. I land on his back, and the two of us fall to the ground while Mom shrieks unintelligible words. He tries to elbow me, but I catch his wrist and twist his arm backward. I lean all my weight on it. He cries out and attempts to roll over, but with one arm pinned behind his back, and my body weighing him down, he can't get enough leverage.

Still lying on top of him, I reach forward with my free hand and grasp his whip, which is an ordinary rope once again. I wrap the rope around his pinned-back arm, but when I try to get hold of his free arm, I find a knife glinting in his grip. I jerk back with a cry as he slashes blindly behind him.

"Calla!"

I look up at the sound of my father's voice.

Taking advantage of my distraction, the man throws me off his back. He leaps to his feet, dodges the sparks Dad throws at him, and dashes across the living room. In seconds, he's up the stairs. Dad shouts and follows after him. I jump up, all set to go after Dad, but Mom wraps her arms tightly around me and gasps, "You're okay. You're okay, you're okay." Her wispy blond hair tickles my cheek as I try to see over her shoulder and up the stairs.

"He's gone," Dad says, hurrying back down the staircase. "What happened? Are you okay?"

"Yes, I'm fine."

"Are you sure?" Mom asks, her shaking hands fluttering near my singed T-shirt before rising to touch my face. "He had a knife. Are you sure you're not … and how did you …" She frowns, her yellow eyes filling with confusion. "You were fighting him. The somersault. Leaping over the couch. Tackling him and pinning him down. How did you do that?"

I bite my lip and stare at the floor. *What do I say, what do I say?*

Dad places a hand on my shoulder. "Calla? What's going on?"

Realizing there's no way out of this other than the truth, I stand straighter, lift my eyes, and look first at Dad, then at Mom. "I want to be a guardian."

Mom lets out a half-sigh, half-wimper. "Calla, not this again—"

"It's what I want!"

"It's *too dangerous*," Mom wails. "We almost lost you once, and I won't go through that again."

"I already know how to fight, Mom. I've been training privately."

"You've been *what?*" Dad says.

"Training. Learning how to fight. To defend myself and protect others."

My parents stare at me, their mouths hanging open in shock. Dad recovers first. "How could you go behind our backs like this and—"

"Because you refused to let me join a Guild, so training behind your back was the only other option."

"And who exactly has been training you?" he demands.

I shake my head. There's no way I'm getting Zed into trouble after everything he's done for me. "It doesn't matter, Dad. What matters is that this is what I've always wanted to do. Not healer school, not chef school, not art school, nor any other profession you've tried to force me into. The Guild. *That* is where I want to be." I grab his hands and look at the pale markings on his wrists. I've always wanted markings like those. Not the deactivated version, of course, but the bold, black lines like those that swirl across my brother's wrists, or Zed's. I look up and meet Dad's eyes. "Please, Dad. You remember what it was like before Mom made you quit. You remember what it's like to save people, to make a difference. You remember how alive it makes you feel when you're—"

"Stop." Mom's commanding voice cuts me off. Most of the time, my mother comes across as annoyingly fragile. Her skinny frame, pale hair, and wide eyes make her appear weak. But beneath her usually gentle exterior is a fierce determination to keep her family safe. A fierce determination that has kept me far from the Guild all these years. "This isn't happening, Calla," she says firmly. "And it isn't just about the dangerous lifestyle of a guardian. It's about the Griffin List. You know that. We've managed to keep your ability a secret all this time, despite the … *incidents* that forced you to leave so many schools."

My jaw clenches. We do our best never to speak of those *incidents*, and Mom knows that. It isn't fair of her to bring them up.

"But if you're working right under the Council's nose," Mom continues, "they'll figure it out. You'll wind up on that list, tagged and tracked like a criminal for the rest of your life."

Ugh, that stupid Griffin List. It always comes back to that. With a frustrated sigh, I cross my arms. "That isn't going to happen, Mom. I can control it now. No one else ever has to find out."

"Find out what?" a male voice says behind me.

I spin around as my half brother steps out of a doorway on the wall. "Ryn!" I hurry across the room and fling my arms around him. I'm not sure why he's here, but I'm glad he arrived in the middle of our argument. He usually takes my side when Mom starts getting unreasonable.

"What happened?" he asks, hugging me tightly. "Are you okay? I came out of a meeting and found a panicked message your mother sent to both me and Dad."

"Seriously, Mom?" I turn back to glare at my mother. "I was handling it."

"You were not—"

"Did you know about the secret training your sister's been doing behind our backs?" Dad says to Ryn.

"What secret training?"

"You should have seen her," Mom chimes in. "Jumping on the furniture, somersaulting, twisting that man's arm around—"

"Hey!" I shout. "Can we please forget about my private training for a moment and focus on the fact that *there was an intruder in our house*?"

"What?" Ryn looks around at the mess, then back at me. "And you fought him?"

"Yes. He tried to kill me, but I—"

"Oh dear Seelie Queen," Mom gasps. "He was trying to *kill* you? And now you want me to let you out of my sight to go play around at the Guild? No. That's not happening. Clearly someone knows what you can do, just like before when you were little, and now they're hunting you down so they can—"

"Mom," I interrupt before she can work herself into a frantic state. "I don't think he was after me. He said he wasn't expecting me. He must have been here for something else, and apparently someone called Tamaria told him it would be easy."

"Tamaria?" My mother's pale face loses its remaining color.

"Yes. Do you know who that is?"

Mom looks at the floor as she slowly shakes her head. "No. I don't."

I glance at Ryn, but he's watching my mother carefully. "Dad?" I say. "Do you know that name?"

"No. Kara, are you okay?" He takes Mom's hand. Her wide eyes are still glued to the floor.

Mom nods, then looks up at Dad. "I was just thinking," she says quietly, "that maybe … maybe Calla would actually be safer at the Guild."

My jaw just about hits the floor. I lean forward. "Excuse me?"

Mom ignores me and continues speaking in low tones to Dad. I can hear every word, though. "If someone breaks in again, it would be better if Calla wasn't here. We could move—we *should* move—but that won't stop it from happening again. And maybe Calla *should* be learning to defend herself properly. Having such a unique Griffin Ability means there's always a risk someone will find out about it. She'll never be one hundred percent safe anywhere. At least at the Guild she'll be surrounded by people who can protect her while she learns the skills to protect herself."

I don't bother pointing out that the whole reason for being a guardian is to protect others, not myself. In fact, I'm so dumbfounded by Mom's sudden change of heart that I can't say anything at all.

Dad pulls Mom to the far corner of the room and lowers his voice so I can no longer hear what they're discussing. I'm not worried about him saying something to change her mind, though. Dad's never been opposed to me joining the Guild. In fact, if it weren't for Mom, he'd most likely still work there himself. He's probably just trying to figure out why she's suddenly changed her mind.

"Calla?" Ryn says. He turns away, motioning to the kitchen with his head. I follow him. He sits down on one side of the table, and I take a seat across from him. "Are you sure about this?" he asks.

"Sure? Of course I'm sure. This is what I've always wanted." I sit back, eyeing him carefully. "Wait, I thought you were on my side."

"I am on your side. If this is the life you want, I'm not going to stop you. I just want to make sure you know how dangerous it is."

"Of course I know how dangerous it is. I'm the one who was locked up in a cage by a psycho Unseelie prince, remember? I've never felt more scared and helpless than I did back then, and I don't ever want to feel like that again." I lean forward. "I don't want other people to feel like that either. I want to protect those who can't protect themselves. And I've been practicing. I saved someone from a kelpie earlier."

Ryn raises an eyebrow. "Your private training includes assignments?"

"Well, not Guild-approved assignments," I mumble, sitting back and scratching my fingernail over the table's surface.

"I see. Well, since I've been on one or two non-approved assignments myself, I don't think there's any reason to mention yours to the Guild."

My lips curl into a smile. "Just one or two, huh?"

"Like I said, we don't need to mention them."

I cross my arms and rest them on the table. "So can you get me into the Guild? Like, with my age group?"

Ryn laughs. "Calla, you can't just skip four years of training."

"But I haven't. I've done the training. I can fight."

"And what about the lessons and tests and exams and all the

other requirements? You have to spend a certain number of hours in the Fish Bowl, and pass a certain number of assignments each year—"

"I can do that now."

"Now?"

"Yes. All the trainees are on summer break for another two months, aren't they? Why can't I do all my Fish Bowl time and assignments while they're away? Then I'll be ready to join them when they return."

"Calla, that's crazy. That's a huge amount of work."

"But I can do it. I can manage."

"Calla?" Dad says, pushing the kitchen door open. He looks back at Mom, who nods to him before heading up the staircase. "We've decided: you can join the Guild."

CHAPTER THREE

I FINISH PACKING ANOTHER BOX OF PAINTING SUPPLIES JUST as the hand mirror on my desk begins playing music. It's a lively melody composed by one of my friends from Ellinhart Academy. At least, we were friends before she started listening to the rumors about why I left my last school. She became distant after that, and I haven't heard from her since summer break began.

I cross the room to my desk and see Zed's face swimming in the mirror's surface. Biting my lip, I consider ignoring the call. I sent him a message last night to say I no longer need his training services, but I didn't go into detail about why. He probably thinks it's because of the embarrassing half-kiss outside my house two days ago. The kiss that makes me want to shrivel up with mortification every time I think of it.

Ignoring his call would be immature, though, and I'm supposed to be showing Zed that I'm not the child he thinks I am. I pick up the mirror and touch one finger to its surface. "Hey," I say with a cheery smile on my face.

"Uh, hi." In the mirror's surface, I see him raise a hand and scratch his hair. "So, I just saw the message you sent last night."

"Yes, um, I have good news." I bounce onto my bed and tuck my hair behind my ear. "I'm finally joining the Guild."

"What?" Zed's eyebrows shoot up. "Are you serious?"

"Yes, it's definitely happening. Well, almost definitely. Ryn's still finding out what the exact process will be, but I'm pretty sure he can get me in. And I know how you feel about the Guild," I add quickly, "so you don't have to be happy for me. But I think it's—"

"Of course I'm happy for you." A relieved smile spreads across Zed's face. "I was thinking maybe you didn't want to train because of … you know, what happened the other evening when—"

"No, of course not." I wave a hand and roll my eyes to show him how silly that would be. "And I'm sorry for making you feel awkward, by the way. I don't know what came over me."

"So … you and I … we're okay?"

"Of course." I give him another bright smile he hopefully can't tell is fake. "I'm over that, don't worry." By 'that' I mean him, and by 'over it' I mean I'm not. But I will be soon. I've got way more important things to focus on now. Important things that include me getting my own guardian weapons, learning how to kick some evil ass, and uncovering dangerous Unseelie plots that threaten to destroy the fae realm. At least, that's what I imagine guardians do once they're fully trained.

I blink as an image of me brandishing a glittering sword while I stand victorious over a fallen foe threatens to sneak past my mental wall and broadcast itself across my bedroom. I push the thought aside as Zed says, "When will you begin?"

"I don't know. Ryn's still finding out details from the Council." And hopefully those details don't include 'Sorry, Miss Larkenwood, we don't accept trainees older than thirteen.' Anxiety tightens my insides. It would be just my luck to have the Guild refuse my application after I've finally got Mom to allow me to join. "Anyway, I need to carry on packing." I hold the mirror in one hand and use the other to wave a pile of sketchbooks into a new box. Pencils scattered across my desk fly back into a glass holder, which joins the sketchbooks in the box. "People will be here first thing tomorrow morning to do the moving spell."

"Moving? Why are you moving?" Zed's expression morphs into that infuriating one he wore when telling me I'm still a child. "Calla, you know you don't actually have to *live* near the Guild you're training at, right? You can use the faerie paths to get there every day."

I bite back the urge to tell him I'm not stupid and that of course I know that. "We're not moving because I'm attending a Guild. We're moving because of the intruder who got into our house the other day."

"Intruder? What happened? Are you okay?"

26

"I'm fine. I managed to fight him off and then he ran away when Dad got home. The point is, Mom freaked out and decided we have to leave. Dad promised to get the latest, most complex security spells, but it made no difference. An hour after it happened, Mom had found somewhere new for us to live."

Zed rubs a hand over his jaw. "That's extreme."

"Yeah, well, that's my mother."

"I don't know how your dad puts up with it."

"Probably something to do with the fact that he loves her," I snap. I'm usually fine with Zed making fun of Mom right along with me, but since he rejected me and probably went straight home to laugh about it with his *girlfriend*, he doesn't get to make snide comments about anyone I care about anymore.

"Uh, anyway," he says. "I just wanted to check that our agreement still holds. You know, now that I'm not training you anymore."

"The agreement where I don't tell the Guild you're still alive with active markings and access to your guardian weapons?"

"Yeah, that."

"Of course I won't tell them. I gave you my word, remember?"

He nods. "Thanks. I appreciate it."

"And I appreciate everything you've taught me. I've come a long way from that scared little girl you met in—" At the sound of a knock on my door, I look up. The door is closed, though, so hopefully the person on the other side didn't hear any of my conversation with Zed. "Gotta go," I say to him. I touch the mirror to end the call, then leave it on my bed while I open the door.

"Ready to join the Creepy Hollow Guild?" Ryn says the moment I swing the door open.

Excitement explodes inside me. "Really? Are you serious? They're letting me in?"

"Of course." He tilts his head forward, giving me that overconfident grin of his. "You didn't doubt I'd be able to make a plan, did you?"

I let out a wordless squeal and clasp my hands tightly together.

"I don't know what you're getting so excited about," Ryn says as he walks past me. He swings my desk chair around and sits. "Guardian training is seriously tough."

"I know." I pretend-swoon onto my bed. "It's going to be amazing."

He laughs. "You might want to look up the definition of 'tough' in the next few hours, or you could be in for a nasty surprise when your training begins."

"I don't care how tough it is. It will still be amazing." I grab the nearest cushion and hug it to my chest as I sit up. "So when do I start? Did you convince the Council to let me join the fifth-year trainees?"

"Hey, it was hard enough convincing them to let you join at all. They gave me their usual story about statistics showing that those who begin training at a younger age make better guardians than those who start later. So I reminded them that your father was an excellent guardian before he left the Guild, and that your half brother is possibly the best guardian the Guild has ever had—"

"You so did not say that to the Council."

"—which means you've clearly got stellar guardian blood running in your veins. Then I told them you've been training in private for the past four years, and they found that very interesting. I even included the story of how you heroically rescued your mother from a dangerous intruder who was bent on killing you both." Ryn pauses as a smile stretches across his face. "They liked that bit."

"So ..."

"So here's the bottom line: You'll be allowed to start with the fifth-year trainees if, by the time the new training year begins, you've managed to pass the final written exam for first, second, third, and fourth year. You'll also need to complete ten different landscapes in the Fish Bowl, ten assignments with a mentor assisting, and ten with a mentor observing."

I stare open mouthed at Ryn. I told him I could manage this, but now that he's saying it out loud, it sounds like an impossible amount of work. "And I need to complete all that in two months?"

"One month.

"*One?*"

"First years get two months over summer break. After that, everyone gets one. Unless you're a particularly enthusiastic trainee, in which case you continue with your own private training during vacations."

"One month," I murmur. "I can do that. I can make it happen."

"Are you sure?"

"Yes. I'll just spend every waking hour either studying or training. It's a lot, but I can do it. And hopefully Mom won't mind me coming home at odd hours after the assignments. I mean, she's cool with this whole guardian idea now, right?"

"Well, I actually spoke to your mother about that." Ryn tilts the chair onto two legs, then lets it drop back onto the floor. "If you're going to pull this off, you need to be completely focused on training and studying. No distractions. Not moving house, or painting, or drawing, or those arguments you and your mom like to engage in at least once a day." He gives me a knowing look.

"Those are called *discussions*," I tell him matter-of-factly.

"Those are called *loud*. I've heard far too many of them."

"So what's your solution?"

"You come and stay with me for the next month."

I pause, gripping the cushion tighter. "Seriously?"

"It makes sense, considering I'll be the one mentoring you until the new training year begins."

"*Seriously?*"

"Seriously."

"THAT IS SO COOL! Oh, wait." My shoulders sag as I realize there's one person, aside from Mom, who might not be wild about this plan. "How exactly does your wife feel about someone else living in the house with you guys?"

"His wife," says a voice from the doorway, "is thrilled to

have you staying with us for a while." Violet leans against the doorjamb and beams at me. "I might even assist with some of your training if I'm allowed to."

"Yes!" I fist-pump the air, then jump up and throw my arms around Vi. "Okay, let me try that reaction again. THAT IS SO COOL!" I shout. "Ryn, you're gonna be the best mentor ever. And I can't wait to come stay with you guys."

"Hey, keep it down." Vi steps into the room and shuts the door. "Don't let your mother hear how excited you are to leave her."

"And I am going to be the *strictest* mentor ever," Ryn adds. "I told everyone on the Council that you'd easily be ready in a month, and I had to convince them I wasn't just saying that because you're my little sister. So I'll be making sure you work your ass off to prove to them that I'm right."

"And to prove it to myself," I add as he stands, "because I *know* I can do this."

"Good. Anyway, I need to meet with my team now and explain that I'm taking on the temporary position of mentor for the next month. They'll have to get on with saving the world without me."

"Whatever." I grab my abandoned cushion from the bed and throw it at him. "You're not really in the middle of saving the world, are you?"

"Apparently he's always in the middle of saving the world," Vi says, rolling her eyes before removing her amber from her pocket to check a message.

"Since it's confidential," Ryn says with an annoying smirk, "you'll never know."

"Fine. One day I'll have top-secret assignments too, and you'll *wish* you knew all about them." I try to look as smug as he does, but the moment is ruined when I remember something important I wanted to ask him. "Oh, hang on." I lower my voice and lean forward. "Did you find any record of someone called Tamaria?"

"Tamaria?" Ryn asks without blinking.

"Oh come on, I'm not an idiot."

"Meaning …"

"Meaning I know there's something weird going on here. Mom was adamant that I'd never attend a Guild—right up until the moment I mentioned the name Tamaria. Then suddenly everything changed. She said she doesn't know anyone by that name, but obviously she's lying. And I *know* you can't stand unsolved mysterious, so I'm pretty sure you went straight back to the Guild and searched their records for someone named Tamaria."

Ryn watches me carefully, the hint of a smile on his lips. "I'm also not an idiot," he says eventually. He leans against my closed door beside Vi and folds his arms. "Who were you talking to when I knocked on your door just now?"

Shoot. How long was he listening outside my room before he knocked? I fold my arms over my chest to mimic his stance. "If you're not an idiot, then you already know."

He nods slowly. "I'm curious. Do I know this private trainer of yours?"

"No. He was never at your Guild."

"Ah, so he's a guardian. Interesting."

Vi elbows him as she writes a reply on her amber and

absently says, "Don't be nosy."

"Thank you," I say to her while mentally kicking myself for revealing that Zed is a guardian. "I'm not telling you anything more about him, Ryn. He's been helping me out all this time, and I don't want to get him into trouble."

"Okay," Ryn says with a shrug. "You know I'm going to find out eventually, though, right? Just like I'm going to find out more about this Tamaria person and who the intruder is."

"So you did look her up," I say with triumph.

"I did. I found three women by that name who've been mentioned in Guild records over the past few centuries, but none of them were involved in any criminal activity. Is there anything you can tell me about the intruder that might help?"

I picture the intruder in his hooded coat. "Well, I'm pretty sure he was a faerie, since he had two-toned hair. Black with dark red, maroon streaks. And his eyes matched the maroon, of course. What was weird, though, was the scar running down his left cheek. Because if he really was a faerie—"

"—then his skin shouldn't scar," Ryn finishes.

"Right. Unless, of course, he was exposed to that metal Prince Zell was so fond of."

Vi lifts her head as Ryn pulls up the sleeve of his right arm and looks at the pale scar that rings his wrist. A memento from an encounter with the Unseelie Court years ago. Vi has one just like it. "Interesting," he murmurs, then lowers his hand. "Thanks. That's helpful."

"So will you tell me if you find out anything?"

"Probably not."

"Ryn!"

"Hey, remember the part about you fitting four years of training assessment into the next four weeks?"

I bite my lip. "Uh huh."

"That starts tomorrow. No excuses and no distractions. So you'd better rest well tonight, because you're about to work harder than you've ever worked before."

CHAPTER FOUR

"I DON'T HAVE ANY SOCKS!" I YELL AS I RUN DOWN THE stairs. "How can I not have any socks, *today* of all days?" I barrel into the kitchen, startling Filigree. He shifts into eagle form and swoops past me, knocking a pile of reed paper off the kitchen table in the process.

"Just transform some of your other clothing," Ryn says as he hurries to pick up the scattered pages.

"What? I don't have time for clothes casting, Ryn. I need actual socks!"

"Take some of mine," Vi says, gathering up the breakfast dishes with a wave of her hand and sending them through the air to the sink.

"Thanks." I turn and dash back up the stairs, then stop halfway. "And have you seen that notebook I made all my summaries in?" I shout back to them.

"Bathing room," they both say at the same time.

"Right," I mutter, continuing up the stairs. I must have left it there when I was studying for my last exam while trying to relax myself in a pool of bubbles.

"Hurry up, Cal," Ryn calls after me. "We're going to be late."

"I KNOW!" I yell back. After my non-stop training and studying over the past month, I received the news that I'd passed everything, danced around Ryn's living room for at least five minutes, then collapsed in an exhausted heap and slept for seventeen hours straight. It was the best sleep of my life, but it meant I ran out of time to move my stuff back home before my first official day at the Guild. So Mom and Dad showed up this morning to wish me well for my first day. Dad went on and on about his first day as a trainee, and Mom spent the whole time looking close to tears. And I'm pretty sure they weren't proud-parents tears. No, they looked more like I'm-terrified-for-my-daughter's-life tears.

When Ryn pointed out that we needed to be at the Guild in forty minutes, they finally left. Things got a little crazy then as I searched my room for all the things I figured I'd need on my first day. When I couldn't locate a single sock, I panicked. How could I wear my new boots without socks? How did I run out of socks in the first place? What kind of guardian *runs out of socks*?

Now, I force myself to walk calmly into Ryn and Vi's bedroom and take a pair of socks from the chest of drawers. Back in my room, I pull them on before stepping into my new boots. They're similar to Vi's boots—the ones I've always looked at with longing—but the heels aren't quite as flat and the laces are blue instead of black. I run my hand through the air from my ankle to my knee and watch the laces do themselves up.

I retrieve my notebook from the bathing room and finish packing my bag. Lastly, I lift the trainee pendant from the bedside table and loop it over my neck. Councilor Merrydale presented it to me the first day I went into the Guild to begin my summer training with Ryn. It's flat and oval-shaped, made from silver, with a clear stone set in the middle. I turn it over and brush my thumb across the engraved name on the back: Calla Larkenwood. This pendant is my security pass into the Guild. It also carried the spell that first gave me access to my own cache of invisible guardian weapons. It has protective charms that make it harder for me to be influenced by dark magic and that aid in healing when I'm injured. When Councilor Merrydale gave it to me, he explained that one day, when I graduate, the pendant will be replaced by the markings on my wrists. The protective charms will be transferred to those markings.

"Cal, come on," Ryn shouts from downstairs.

"Coming!" I drop the pendant against my chest, then grab my bag off the bed. After slinging the strap over my shoulder, I hurry downstairs.

"Oh, wow," Vi says as she walks from the kitchen into the living room with her eyes glued to Ryn's amber. "Are these Calla's results from the fourth-year exam? They're a—"

"Aaand I'll take that," Ryn says, deftly swiping the amber

from her hands as he walks past her. "Confidential, remember?" He kisses her cheek before pushing the amber into his pocket, then grabs a mug from the coffee table and downs its contents.

"Why does everything interesting have to be confidential?" I demand, jumping down the last two steps.

"And since when do you follow the rules, Ryn?" Vi asks with a teasing smile.

Ryn sighs, looks at me, and asks, "Do you have everything?"

"I think so. Notebooks to write in, that textbook Vi said was really useful, clothes for training in, snacks for lunch time, that letter you gave me from the Chief Examiner, and my—"

"So, basically, you're completely overprepared."

"Ryn!"

"Ryn, that's not helpful," Vi says as she crosses the room to the hallway. "You know how nervous she is for her first day."

"Of course I know. I can feel it. She's being ridiculous, though, since she has nothing to be nervous about."

With a groan, I push past my insensitive brother and head for the hallway. "Are you coming with us, Vi?" *Please, please, please say yes.* I need someone who actually gets how important this day is to me.

"I'm sorry, I can't." Vi gives me an apologetic look as she removes a weapons belt from the hallway cupboard. "I need to be Underground in fifteen minutes to set up that workshop for new instructors. Besides, if you want to make a good first impression today, walking into the Guild with me at your side isn't going to help. You know how they feel about me."

"Don't be silly." Ryn strides past us and raises his stylus to the hallway wall. "They love you."

"Right." Vi secures the weapons belt around her waist with a loud click. "Do they use the words 'Guild traitor' for everyone they love?"

"Well, no, but you're married to the Council's newest and sexiest member, so they can't really hate you, can they?"

"Fantastic," I say, grabbing Ryn's arm and facing the doorway he just opened. "Now that I've had to listen to my brother call himself sexy, can we please go?"

"We can." He blows a kiss to Vi and says, "Have a good day, my sexy Guild traitor."

Shaking my head, I tug Ryn into the darkness of the faerie paths.

"So," he says, "calling you ridiculous didn't help your nerves?"

"No."

"I'm sorry. I was trying to make you see you've got nothing to be nervous about."

"Shh, I'm trying to focus." I picture the small entrance room next to the Creepy Hollow Guild's main foyer. We step out and find a guard standing there. He scans the markings on Ryn's wrists with his stylus, then does the same to my pendant when I hold it up. "Thank you," I say, giving him a wide smile. I still get excited every time I arrive here.

The guard steps aside and allows us to pass through the door and the curtain of invisible magic that exists there. It's meant to detect dangerous magic, strange enchantments, and other threats. In the main foyer, I look up and admire the swirling cloud of protective enchantments in the domed ceiling as Ryn leads the way across the marble floor. We reach the grand staircase. An emerald green carpet that never seems to get dirty covers the stairs. The wooden banisters are decorated with carvings of curling patterns. I run my fingers over the grooves as we climb.

"So we're meeting with Councilor Merrydale, right?" I ask.

"Actually, Head Councilor Bouchard is here. I got the message this morning."

"*Head* Councilor?" My anxiety kicks up a level. "Like, the bigwig in charge of *all* the Councilors?"

"That's the one. He's based at the French Guild, but he visits the other Guilds periodically to check on things. I guess it's our turn today."

I clench one fist and press it against my lips. Why, why, why did he pick today? I'm nervous enough as it is without having to meet some scary Head Councilor.

"Hey, it's fine. Don't panic." Ryn reaches for my free hand and squeezes it. "Trust me, there's nothing intimidating about this guy. He'll introduce you to your mentor and explain a few things. That's it."

I lower my fist to my side and release it, breathing out slowly. "Okay. You're right. I'm sure I have nothing to be nervous about."

"Of course I'm right," Ryn says, flashing me a grin.

We continue climbing the stairs until we reach the floor housing the Council members' offices. "Are you getting an office up here?" I ask.

Ryn shakes his head. "They offered me one, but I declined. Since I'm still leading a guardian team and don't have many

Council responsibilities yet, I'd rather continue working on the same level as my team members." He looks over his shoulder, then adds in a low voice, "It's far too boring up here."

If nerves weren't currently twisting my face into a pained expression, I'd probably smile at that. We stop beside Councilor Merrydale's office, and Ryn knocks while I take another slow breath that does absolutely nothing to calm the building anxiety in my stomach.

"Enter," calls a high-pitched voice that definitely does not belong to Councilor Merrydale.

"Leave your bag outside," Ryn says. I let the bag slip to the floor as he opens the door. He lets me walk in ahead of him. Behind the large desk I've become accustomed to seeing the cheerful Councilor Merrydale sitting at, I find a short man with slicked-back hair arguing with a woman I've seen several times near the training center. The man is one of those unfortunate male faeries whom nature decided to grace with a feminine color. Looking into his annoyed pink eyes, I'm reminded for a moment of a rat.

Focus, Calla!

Next thing I'll ruin everything by projecting an image of Councilor Bouchard scurrying around on the floor. Something tells me I wouldn't be able to explain that one away without landing myself on the Griffin List.

"So this one is the fake?" Councilor Bouchard asks the woman in accented English. He waves a bronze bangle decorated with clockwork parts and green gems in front of her face before smacking it down on the desk. "And you do not know how long the real one has been missing?"

"No," the woman says. "It's an exact replica. And the alarm was never—"

"And why was it here? Do you not know the procedure? Artifacts such as this must be sent to the vault at the Seelie Court."

"Harmless artifacts, yes. But as I've already explained to you—"

"No." Councilor Bouchard holds a hand up as if silencing a child. "No more explaining. I will be downstairs in ten minutes to address your entire department."

The woman snatches the bangle from the desk and strides past me, her lips pressed together in anger.

Councilor Bouchard crosses his arms and turns his pink gaze to me. His eyes widen briefly as he takes me in. It's a reaction I'm used to. Faeries come in all colors of the rainbow, but, as I've discovered after attending seven different schools, gold isn't a common one. In fact, I've never met anyone with hair and eyes the same color as mine. "And who are you?" he asks in a way that leaves me feeling like I'm wasting his time simply by standing here.

I try to answer, but my voice gets stuck somewhere at the back of my throat, and all I can think is that I'll never trust Ryn again when he tells me someone isn't intimidating.

"This is Calla Larkenwood, sir," Ryn says. "She's the new trainee starting with the fifth years this morning. We were supposed to meet with Councilor Merrydale, but I received a message saying I should bring her to you instead since you're here today."

"Oh, yes, yes. Miss Larkenwood." Councilor Bouchard sifts

through the papers on the desk before lifting one and frowning at it. "Private training. Passed all requirements as set forth by the Council. Excellent results for all written examinations. Some trouble with guardian weapons." He lowers the page and looks at me. "You know you cannot be a guardian if you cannot use the weapons."

I clasp my hands to stop my fingers from twisting together. I clear my throat to make sure my voice works this time. "Yes, sir, I know that. But I can use the weapons." Figuring out how to pull invisible weapons from the air was the hardest part of my training. In the beginning, I'd stop in the middle of fighting so I could fully focus on picturing and feeling for the required weapon until it materialized in my hand. By that time, of course, Ryn would be staring at me with a bored expression while saying something like, "I've killed you three times already." It took a lot of practice for me to get to the point where pulling weapons from the air felt more like instinct than effort. In fact, I'm still not entirely sure I'm there yet.

"You can use them?" Councilor Bouchard says. "Oh good. Please show me a sword."

"I—I must—You want to see a sword?"

"Yes. Hurry up, I haven't got all day."

My right hand twitches, but I can't seem to picture the sword. All I can see are those impatient little rat eyes, boring into me. Labeling me not good enough. A failure.

Come on, Calla. See the sword. Feel the sword. Make it—

Ryn tugs me against his chest, wraps an arm around me, and brings a knife to my neck. Jolted out of my frozen state, I reach forward and slash my hand through the air as if with a sword. Halfway through the motion—and to my great relief— a sword glittering like a thousand stars welded together appears in my hand. Ryn steps swiftly away from me, and I'm left with adrenaline coursing through my body and a glowing sword in my hand. It disappears when I release it, leaving a trace of sparkles in the air that vanish seconds later.

Councilor Rat-Man-Bouchard blinks, then says, "I suppose that is good enough." He turns back to the page in his hand. "Your mentor is Olive Stockland. I'm sure she can take things from here." He waves a dismissive hand at us before searching through more papers on the desk.

I turn and just about run for the door. Ryn follows close behind me and pulls the door shut. I pick up my bag, fix him with a glare, and whisper, "What happened to that guy *not* being intimidating?"

Ryn pulls me away from the office and down the corridor. "What happened to you being able to use the weapons?"

"I can use them. Sometimes I just need some ... en-couragement."

"Like a knife to your neck?"

My bag strap slips, and I pull it back onto my shoulder. "Yes," I say with a sigh. "I think I froze or something. He was staring at me with those weird little pink eyes, and I couldn't focus enough on the weapons. So thanks for kicking my brain into action."

"You're welcome." We head back down the stairs. "And I'm sorry about Councilor Bouchard," Ryn adds. "He's usually pretty tame, but something's obviously caused him to lose his temper today."

"Well, hopefully my new mentor has more patience than the Head Councilor."

"Hmm." Ryn directs me down the second floor corridor. "I'm not sure 'patient' is the word I'd use to describe Olive Stockland."

"Oh dear." This day just keeps getting better.

"Hey, stop stressing about everything. I'm sure the two of you will end up besties."

I punch Ryn's arm. "I'd like to remind you that I have no besties."

"So here's your chance to make one." Ryn stops and spreads one arm out toward the closed door in front of him. "All the best, baby sister. I'll see you later."

My stomach plummets. "You're leaving me?"

"I am." He gives me a brief hug. "Time for you to do this on your own."

CHAPTER FIVE

AFTER CLEARING MY THROAT AND PULLING MY SHOULDERS back, I knock on Olive Stockland's door. Ryn is right. He got me into the Guild, he spent all summer training me, he quizzed me before every exam, and he saved me from making an idiot of myself in front of the Head Councilor. So now it's time to step up and do the rest of this on my own. It's time to prove I have just as much right to be here as every faerie who's spent the past four years—

"Come in!"

Okay, time to focus.

I place my hand on the doorknob, then hesitate as it hits me: I'm about to meet my mentor. My *guardian mentor*. This is really happening! I twist the knob and push the door open.

Olive's office is a mess. The desk is invisible beneath piles of reed paper, several knives, some dirty mugs, and a broken crossbow. Her chair is piled with boxes, and the chair on my side of the desk has a plate of something that was probably breakfast sitting on it. On the right side of the room, a tall woman—Olive, presumably—is stacking books on the highest shelf of a cabinet that reaches the ceiling. She flicks her right hand in a repetitive motion, causing the books to fly one by one from her left hand onto the shelf.

When she's done, she steps back, pushes stray wisps of short hair away from her face, and looks at me. "Yes?"

My hand tightens around my bag strap. I clear my throat once more. "Hi. Good morning. I'm Calla." When she does nothing more than place her hands on her hips and blink at me, I add, "Calla Larkenwood. Um, I'm the new trainee starting with the fifth years. You're … my mentor?"

Olive lets out a puff of air and gives me a grim smile. "Wonderful. As if I don't have enough on my plate already, I now get to mentor yet another trainee. And, to make matters worse, it's a trainee who thinks she can skip four years of hard work and start at the end."

"I …" I pause with my mouth partially open, stunned by her immediate hostility.

"Well?" she says. "Do you have anything to say, or is that vacant expression something I should get used to?"

I snap my mouth shut and turn my gaze to the floor in humiliation. Why, why, *why* did the Council have to give me a mentor who doesn't think I should even be here? Or do all the mentors feel this way about the new trainee who 'thinks she can skip four years of hard work'? An ache behind my eyes warns me that tears are on the way. I blink several times until I'm certain the tears won't surface. I've had practice in this department. I've dealt with people like this before. And, while it isn't ideal to have a mentor who thinks I'm nothing but a waste of her time, I can make it work if I have to. It's what I've done at every other school.

I place my bag on the floor and cross the room. After removing the plate of congealed food and balancing it on top of a pile of reed paper, I sit on the chair. "It doesn't matter if you don't like me," I tell her. "I'm used to people not liking me, or avoiding me at all costs, or looking at me like I've got dangerous Unseelie blood running in my veins. It doesn't change the fact that I've already proved to the Council I belong here, and it doesn't change the fact that I *am* going to become a guardian."

She blinks again but recovers quickly. "Well, I don't know what you're sitting down for then. Your first lesson started two minutes ago."

"What?" I stand quickly, forgetting that I'm supposed to be portraying an air of composure.

"Oh, I'm sorry, are you too high and mighty to bother with reading your timetable?"

"I don't have a timetable. Aren't you supposed to give that to me?"

Her glare becomes frostier. "I have enough people telling me how to do my job without Miss High-and-Mighty adding her two cents to the mix." She yanks open a drawer on the other side of the desk, peers inside, and removes a scroll. "Here." She strides past me, pushing the scroll into my hands as she goes. "Timetable, locker instructions, code of conduct, rules, and other things I don't have time to explain. Follow me."

I spin around to find that she's already left the office. I grab my bag and hurry after her.

"The first part of fifth year consists of lessons, physical training and assignments," she continues as we head down the corridor at a brisk pace. "Some assignments are written, but most are out in the field. Initially I'll be observing some of those assignments, but you'll soon be doing solos. For both kinds, you'll report to me before and after. Any questions?"

"Uh—"

"Good," she says as we reach the stairs. "In a few months, lessons will end, and you'll spend all your time on physical training, solo assignments, and the occasional written assignment. Every kind of assignment earns you points. Points go toward your ranking. The rankings are displayed on a notice board in the training center, but all rankings will be removed several months before the end of the year as final rankings remain confidential until graduation."

"Do points carry over from previous—"

"That's the entrance you'll come through every day." She points across the foyer to the guarded entrance room as we reach the bottom of the stairs. "It's the only part of this Guild accessible from the faerie paths. Make sure you wear your trainee pendant every day. You won't be allowed in without it."

Several questions come to mind, but I'm almost certain Olive will ignore me if I attempt to ask them.

"The dining hall is down here," she says as we reach the other side of the foyer and enter a familiar corridor. "You're welcome to eat all your meals there, unless, of course, Guild food isn't good enough for you."

"It's—"

"Further down on the right is the training center, which I sincerely hope you're familiar with by now. At the end of the corridor are the trainee lockers, and here on the left—" she stops beside a door that stands ajar "—we have the lesson rooms."

Nervous adrenaline shoots through me as I hear voices on the other side of the door. Trainees are in there. My class. My fellow fifth years. People who've been friends for years. People who, just like Olive, might not want me here.

"Now." Olive folds her arms and looks down at me. "I know the only reason you're here is because your brother sweet-talked the Council into letting you do some kind of elaborate month-long audition. And I—"

"It wasn't an audition," I protest as indignation rises within me. "There were exams and assignments, and I passed every—"

"And I don't like people who think they're better than the rules we've all worked so hard to put in place," she continues.

"But I haven't broken any—"

"I also don't like to be interrupted."

I open my mouth to point out that she's doing just as much interrupting as I am, but I decide against it. I'd rather not make this conversation worse than it already is.

"But you're here now," she says, "and there isn't much I can do to change that. So I have only one more thing to say to you." She leans closer. "Don't embarrass me." After a threatening pause, she straightens and walks away.

I stare at the door in front of me, frustration giving way to fear. Questions assault my mind as I raise my hand to the door. Do the trainees inside this room know about me already? Not just that I'm joining them, but do they know who I am? Have they heard the stories? The rumors? Do they know about the *incidents*?

I tell myself it doesn't matter what these trainees have or haven't heard. I focus on my mental fortress, making sure every thought is locked firmly within its imaginary walls. Then I push the door open—and the eyes of about twenty trainees fall on me. I'm too nervous to look directly at any of them. All I'm aware of is the sea of colors—blue, purple, red, palest green, and a dozen others—and the sudden hush in the room.

"Ah, here she is," says the man standing at the front of the room. "This is Calla Larkenwood, everyone. Welcome, Calla." He gives me a smile that appears to be far more genuine than the one Olive gave me. "I'm Irwin, and these are the fifth-year trainees. I've already mentioned to them that you'll be joining us, and they're excited to include you in their group." He gives the class a pointed look, which clearly means that no one in this room is excited to include me in anything.

"Um, thanks," I mutter. I spot an empty desk and head straight for it, keeping my eyes down. I slip into the chair and let my hair fall forward over my shoulders, shielding my face from the stares I have no doubt are still pointed at me.

"Anyway, as I was saying before you came in, Calla," Irwin continues, "we're beginning the year by taking a more detailed look at Guild history directly after the fall of Lord Draven." I hear several groans from around the classroom. Irwin looks unimpressed. "Come now, people, this is your history. *Your* history." He points a finger at a girl in the front row. "And yours. And yours." More pointing. "You lived through it. Some of your parents helped shape it. And when you're working for the Guild one day, you'll need to understand exactly what went into restructuring our government and our laws, what measures were put in place to prevent another fall, what policies and regulations were changed, how the PCAIM Commission worked, why the Griffin List came into being after we discovered where all the Gifted got their abilities from, why the reptiscilla guardian petitions were unsuccessful—"

"Haven't we done all that already?" a guy in the second row asks, interrupting Irwin's long list. I can't help agreeing with him. I definitely remember a question in my exam last week about reptiscilla guardian petitions.

"Yes, it's all been mentioned before, but we're going into more detail on everything. So." He claps his hands together. "Please turn to page seventeen."

The sound of rustling pages fills the air. I glance around and realize for the first time that almost everyone else has a textbook in front of them. It's a textbook I decided not to bring with today because Ryn assured me no one ever starts lessons on the first day. I guess he was just as wrong about that as he was about Councilor Bouchard.

I'm about to swallow my embarrassment and raise my hand when a book plops onto the empty desk joined to mine and a girl slides into the chair. "I thought you might want to share," she says, pulling her chair in and smiling at me. Her red eyes are a little scary, but her smile is friendly enough.

Relief courses through me along with the realization that not everyone in this classroom feels the same way Olive does. "Thank you," I whisper as Irwin begins reading from the textbook.

"Sure. I'm Saskia, by the way."

She turns to the correct page, and I scan the heading. *Pardon for Those Who Committed Atrocities Under the Influence of the Mark.* I try to focus as Irwin drones on, but I keep getting the feeling that people are watching me. Including the person whose textbook I'm trying so hard to concentrate on. I lift my gaze. A smile flashes across Saskia's face before she returns her gaze quickly to the textbook. I look around and get the same reaction from several other trainees. Well, not the smile, but the hurried turning away of heads.

Focus, Calla. Read the text. Listen.

When Irwin reaches the end of the section, which was four very long pages, he gets a debate going back and forth across the classroom. There are strong opinions on both sides of the divide. Some agree that no one should have been held accountable for actions they had no control of during Lord Draven's reign, while others believe there should have been some form of punishment for everyone who carried out his orders, even though they were 'brainwashed' at the time. I listen carefully, keep my head down, and hope I don't get called upon to participate.

When the debate starts getting personal, with people shouting about the guilt and emotional turmoil their mother or brother or neighbor has to live with every day—"Surely that's punishment enough!" a guy from the front row yells—Irwin brings it to a close. We're told to report to the training center for the next three hours. After lunch we'll be back here for another lesson with a different mentor.

Chatter rises, along with the scraping of chair legs against the floor. Saskia's textbook slaps shut before scooting toward the edge of the desk and dropping neatly into her bag. I stand, feeling the stirring of nerves in my stomach again. Surviving a lesson was easy enough; now I have to survive three hours in the training center. Three hours that most likely involve one-on-one combat with someone from this room who wishes I wasn't here.

Well, I suppose it'll be like fighting a real opponent then.

Saskia stands and lifts her bag onto the desk. "You don't look the way I imagined," she says, tilting her head to the side and examining me.

"Oh."

"I've never met anyone with actual gold in their hair." She pulls her own hair over her shoulder and twists it around and around, the red and brown strands tangling together. "I suppose it's just another thing that makes you different."

Different. Yeah. Not something I want to be. "Um, thanks." Her probing gaze makes me uncomfortable, but that bright smile is back on her face, so I figure I should take the opportunity to try and make a friend. "And thanks for coming to my rescue with the textbook."

"Oh, sure, of course. Any excuse to sit next to you." She leans closer and lowers her voice. "I wanted to be the first to ask you about the boy and the bicycle."

"W-what?" A slow chill creeps up my spine. The boy and the bicycle. Incident Number Four.

"You know," she says. "That boy at the healer school who suddenly started riding his bicycle in frantic, weird patterns because he was convinced he was riding through a maze with some terrifying creature chasing after him."

I do know. I wish I didn't, but I do. "That's ... not really ..."

"My mom's a healer, you see, so she heard about it from her friend who teaches at the school you were expelled from. She said your mom's an Unseelie faerie who taught you dark magic so you could make that guy go crazy as punishment for teasing you. She said I have to stay away from you. I told her she was being ridiculous, of course, and that I'd find out the real story from you."

"I don't have Unseelie magic," I say automatically. "Neither does my mother."

"Oh, yeah, of course not. I mean, there's no way the Guild Council would let you in here if you did. But everyone knows weird stuff happens around you. So I just want to know how you do it."

I glance around. Irwin is gone, and only a few stragglers remain, quietly gathering their things. I resist the urge to hug my arms tightly around my middle. "I don't do anything," I say to Saskia.

"Come on, share your secret. Otherwise everyone's going to think you *do* know dark magic."

I step closer to her. "I don't have a secret," I say firmly, "and I don't know any dark magic."

She shrinks away from me as though in fear, but I can see a triumphant gleam in her crimson eyes, and I get the feeling this is the reaction she was aiming for all along. "So it's true then. You do know dark, Unseelie magic, and the only reason the Council let you in here is because your brother's now one of them so he can cover up your secrets." She steps backward and raises her voice to add, "I guess we'll have to stay away from you after all."

CHAPTER SIX

TEN MINUTES LATER, AFTER QUICKLY CHANGING INTO MY training gear and taking a few moments to push down the anger beginning to boil deep inside me, I join my classmates in the vast hall that serves as the training center. Most of them have already moved to various stations around the hall—running, balance practice, high bars, stick fighting—but a few are still standing in front of the notice board examining the schedule. I move closer so I can read the names on the list. Two girls step hurriedly away from me, whispering to one another. Rather than shouting out that I'm actually *not* contagious, I pretend I didn't notice.

I locate my name on the schedule and find my three hours of training divided into Climbing, Target Practice and Fish Bowl (Solo). My heart lifts at the sight of that small word in brackets. Thank goodness I don't have to fight any of my fellow trainees just yet.

"Can't I swap with someone?" Saskia's annoying voice carries over the general hum of activity around me. I glance to the side and see her speaking to a woman standing by the door. "I don't want to be next to her," Saskia whines. "Don't you know how dangerous she is?"

It doesn't take a great deal of intellect to figure out who Saskia is talking about. I clench my fists and head for the far side of the hall. The climbing area is made up of trees, ropes, a cargo net, and various types of walls. The cargo net is the most difficult. I had to race Ryn up and down almost every day during my summer training, and I never once managed to beat him.

I choose a spot on the wide mat in front of the rock wall, sit down, and reach for the bracelet on my arm. Attached to the chain is a hollow bead used for storing items that are shrink-safe. I remove the bead and hold it in my palm while saying the words to enlarge it. When it's reached its maximum size, I twist to open it. I take out my fingerless climbing gloves and pull them on before shrinking the giant bead and returning it to its place on my wrist. Then I spend a few minutes stretching. I'm about to jump up and start on the rock wall when a dark-haired girl sits down beside me.

"Hi," she says. "I'm Gemma."

I watch her warily. She seems friendly, but then, so did Saskia before she started accusing me of dark magic. "Look," I say with a sigh, "if you're here to ask about my Unseelie mother or if I can teach you how to make your ex-boyfriend go nuts, you're wasting your time."

Her eyes widen slightly. "Oh, you mean like Saskia?" She rolls her eyes. "Don't worry. I don't believe any of that. Saskia doesn't actually believe any of the nonsense she's spouting either. She's just ticked off that the Council let you join us. Her cousin wanted to join the Guild when he was fifteen, and they didn't let him. But that was because he didn't pass any of the entrance tests they gave him, so it makes complete sense. You obviously did, so that's why you're here." Gemma stretches her legs out in front of her and reaches forward to touch her toes.

Still uncertain of where I stand with this girl, I say, "And you don't think I should have started at the bottom? In first year?"

"Well, you've been trained privately, haven't you?" She straightens, then leans to one side and stretches the opposite arm over her head. "And you passed all the exams the Council gave you during summer break, right?"

I nod slowly as suspicion weaves its way through my mind.

"Yeah, so then you're hardly any different from the rest of us."

I cross my arms. "How do you know about the private training and exams?"

"Oh, my mom's in the admin department here." Gemma rolls her shoulders a few times. "Not the most exotic of jobs, but she knows more about what's going on than most of the—"

"Heeey, ladies." A tall guy skids across a shiny section of the wooden floor and drops onto the mat beside Gemma, almost knocking her over. "So," he says, beaming at me. "You're the new girl. The one who makes weird stuff happen to people. I was—Ow!" he exclaims as Gemma smacks him across the head. "What?"

"Don't be nasty."

"I was just joking. You know, lightening the mood."

Gemma shakes her head. "This green moron over here is Perry. And this blue—" she says as a shorter, stockier guy takes a seat on her other side "—is Ned." Ned gives me a shy smile, which I return hesitantly.

"Um, I thought it was rude to refer to people by their color," I say.

Gemma shrugs. "We're friends. We don't mind."

"So, Calla," Perry says. "Tell us about yourself." The three of them stare while I blink awkwardly at them.

"This is weird. I kinda feel like I'm in an interview."

"You are," Perry tells me. "We're interviewing you for the position of Friend."

"Friend? Really?" It's a nice thought, but after my experience with Saskia, I can't help wondering if Perry, Gemma and Ned have another agenda. "I thought we were supposed to be training now."

"Nah, don't worry about that." Perry leans back on his hands. "Nobody gets serious about anything until at least the second session. Well, except the overachievers."

"Plus the Head Councilor's visiting today," Gemma adds, "so no one's paying attention to us. They're all running around the rest of the Guild trying to keep up appearances—"

"A little difficult when a valuable item has just been stolen from the artifacts level, wouldn't you say?" Perry interrupts, his eyes widening and eyebrows climbing.

"Hey." Gemma nudges his arm. "You're not supposed to know about that."

"*You're* not supposed to know about that," Perry says, "but your mom tells you every—"

"Would you prefer me *not* to pass on all the interesting bits of information I—"

"Guys," Ned says.

"Right, sorry." Perry returns his gaze to me. "We tend to ramble at times."

"How about *all* the time," Ned mutters.

"You know what?" I say to them, pushing myself to my feet. "I probably don't fit into the overachiever category, but I do feel like I need to prove I belong here, so … I'm gonna get on with climbing this wall." I hurry away from them before they can say anything else. I know I'm being rude, but I can already predict how this will end. There are only two options. Either these people are being over-friendly because they want something, or they're being over-friendly because, well, they're genuinely friendly people. And if that's the case, it'll hurt a whole lot more when they decide I'm not worth hanging out with after all.

I stop at the foot of the rock wall. Painted along the bottom are ten small clock faces. No one else is climbing here, so I pick one in the middle. I touch the clock, the painted second hand begins moving, and I start climbing. I move as quickly as I can, reaching for handhold after handhold, never slowing for a break, never allowing my fingers to slip. I slap the ceiling with my hand, then begin the descent without a moment's pause. I feel the way with my toes. Down and down and down, until eventually I drop to the floor. I smack the clock face, then stand back as smoky black numbers float into the air.

Darn. Not my fastest time. I can certainly do better.

I glance briefly over my shoulder to see if Gemma, Perry and Ned are still sitting on the mat, but they're gone. It's a relief to know no one's watching me.

I climb the rock wall a few more times, then the tallest tree, and then give the cargo net a go. I navigate the squares of knotted rope as quickly as a I can, but the smoky black numbers that rise off the painted clock face when I'm done tell me I'm nowhere near Ryn's time.

For my second session target practice, I'm not alone. I've got Saskia on my left and a guy on my right. Saskia's throwing knives—and doing an excellent job of it—while the guy practices with a bow and arrow. They're both using their guardian weapons, which means I should probably do the same. I roll my shoulders, pretending to loosen up while focusing on the sparkling throwing star that's part of my invisible collection of weapons.

Come on. See it, feel it, pull it right out of the air.

Finally, after plenty of internal instruction, I grasp the air and find a throwing star between my thumb and forefinger. I pull my arm back, line up my elbow, then bring my hand down fast. The star hits the target almost exactly in the middle. I allow myself a quick smile. There's a reason I've practiced this particular weapon more than anything else: it's always been my favorite.

Once I get going, it's easy to keep pinching the air and finding a new throwing star in my grip. The target is enchanted so that seconds after a weapon strikes it, the weapon vanishes. It makes for an uninterrupted practice session.

When the hour is up, I head for the Fish Bowl feeling pleased with myself. Aside from the throwing stars, I practiced with several other knives from my guardian collection, and I did a pretty good job. Not as excellent as Saskia—I kept track of her performance from the corner of my eye—but good enough to show anyone who might be watching that I know what I'm doing. Hopefully any rumors that I don't belong here will soon die.

I hang around the edge of the giant white orb known as the Fish Bowl, waiting for the setting designer to tell me I can go in. She's standing on a platform above the orb with an amber tablet in one hand. She makes a few notes on the tablet with her stylus, then calls out, "Next trainee, you're up."

I step forward and push my way through the wispy white tendrils, wondering what I'll find inside the orb today. I've enjoyed most of my Fish Bowl experiences. Some were solo like this one, where I was required to fight against the environment inside the orb, while in others, I had to fight an opponent. I've been chased through a jungle by nameless creatures, I've fought Ryn on a ship in the middle of a stormy sea, I've outrun flowing lava from an erupting volcano, and I've swung through a forest of vines while fighting off a hippogriff attack. All without weapons or magic. That's the Fish Bowl rule.

The vapors around me disappear, and my ears are assaulted by the crashing of brick and concrete against tar and the rumbling of the earth as tremors race through it. The ground shudders, causing me to lose my balance. I grab onto a street light before I fall, my eyes darting around as I take in my surroundings. I'm on a city street surrounded by crumbling high-rise buildings. Crushed cars and giant pieces of rubble litter the road. I hear a scream. In the distance, a small girl stands in the middle of the road.

I have to get to her.

I push away from the street light and jump onto the nearest car. A shadow passes over me, and I hop onto another car as a broken piece of building crashes onto the spot I was just balancing on. I clamber over and around more rubble, dodging falling items and struggling to keep my balance as the ground shakes. The girl screams again, but we're separated by more cars and the shattered wreckage of a giant word that must have been attached to the side of a building not too long again.

Then I see my way to the girl. A concrete pipe. Cracked, but still intact. Looking through it, I see her on the other side. I run to it, telling myself how easy it will be to crawl through and get to her. I place my hands on either side of the opening and get ready to crouch down.

But I can't. I can't, I can't, I *can't*. Panic sets in as I imagine the concrete closing in on me, squeezing tighter and tighter, trapping me until there is no air, no light, no way out. My throat constricts. My breath shortens.

I back away, forcing myself to breathe deeply in and out. I'll navigate the deadly shards of broken building signage if I have to, but I won't crawl into that tunnel. I hurry away from it. The ground shudders once more. A jagged line races toward me, splitting the road in half. I jump out of its path and land against the side of a car. The concrete pipe rolls to one side, and the sign slides to the other. I see the girl clearly now, further ahead and on the other side of the chasm that divides the road. Behind her, a car goes up in flames. The shuddering ground keeps tilting, its gradient increasing, and the burning car and surrounding rubble begin rolling toward the girl.

I run at the chasm and leap with all my might. I need to knock the girl out the way. I need to reach the other side of the chasm. But it's wider than I thought, and instead of landing on the other side, I find myself falling, falling, falling. Arms flailing. Darkness growing.

And then it's all gone. I'm lying on my back blinking up at the white wisps of the Fish Bowl's surface, my body shaking and my breath coming in quick gasps. I sit up and look around the empty orb.

I've failed. Day one as a real trainee, with who knows how many of my classmates watching on, and I've failed.

Dammit.

I pound my fist against the floor before standing. That stupid concrete pipe. Why did that have to be the only way to the girl? Why did I have to *freeze* instead of calmly crawling through it? Surely I'm old enough now to move past this ridiculous fear.

Apparently not.

I stride toward the edge of the orb and push my way through the vaporous barrier. On the other side, I try not to meet anyone's gaze. Why are people standing around? Don't they have their own training to do?

"Do you want to go again?" someone calls to me. I look around and up and find the setting designer peering down at me with raised eyebrows. "You've still got plenty of time left in this session," she says.

"Uh, no." I back away. "I'm feeling a little lightheaded. I'm just going to ... sit down." I turn and almost walk into Saskia.

"Wow, that was impressive," she says as I jerk to a halt. "You lasted, what, a whole two minutes?"

"Stop being such a troll, Saskia," Gemma says, walking up to us with her arms folded over her chest.

"Hey, I'm just stating the facts. Miss Nepotism wants us to believe she's guardian material, but she can't even make it through a solo experience in the Fish Bowl."

"Miss Nepotism?" I demand. I'm frustrated enough as it is without this girl implying that the only reason I'm here is because my brother is on the Council.

"Yeah, you know, it means—"

"I know what it means," I snap. "And I'll have you know that the Council—*before* my brother was invited to be a member—laid out a long list of requirements for me, and I passed *every single one*. So I have just as much right to be here as you do."

"It's not the same," she says sulkily.

"Fine." I grit my teeth to keep my temper in along with the images of me knocking Saskia clear across the room. *Don't let anyone see that. Do NOT let anyone see that.* After making sure the disturbing images aren't about to be broadcast across the training center, I ask, "What exactly is it going to take to make you accept that I belong here?"

She purses her lips and taps her chin. "Well, there is the initiation the rest of us went through."

Gemma throws her hands up. "That's so stupid. She doesn't have to do that."

"Stay out of this, admin girl," Saskia says, sending a venomous glare Gemma's way.

Gemma turns to me, shaking her head slowly, probably trying to communicate that I don't have to do this. But if it's nothing more than a silly initiation for first years, then it can't be that difficult. And if everyone else did it, I want to do it too. I bite my lip, then say to Saskia, "Tell me more about this initiation."

Gemma groans and walks away as a slow smile creeps onto Saskia's lips. "Come to the old Guild ruins tomorrow night at nine." She leans closer. "If you think you can handle it."

CHAPTER SEVEN

IT'S SIXTEEN MINUTES TO NINE THE NEXT NIGHT WHEN Mom knocks on my bedroom door and asks if she can come in. A quick wave at my closet brings my robe sailing through the air. I pull the blue fabric swiftly over my clothes before opening the door. I give Mom a sleepy smile.

"All settled in?" she asks.

"Yes, I think so." I moved my things back home yesterday afternoon after Olive dismissed me with an annoyed "I thought I told you not to embarrass me. Get out of my sight now." I spent last night and this evening unpacking my belongings. This place doesn't feel like home, though. It's hotter and smaller and creakier than our place in Woodsinger Grove, which is the only home I've ever known. Thanks to Mom and her paranoia, we'll never live there again.

"Well, it's nice to have you back," Mom says with a smile. She wanders past me and brushes her hand over the pencils on my desk. "How were your first two days? You haven't said much so far."

"Oh, you know, I'm just tired from all the busyness." I pull back my bed covers and climb into bed. "But it's been good. Great to finally be there as a real trainee." I haven't told her about my disappointments: disinterested mentor, unfriendly classmates, and failed Fish Bowl experience.

"And … you feel safe there?"

"Of course. It's probably the safest place to be outside of the Seelie Court." After the Destruction and Lord Draven's reign, the new Guild Council made sure no one would ever break through the Guild's magical protection again.

"That's good," Mom says, leaning against my desk chair. "You might not be safe here at home, but at least most of your time will be spent at the Guild now."

I don't point out that a lot of my time will be spent *outside* of the Guild on assignments. Instead, I say, "We're fine here, Mom. After all the protective charms Dad got for this place, it's probably as secure as the Guild."

"Yes, well, let's hope so. He certainly paid a lot for some of those charms." The dazed look I've become familiar with over the years crosses Mom's face before she shakes her head and turns away. She turns in a full circle, then pulls the chair out and sits.

Sometimes I wonder if my mother is just a little bit crazy.

"I should probably get to sleep," I say, adding in a yawn for good measure. "I need to be up early. Looks like most trainees eat breakfast at the Guild, so I was planning to join them if … you don't mind?"

Mom nods as she stands. She tucks a wisp of pale yellow hair behind her ear. "That's fine." I can imagine what she's thinking. That I'll be safer eating breakfast at the Guild than eating breakfast at home, or something silly like that.

She kisses my forehead—which makes me feel far younger than I am—and leaves. The door creaks shut behind her. I rest my head on a pillow and listen to her footsteps as she descends the stairs. When I can no longer hear her, I sit up. The enchanted clock hanging above my desk tells me I've got nine minutes until I need to be at the old Guild ruins. I painted the clock myself while I was at Ellinhart Academy. It's an abstract mishmash of numbers, but I bought a charm that superimposes the time in shining gold digits over the painting.

I remove my robe to reveal long dark pants and a dark tank top. If this were an assignment, I'd cover up my pale arms, but it's too warm tonight to bother with that. I step into my boots, which lace themselves up as I grab my trainee pendant from beside my bed. The boots aren't helping with the heat, of course, but I don't feel guardian enough without them. I return the robe to the colorful section of my closet—a section I won't be using much anymore—and check that my door is properly closed. Then I open a doorway to the faerie paths on the wall beside it.

I picture the overgrown ruins of the old Creepy Hollow Guild. It existed for many centuries before Lord Draven destroyed it a decade ago. It was an enormous structure, concealed by exceptionally powerful glamour magic. Draven's magic turned out to be more powerful, though. When the Guild exploded forth from the single tree it was hidden within, it demolished a large part of the forest. I never saw it back then, but I trained in the area recently with Ryn, and Zed took me there a few times during our years of private training. The forest has regrown within and around the ruins, reclaiming the area as its own. Trees pushed their way through, moss gathered on the stones, and vines crawled over fallen pillars and splintered wood.

I walk out of the faerie paths and onto the ruins. The leafy treetops filter out most of the moon's light, but glow-bugs and sprites with tiny lanterns always hang around here, and one of the varieties of creeping plants glows at night, further lighting up the area. I climb over and between cracked and crumbling obstacles, looking out for Saskia. Part of me wonders if she's lured me here to meet some wild and dangerous creature instead of her, but then I hear her voice.

I look around and find her leaning against a fallen stone statue of a pegasus. The majestic creature has no head and only one wing and is riddled with cracks. Beside Saskia is a guy I recognize from our class. "There you are," Saskia calls to me. "I thought you might be too afraid to show up."

"Why did you think that?" I ask, heading toward the two of them. "It's not as though I'm late."

"Whatever." She folds her arms over her chest and stands up straighter. "This is Blaze. He's the one who came up with the initiation idea in our first year."

"Hey," Blaze says. "So I heard you're willing to do whatever it takes to prove you're one of us instead of some artsy freak."

I look at Saskia. Clearly she did some editing when reporting our conversation to Blaze. She raises an eyebrow, as if daring me to contradict her. I remind myself not to let this girl and her pettiness get to me before turning my gaze back to Blaze.

"Did everyone in your year do this initiation?"

"Yes. Even the skinny nerds. Initiation isn't allowed by the Guild, but this was all off the record, of course. We had our own ranking system too. We paired people up and made them race against each other to complete the task. It made our first few weeks as trainees a whole lot more fun than they would have been otherwise."

"It was rather thrilling," Saskia says, grinning at the memory.

"So what is this task?"

"You need to go Underground to Sivvyn Quarter, retrieve an item—anything. A book, jewelry, whatever—and bring it to us at one of the Underground clubs to prove that you did it."

I look from Blaze to Saskia, then back again. "That sounds like a stupid task."

The smirk on Blaze's face turns to a glare. "Sivvyn Quarter is a residential area. That's what makes it a challenge. You won't just find something lying around. You actually have to break in to someone's home and take something—without getting caught."

"So you want me to *steal* something? Doesn't that go against the very essence of who we are as guardians? We're supposed to do good, not bad."

Saskia lets out an exaggerated groan. "Jeez, Calla. Do you take everything in life so seriously? It's just a game. And you don't *keep* the item. You take it back."

"That's the second part of the challenge," Blaze says. "Returning the item without getting caught."

"And what's stopping me from simply going home, fetching a necklace from my own bedroom, and bringing it to you?"

Saskia holds up a narrow strip of leather. "Tracker band. Your mentor probably hasn't given you one yet, so you'll be using mine." She steps closer, wraps the band around my wrist, and clips it closed.

I touch the soft leather. "I assume you have access to one of those replay devices for tracker bands?"

"Obviously," Blaze says. "My mentor never locks his office."

"So, are you in or out?" Saskia asks. "And remember that 'out' means you're obviously not guardian material."

I watch two sprites flit hand in hand past us while considering this 'initiation' challenge. *Steal something from Underground.* The stealing part should be fairly easy, aside from the fact that I don't agree with it. It's the Underground part I'm worried about. I've never been down to the vast network of tunnels that run beneath Creepy Hollow, but I can imagine them. Narrow. Dark. Earth closing in around me. My chest constricts just thinking about them.

I push my panic down, telling myself the tunnels can't be that bad. 'Out' isn't an option if I'm hoping to be accepted by my classmates. And while I don't *need* acceptance, it'll make my time at the Guild far easier. A time that could very well last decades—centuries, even—since I plan to be a guardian for the rest of my life. Which means I need to get along with the people I'll be spending every day working beside.

"I'm in."

CHAPTER EIGHT

"GREAT." SASKIA GRABS MY ARM WHILE BLAZE OPENS A doorway to the faerie paths. Before I have a chance to say another word, I find myself stepping out of the darkness into a tunnel. Fortunately, it's a lot larger than the concrete pipe I faced earlier today. I expect to feel earth beneath my boots, but the ground is covered by large, flat stones, spaced closely together. Some glow yellow, bringing a warm light to the enclosed space.

"Sivvyn Quarter is that way," Saskia says, pointing over my shoulder. "We'll be down this side, at Club Deviant."

"Club Deviant?"

"Pretty easy to find. Just tell the faerie paths. They'll take you close enough."

"And … what kinda of fae am I likely to run into in Sivvyn Quarter?"

"All kinds," Blaze says as he drapes an arm casually around Saskia's shoulders. "That area doesn't belong to any particular group of fae."

"Oh, and just remember not to tell anyone you're with the Guild," Saskia adds. "You'll probably end up dead."

My eyes widen. "It's that bad?"

"Yeah, well, you know what happened after the reptiscilla petitions were denied."

I do. After the Council made it official that the Guild would never be open to anyone but faeries, there was a riot. Two guardians ended up dead, along with five reptiscillas. "I remember," I say with a nod.

"Then you know that reptiscillas hate guardians even more now than they did before the Destruction."

"Along with every other kind of fae," Blaze adds. "They think we tricked them. Used them to defeat Draven, then laughed in their faces when they wanted to join our Guilds and become guardians like us."

"Okay, I get it. They all hate guardians. I'll be careful." And if I'm somehow found out, I'll mention Vi's name. She and a handful of other guardians have been on the reptiscillas' side from the beginning, so hopefully they don't hate her—or anyone related to her.

"You might want to change your clothes then," Saskia says, her eyes brushing over my outfit. "Unless you want to be the only one wearing plain black in Club Deviant. No one would *ever* guess you're with the Guild then." With a self-satisfied smile and a haughty tilt of her chin, she grasps Blaze's hand and spins around. "Come on. Let's at least get some fun out of this evening."

Blaze pulls her against his side and presses a loud kiss to her cheek as they walk away. I head in the opposite direction, trying to ignore the echo of Saskia's giggles. The tunnel isn't straight, and every time it curves to the left or right, I wonder if I'll meet someone around the bend. I haven't gone far before I notice a distant sound. I can't make out what it is as first, but as the noise grows louder, I decide it must be the rattle of wheels over the stone-covered ground.

I'm proven correct as the tunnel curves and widens, and a wooden cart, its contents covered by a blanket, comes into view. It's pushed by a tall elf dressed in tight green pants and a green waistcoat. He slows when he sees me, but soon regains his speed. His eyes remain trained on me as we draw near to one another. His eyebrows—pierced with a row of silver rings—draw together.

As we pass each other, I point my eyes forward and tell myself not to run. That would look suspicious. I quicken my pace slightly, but keep it to a walking speed. *Don't panic. Don't run. Nothing is wrong.*

The rattling of the cart stops.

A shiver runs up my arms. Why has the elf stopped? Is he watching me? Is he coming after me? I long to look over my shoulder, but I don't want it to appear as though I have anything to be concerned about.

Keep walking. Keep walking, keep walking.

The cart rattle starts up again. I risk a glance over my

shoulder. The elf and his cart are moving in the opposite direction. A few moments later, they disappear around a curve in the tunnel.

I release my anxiety in a long, slow breath. Then I remove my stylus from my boot and prepare to alter my outfit. I'm certainly no clothes caster, but I know a few basic spells from an introductory course I took at Ellinhart. In my first year there, I tried out everything from painting, drawing and sculpting to fashion design, interior design and architecture. I almost failed the architecture section, but fashion design was fun.

I remove my boots, then run my stylus from the bottom of my pants all the way to the top of my thighs, watching the fabric disappear until I'm wearing shorts that are shorter than anything my mother would approve of. With another couple of spells written across my clothing, the shorts become bright blue and the tank top becomes the peachy pink of an early morning sky. I ruffle my hair up, pull my boots back on, and get moving down the tunnel. When I pass two reptiscillan girls, neither gives me more than a disinterested glance.

After another few minutes of walking, the tunnel widens before coming to an intricately carved stone archway. Curling letters painted onto the top of the stone structure spell the words *Sivvyn Quarter*. Beyond that, the tunnel forks into three separate lanes. With no indication of which one might be the best option, I choose the middle lane.

Glowing stone tiles continue to light the way as I walk. I pass a door on the left, and then another on the right. Presumably these doors lead into homes, but how am I supposed to break in? And what if I find someone on the other side? Am I supposed to grab something and run? I place my ear against the next door I come across and hear voices within. I move on. The next home I come to is silent, but I can't bring myself to attempt anything. Breaking in just *isn't right*. How can Saskia and Blaze expect me to do this? I continue along the tunnel, trying to figure out what to do.

And then I smell it. Sharp but familiar, it makes me feel instantly at home. It's the smell of the art studio back at Ellinhart where I spent many hours on my own, absorbed in my work. It's the smell of our living room every time I brought home a newly finished canvas.

Paint.

Different kinds, their scents mingling together in the air. I stop beside the only door in the vicinity and listen. No sound comes from within. Perhaps it wouldn't be so bad to just sneak in, grab a paintbrush, and leave. I carefully try the handle, but, as I expected, the door doesn't open. I try the simple spell for turning a lock, but nothing happens. Obviously an enchantment to prevent tampering. I place my hands on my hips and stare at the door as I consider what to try next. As far as I know, only glamoured faerie homes are protected against un-authorized entrance via the faerie paths. After all, only faeries can travel that way. Which means if I could just *see* what's on the other side of this door, I could get to it.

I crouch down and peer through the keyhole. In the dim light, I can make out the arm of a couch along with the blue and brown striped cushion leaning against it. I can't see much else, but that's all I need. I open a faerie paths doorway on the door itself and walk into the darkness. It closes up behind me while I imagine the room. I picture it *right here*, only feet away from me. I look down, imagine the striped cushion beneath me, and will the faerie paths to open. Light appears below my feet. I drop out of the darkness and bounce onto the couch.

Well, that was surprisingly easy.

I stand and look around the cosy living room. The source of the dim light is a tall lamp in the corner of the room, covered by an old-fashioned lampshade with tassels hanging from its scalloped edge. The furniture looks just as old, as does the rug on the floor. This is probably the home of some old lady. The artwork, however, seems out of place here. Canvases drenched in streaks of bright color fill the room. Some are hanging, while others lean against the walls. A blazing sunset; rainbow-tinted spray rising from a waterfall; a woman wandering across clouds of pink, orange and mauve; sprites dancing in the rain. I drink in their beauty, thinking I could stare at them forever. They're so much better than anything I've ever done. So much more *alive*.

Surprisingly, the paint smell is far less noticeable inside here. When I see the large nimph lily sitting on a low table in the corner, it makes sense. Nimph petals absorb odors in the surrounding air while giving off a fresh scent. They're collected by faeries in the exotic province of Driya and enchanted to remain alive. My second-year painting teacher had one in her office at Ellinhart.

Focus, Calla.

Right. I'm here to take something and leave. I blink and look around with renewed purpose. An old writing desk standing against one of the walls is covered in small items that should be easy to take. Jars of different colored pencils, reed paper scrolls, several books, a strange device that looks like a metal pen with coils, springs and screws attached to it, and a miniature ship sailing on an enchanted stormy sea inside a glass bottle. Small note-sized pages with quick pencil doodles litter the desk, and an unfinished charcoal drawing of a horse sits to one side.

Then my gaze alights on something I recognize: a bronze bangle covered in green gems and clockwork cogs and gears. A bronze bangle I saw in Councilor Merrydale's office just this morning. A fake, Councilor Bouchard had called it. An exact replica, the annoyed woman had told him. Which means that the bangle on the table in front of me, the bangle with stones that shimmer like hot coals in a green fire, is the real thing.

"No way," I murmur, my heart picking up speed as excitement races through me. Is it possible I can complete Saskia's silly initiation *and* retrieve an important artifact that was stolen from the Guild—all in one night?

I hear a click from the door behind me.

Shoot!

I grab the bangle and spin around as the door handle turns. I have to hide—or extinguish the light—or open a doorway back to the—

Too late. The door swings open, and instead of a reptiscilla or a dwarf or any of the strange halfling creatures I might have expected to find down here, in walks a faerie. A rather good-looking one at that. His eyes are pale but bright, and they land on me immediately. He frowns. His hand tenses on the jacket slung over his shoulder, and his gaze darts around the room before returning to me.

"Who are you?"

A valid question, and one I'm entirely unprepared to answer. The hand hiding behind my back clenches the bangle. I wonder how quickly I can get my stylus out of my boot and open a doorway. "I'm … an admirer of your art."

"I see." Slowly, and without removing his eyes from me, he closes the door behind him.

Damn, that's not good.

He takes two steps forward and drapes his jacket over the back of an armchair. As he crosses his arms, I notice the dark outline of a phoenix tattooed across his upper right arm. A twisting vine of thorns snakes down his left arm.

"Why do you look familiar?" he asks, snapping my attention away from his body art and back to the fact that I've just been caught breaking into his home.

"Familiar?" I laugh, attempting to make it sound carefree rather than panicked. "Have you met many gold faeries?"

"No," he says. "I haven't."

My hand twitches, preparing to dive for my stylus. Something tells me I won't be able to reach it before he reaches me, though. Which means I'll have to fight my way out of here. Or put up a shield strong enough to hold him back while I open a doorway. Or … the other option. My secret weapon.

"How did you get in here? The door has some powerful protection on it."

"I guess I'm just that good," I say as I begin drawing power from deep within me. The simplest way out of here is with a shield. I just need a few moments to gather a sufficient amount of power to make it a strong one.

The man looks amused. "Just that good, huh? I doubt it. You're a faerie, which means the most likely way you got in here is through the faerie paths. But this home has no name or number for you to whisper to the paths, and I've taken great care to make sure there are only two other people who know what the inside of it looks like. So how did you get in?"

If I wasn't in such a dangerous situation, I'd probably roll my eyes. This guy thinks he so clever, yet it took me less than a minute to get in here. "You might want to block your keyhole," I tell him.

"It is blocked. No magic can get through it."

"Well, I guess you forgot about light." And with that, I throw up my arm and raise a shield of invisible magic between us. Still gripping the bangle in one hand, I drop down, retrieve my stylus, and—

A wave of power knocks me backward. I crash into the desk chair before landing on the floor. My shield is gone, the man is striding past the couch toward me, and I'm blinking in confusion. How the freak did he call upon so much power so quickly?

He's only feet away from me when my recent training kicks in. I grab a throwing star from the air—which, miraculously, is there the second I need it—and throw it at him. It nicks his arm as he dodges to the side. I scramble to my feet and launch myself over the couch. I run for the door, but nothing happens when I twist the handle.

"Not only an *art admirer*, but a guardian and a thief as

well," the man says.

Knowing now that there's only one way out of this, I spin around—and let go of my mental wall.

It crumbles into imaginary dust as I focus hard on showing this guy exactly what I want him to see. I picture a dragon breaking through the door behind me. In my mind's eye, I see the dragon's powerful talons rip the door apart and fling it to the side, knocking me out of the way in the process. The dragon lumbers into the room, letting loose scorching flames. It grows larger and larger until its head brushes the ceiling and all the furniture in the room is not only burning, but crushed against the walls. The man jumps out of the way and flattens his body against the wall. He holds his hand up, probably to do some kind of magic that will have no effect whatsoever on the imaginary dragon, while edging toward the splintered, burning remains of the door.

With his attention no longer focused on me—at least, not the real me—I can safely get out of here. I turn and hold my stylus up to the door. Gritting my teeth and breathing hard against the effort of holding together such a detailed scene in my mind, I quickly write the words to open a doorway. I step into it and wait for the darkness to close up behind me before finally releasing the image of the dragon and the destroyed living room. Weariness tugs at the edges of my mind, but I can't give in to it just yet.

I push the bangle onto my left arm and think of Club Deviant. Since I have no image to hold onto, I repeat the words in my mind until the darkness ahead of me lifts and the silence pressing against my ears gives way suddenly to a hammering beat and a magically enhanced repeating melody. Just outside the faerie paths, fae of all kinds dance and sway beneath a lingering haze of sweet smoke.

Don't hesitate. Be confident. Pretend you belong here.

I push the bangle further up my arm and walk into the club. It isn't as packed as the few clubs I visited back at the beginning of my Ellinhart schooling when I still had some friends. I don't even have to push past anyone to get to the bar area. I perch on a stool and look around for Saskia and Blaze. They're not at the bar, and I don't see them on the dance floor. Darkened booths line one side of the club, but something tells me I probably don't want to take a closer look into any of them.

A reptiscillan man leaning against the other end of the bar seems to be watching me. Or is it someone behind me? Not wanting to encourage him, I avert my eyes and angle my body away from him. I eye the bottles of varying shapes, sizes and colors behind the bar. Should I order a drink? How long do I need to wait for Saskia before I can call an end to this initiation thing? Surely I've proved myself by now. She'll be able to see from the tracker band that I broke into someone's home, took an item, and—

Oh, shoot.

I projected while wearing a tracker band.

No! How could I be so stupid? I stuff my hands beneath the bar's counter, as if that might hide the evidence that's wrapped around my wrist. Then I pause in my panic. Exactly what information will show up on the tracker band? When Saskia and Blaze hold it under a replay device, they shouldn't be able to see the dragon. After all, the dragon was never there. So instead they'll see a guy who suddenly began fighting off nothing, and that'll only serve to fuel the rumors that I can somehow make people crazy.

Fantastic. So I'll still be an outcast, but at least I won't be on the Griffin List. Unless … what if a mentor sees what's on the tracker band? What if a Councilor sees it? What if everyone at the Guild starts to think I have a special ability to make people go insane, and I wind up on the Griffin List anyway?

Stop panicking!

The solution is simple. Take the tracker band off and destroy it. That way no one will ever—

"Do you have a death wish?" The owner of the intrusive voice slides onto the stool beside mine and into my personal space. "What are you doing in a club owned by the number one guardian hater in Creepy Hollow?" he demands.

I lean away from him, my eyes traveling up tattooed arms to the same face and eyes I was admiring not ten minutes ago. Eyes that are now narrowed in anger. I shrink further away from him, my right hand gripping the bangle on my left arm. "What do you—Wait, how did you find me?"

"Word travels quickly when silly young guardians decide to risk their lives Underground."

"I'm not a silly—"

"No, you're a thief."

"*I'm* a thief? You're the one who stole the bangle in the first place." I raise my bejeweled arm and wave it at him. "I'll be returning this to the Guild, and there's nothing you can do to—

"You *put it on?*" He slips off the stool and takes a step back. "What the hell is wrong with you?"

I look from him to the bangle and back again, wondering if I should be alarmed. I haven't felt any different since I pushed the bangle onto my arm, though. Perhaps this is a trick to get me to take it off. "There's nothing wrong with me," I tell him as I stand. "And since this club is apparently owned by someone with an intense hatred for guardians, I think I should go."

"Wait." He steps closer, and I bring my hand up fast, sending sparks dancing through the air toward him. He ducks out of the way, then raises his hands, gesturing surrender. "Just give me the bangle," he says, "and I'll let you go."

"*You'll* let *me* go?" I say with a confidence I don't feel. "Have you forgotten the dragon already?"

"Have you forgotten the power that knocked out your shield in an instant and swept you to the ground?"

I haven't. That's the problem. *Don't show fear, don't show fear.* I just need to keep talking long enough to come up with a projection that can get me out of here. "That was hardly power," I say casually. "Why don't we have a second go, and you can show me if you've got any power left after—"

"This isn't a game, little guardian." He closes the distance between us and grabs my arm. "Someone is coming for that bangle, and you don't want to be here when he arrives." Up close, I see that his eyes are a very light grey-green that doesn't seem to quite match the color highlighting his brown hair. They're beautiful eyes. I could stare at them for ages if I wasn't currently trying to get away from this guy.

I try to wrench my arm from his grip, but he's far too

strong. "If you want it so badly, *old man*," I say to him through gritted teeth, "then why haven't you taken it already?"

"Because, silly girl," he says, leaning even closer, "I'd have to cut off your arm."

A chill runs through me, but I do my best to forget his words and focus instead on the projection I've decided on. I don't have enough energy for anything as detailed as the dragon, and he probably wouldn't fall for something like that a second time. Instead I imagine myself slowly raising my left arm. "Fine," the imaginary version of me says. "You can have it." In my mind, I see myself slipping the bangle off my arm. I hold it between us, waiting for the moment when he releases me.

"Thank you," he says, somewhat warily. He lets go of my arm and reaches for the bangle. The bangle that isn't there. Imaginary me throws it with all her might over his shoulder. With an angry groan, the artist spins around and dashes after it.

I turn and run in the other direction—but a large bald man is moving toward me. "You!" he bellows. "You are the one. The gold they told me about. The *guardian*."

What? I glance around, seeking the best escape route. But before I can move another step, I'm surrounded. An elf on each side, and another behind me. They grab my arms and tug me roughly after the bald man, who's heading through a door behind the bar.

"I will not have guardians in my club," he calls over his shoulder.

"But I'm not a guardian," I protest.

The man stops and looks over his shoulder. His eyes—fiery orange with narrow vertical pupils—glare at me. "They said you'd say that," he snarls, revealing a forked tongue. *Drakoni*, my mind whispers to me.

"Look," I say to him, struggling against the elves until I manage to raise my arms just enough to show my bare wrists. "No guardian markings."

"Trainee," the drakoni man spits. "Same thing."

How does he know that?

He strides along a passageway, and I'm dragged after him into a dim, smoky room where two men are sitting at a round table, drinking amber-colored drinks and playing cards. They're laughing about something, but they look up as the elves push me roughly into the room. One of them leers at me, while the other—

"Zed?" Relief and confusion collide, making me light-headed. For an odd moment, the room seems to vibrate. "What … what are you doing here?" *In the company of Creepy Hollow's biggest guardian hater?*

The room vibrates again.

"TAKE IT OFF!" a voice yells from somewhere behind me. At the sound of running footsteps, I look over my shoulder past the elves. I see the artist, but he blurs as the vibration around me intensifies. A shock wave ripples through the air, and with a loud *whoosh*, everything around me vanishes.

And then reappears with a jolt.

I blink.

This isn't the room I was in a second ago. This is my bedroom at Ryn's house. All my things are here, despite the fact that I moved everything out this afternoon. Aside from a faint green tinge overlaying the scene, everything looks the same as it was when I lived here. My clothes peek out of a half-open drawer. My work is spread across the desk. My trainee pendant hangs on the closet doorknob.

I turn slowly on the spot as my heart pounds heavily in my chest. Then I see the person sitting on the bed—and I completely freak out.

The person is me.

PART II

CHAPTER NINE

I STUMBLE BACKWARD AND FLATTEN MYSELF AGAINST THE wall, but the me on the bed doesn't seem to notice. How is this happening? How am I *looking at myself*? For a moment I wonder if I'm projecting this entire scene, but that can't be right. I'm not imagining this. I'm not controlling it. This is *real*.

Footsteps sound in the corridor, and Vi pokes her head into the room. "I know you're studying," she says, "but feel free to join us whenever you want."

The other me groans and covers her face with a textbook. "The food smells so good," she says from behind the pages. "I wish I could come down now."

"Not much longer to go, and you'll be done with all this extra work," she says with a smile. "I'll shout when dinner's ready. You can join us then."

She disappears, leaving me with a sense of déjà vu so strong it almost knocks me over. This conversation has already happened. Last week sometime, while I was studying for a written exam. Which means I'm currently standing in ... the past?

How the freaking heck did I get to the past?

The bangle.

I grab the decorated band of bronze and try to tug it off, but it won't move. "Come on," I mutter, pulling harder. Realizing I've spoken out loud, I freeze and look at the girl on the bed. She shows no sign of having heard me. I get back to my attempts at prying the bangle off my arm, but it's no use. It won't budge.

With a groan of despair, I hurry out of the room and downstairs. I don't know how to get myself back to the present, but standing in my bedroom tugging at my arm clearly isn't helping. I arrive in the living room as Ryn opens a doorway on the wall and welcomes his friends, Jamon and Natesa. This is the night they came for dinner along with Raven and Flint, who are already sitting on a couch playing with their three-month-old son. I remember making fun of Ryn when he told me he and Vi were hosting a dinner party. "You're so not the type to host *dinner parties*," I told him.

As Jamon and Natesa's five-year-old daughter skips across the room to play with the baby, I move closer to everyone. "Hello?" I say loudly, knowing before I open my mouth that it's unlikely anyone will hear me. As I expected, not a single person in the room pays attention to me. The adults sit, and Vi walks out of the kitchen, directing a line of drinks through the air. I raise my arm in front of her as she passes. She walks right through it.

A chill rises across my skin. I'm nothing more than an observer here, unable to influence my surroundings or communicate with anyone around me. Wait, what about my amber? Perhaps I can communicate with someone in the present. I slip my fingers into the top of my left boot and draw my amber out. I swipe my finger across its surface, but nothing happens. I remove my stylus and use it to write on the amber, but no words form there.

Dammit.

And the faerie paths? Where would they take me if I opened a doorway now? To somewhere else in the past? I walk to the nearest wall to write on it, but my hand simply passes through when I lean my wrist against it.

Frightened, I snatch my hand back. I try to write a doorway spell into the air, but I have as much success as if I'm writing with an ordinary stick.

I'm trapped. Trapped within this green-tinted world in the past. I clutch my head in my hands and try not to panic.

"Hey, I heard you're on the Guild Council now," Jamon says, obviously to Ryn. "Condolences, man."

Ryn groans. "I know. I wanted to turn down the offer, but Vi convinced me not to."

I raise my head at that, puzzled by Ryn's words. I thought becoming a member of the Council was a *good* thing.

"Well," Violet says, sitting beside Ryn and tucking her legs beneath her, "since we decided you'd be the one to stay with the Guild, it makes sense for you to accept a position on the Council. We want to know as much as possible about what's going on there, and we'll only know that if you're working near the top."

"I know." Ryn lets out a dramatic sigh. "I'm happy to take one for the team."

Take one for the team? I thought my brother *liked* working at the Guild.

"Oh, I need to take this," Ryn says, reaching forward as a small mirror lying on the coffee table lights up. "It's probably about the protest."

"Protest?" Raven asks as Ryn heads to the kitchen. Before he disappears through the door, I catch a glimpse of my father's face on the mirror's surface.

"Another Griffin List protest," Vi says. "The Guild's managed to keep it quiet so far. They don't want it getting out of hand like last time."

"Oh, is it to do with that man who's on trial at the moment for attempting to blackmail a Council member to keep his wife's name off the list?"

Vi nods. With my distress replaced by curiosity for a moment, I follow Ryn to the kitchen. Dad doesn't work for the Guild anymore, so why is he talking to Ryn about a protest the Guild is trying to keep quiet?

"You're putting me in an awkward position here, Dad," Ryn says as I walk into the kitchen. The mirror is on the kitchen table, and Ryn's leaning over it.

"I know," Dad says. "I hate involving you, but I'm worried that with this trial going on, and the Guild looking into any hint of corruption, it won't be long before someone starts wondering about Calla."

What?

"All I'm asking is that you make sure there's no record of the bribes anywhere."

Bribes? What bribes?

"There was more than one?" Ryn says after a pause.

No, no, no. What has Dad done? What kind of bribes did he have to make in order to keep my incidents quiet? What if he gets caught? What if he has to go to prison just because he tried to keep me safe? I couldn't live with that kind of guilt. I couldn't—

Vibrations. A shock wave. Ripples and a whoosh and—

I'm standing in the back room of Club Deviant again, breathless and nauseous. Zed looks horrified, the elves are backing away from me, and running footsteps are still coming down the passage. A hand grabs my arm. "Close your eyes," the artist says.

"W-what?"

"Close your eyes!"

I do. On the other side of my eyelids, something flashes bright white, followed by a rumble-crash that sounds like thunder. Then I'm stumbling and running. I open my eyes as the artist pulls me along the passageway and back into the club. I think about tugging my arm free and making my own escape, but his grip is too strong. Past the dancers, out the door, down the tunnel.

He stops and turns to face me. "No more mind games. Give me the bangle."

"They—they're going to find us," I gasp, peering over my shoulder.

"They're temporarily blinded. They won't be finding anything for the next few hours. Now give me the bangle."

I face him. "Even if I wanted to, I can't get it off."

He lets out an impatient breath of air. "Of course you can. It's only when you're in the past, using its power, that you can't remove it."

"And … you can't take it off me?" I ask, moving another step away from him. Another wave of nausea rolls over me, but I breathe deeply against it. "You said you'd have to cut off my arm to get it."

"Correct. And I'd prefer not to do that, so just give it to me. You saw what it can do. Time travel is extremely dangerous in the wrong hands."

"Exactly." I take another step back. "That's why I need to return it to the Guild."

He makes an irritated noise. "It will be stolen again if you give it back to them."

"So don't steal it then, and everything—"

"Not by me."

"By me," a voice says behind me. I whirl around and find a man standing a few feet away, a doorway in the air melting closed behind him. "Give me back my power," he says. Sparks ignite from his fingers and zigzag through the air toward me. I throw myself to the side. My shoulder hits the tunnel wall as the sparks fly past me.

Throwing star.

I reach for one and fling it at my attacker. I needn't have

bothered, though, since he's now locked in a battle of sparks and knives and whirling wind with the artist.

"Oh! There she is!"

I jump away from the tunnel wall as a doorway materializes beside me. I wrap my hand around air and find a glittering sword in my grip a moment later. I'm about to slash at my newest opponent when I realize who it is.

"Calla, come on!" Perry shouts, holding his hand out to me.

I let go of the sword and grab his hand. He tugs hard, and I fall into the darkness with him.

CHAPTER TEN

I STUMBLE OUT THE OTHER SIDE OF THE FAERIE PATHS AND onto the old Guild ruins along with Perry and Gemma. "Are you okay?" Gemma asks immediately.

I pull the bangle off my arm and drop it on the ground as if it burns. I raise my hands and press my fingers to my temples. "I'm ... so confused."

The drakoni club owner somehow knew I was with the Guild.

Zed seems to be a friend of his.

A piece of jewelry sent me back in time.

Dad's involved in illegal bribery.

The artist whose house I broke into saved me, then threatened to cut off my arm.

A random guy who wants to steal the bangle—*again,*

apparently—showed up out of nowhere.

And then a couple of trainees appeared in exactly the right place to rescue me from the whole mess.

What. The heck. Is going on?

"We heard Saskia and Blaze plotting this afternoon," Gemma says. "That's how we knew where you were."

I lower my hands and look at her through the dim moonlight. "Plotting?"

"Yes. Plotting an initiation that sounded a whole lot more involved than ours was. When we were in first year, most of us found the idea of simply *being* Underground scary enough. Two guardians had recently been found dead down there, and the Guild never figured out what happened, so it was pretty much the most dangerous place for us to go."

"Which is why that idiot Blaze decided we should all take a trip down there as an initiation ritual," Perry says.

"And since he was the biggest, meanest idiot," Gemma says, rolling her eyes, "the rest of us figured we couldn't say no. We didn't use the faerie paths. Blaze found one of the entrances, and we each had to go down one by one and stay there for ten minutes."

"Well." I cross my arms. "That sounds a whole lot simpler than what I just went through."

"Yeah. We heard the whole ridiculous plan in the library this afternoon," Gemma says.

Perry leans closer to me and whispers, "Guild Library," as if sharing a secret. "Excellent spot for eavesdropping. You'll discover this soon."

"Yeah, so they were hoping you'd either get caught while

breaking into someone's home," Gemma says, "or that their anonymous tip to Club Deviant's owner would get you in trouble with him. And by 'trouble—'" she glances at Perry "—I think they meant something a lot worse than just getting kicked out."

I press my lips together as anger heats my blood. I've wound up an outcast at every school I've been to, but no one's ever tried to get me killed before. What is wrong with Saskia?

"We tried to find you at the Guild after we heard everything, but you'd left already. I asked your mentor for your amber ID so I could get hold of you, but the moment I mentioned your name, she looked at me like I was a pile of goblin droppings."

"Yeah, she's super friendly."

"And we couldn't find your brother either," Perry adds as he pushes himself up onto a wall. "So we figured the next best thing would be to try find you Underground before you got yourself into too much trouble. We wandered around Sivvyn Quarter for a while, then kept opening doorways near Club Deviant until you finally showed up."

"Wow. You went to a lot of trouble."

Perry shrugs and swings his long legs, kicking his heels against the wall. "The bill's in the mail."

"Perry!" Gemma elbows him. "Don't be such a butt-head."

"What?" His eyes widen in defense. "Obviously I'm joking."

I feel the hint of a smile on my lips. "Well, thank you for pulling me out of there. I appreciate it."

"Sure." Gemma beams at me. "That's what friends are for, right?"

Friends. Right. I look down. The bangle lies on a rock beside my left foot. I can't tell if it's a trick of the moonlight or some kind of magic, but the green stones seem to be glowing. "Being friends would be great," I say, "but I don't want to waste your time."

"Why would you be wasting our time?" Perry asks.

"It's just ... people don't generally want to be friends with me."

"Because ..."

"They're scared of me. And soon you will be too. You'll hear more and more stories about me, stories that will freak you out, and you'll decide it's a whole lot safer *not* being my friend."

"We already know about the boy and the bicycle," Gemma says. "So what? He went crazy. Doesn't mean it was your fault."

"Everyone knows that story," I say. "It got out pretty quickly. I'm referring to all the others."

"Others?"

"Yes. There are other stories." I fidget with the frayed edge of my make-shift shorts.

"And ... are they true?" Gemma asks carefully.

I bite my lip. I can't tell them everything, but I don't want to lie to them either. "The truth is that I've never made anyone crazy. I've never used dark magic, and my mother isn't an Unseelie faerie."

"Well, that's all we need to know then," Perry says, clapping his hands together as if that settles the matter. "Interview over. You'll receive a formal offer of friendship in the mail."

Gemma rolls her eyes and pushes him off the wall.

* * *

Exhausted from projecting the detailed dragon scene, I collapse into bed late on Tuesday night—after hiding the time-travel bangle at the back of my sock drawer next to the necklace from Zed that I plan never to wear—and then proceed to oversleep the next morning. I'm lost in a deep, faraway sleep when Mom bangs on my door to ask if I'm still planning to have breakfast at the Guild. I get dressed in record time, ignore the three amber messages I received from Zed during the night, and just about run out of the faerie paths into the entrance room at the Guild. After the guard scans my pendant, I hurry toward the dining hall. I'm almost there when I realize I didn't bring the bangle. I slow down, wondering if I should go back home and get it, but then decide not to. I haven't figured out yet if I should take it directly to someone, or if I should return it anonymously.

My amber tingles in my back pocket as I reach the dining hall door. I thought my brief journey back in time had ruined it, but it started working again during the night. I pull it out and read the latest message from Zed.

Please let me know you're okay. I don't know what you're mixed up in, but you know I'm here for you if you need my help.

With an annoyed huff, I lean against the wall outside the dining hall and quickly scribble a reply with my stylus.

What I'm mixed up in? What about what you're mixed up in? Drinking and playing games with dangerous Underground people. Is that a recent development, or have I just never known about that side of you?

Like I never knew about your girlfriend, I add silently, a dull ache settling in my chest. I haven't had much spare thinking time recently, but in the moments when my mind hasn't been occupied with Guild history or potions details or fighting tactics, it's turned—annoyingly—to Zed. I know I stand no chance with him, but I wonder if, some time in the future, he might see me differently.

Stop being an idiot. Forget him and move on.

Attempting to take my own advice, I drop my amber into my bag and walk into the noisy dining hall. It's about half full. Most of the occupants appear to be trainees, but I spot some mentors and a few older guardians. I'm about to walk to the table where Perry, Gemma and Ned are seated, but then I spot Saskia two tables away from them. The ache of Zed-rejection morphs into the burning heat of anger. I march across the room, my fingernails pressing into my palms as I clench my fists.

Saskia takes a sip of something from a mug before noticing me. Her eyebrows jump up in surprise as she lowers the mug. "Oh, look who survived initiation."

I'd love to slap her but I manage to hold myself back. "You nearly got me killed."

"What? Me?" She pretends to look hurt. "I would never do anything like that."

"I could have you expelled for what you did."

"Oh, well, you know all about expulsion, don't you. I guess I should be afraid."

Angry images flicker at the edge of my mind, threatening to break free. I force them back. "When exactly do you plan to grow up, Saskia? In a year's time we'll all have graduated. We'll be working here. We'll be *professionals*. Are you still going to act like a five-year-old then? Are you still going to attempt to sabotage the people you're meant to be working *beside*, not against?"

Saskia looks around at the other fifth-years at her table. "Not all of them. Probably just you."

"*I'm not your enemy*," I force out between my teeth. "I'm here for the same reason you are: to save people. To stop criminals. To see justice served."

I spin around and head for Perry's table, only realizing now how quiet the dining hall has become. Keeping my eyes on the empty space next to Gemma, I move as quickly as I can without running. I climb over the bench and sit as Perry starts clapping. "Well done. That was quite a speech. Here, have a cinnamon twist." He removes one from Gemma's plate and places it in front of me.

"Does Saskia really have to be so childish?" I ask. "I know she's annoyed that I didn't have to start in first year like everyone else, but haven't I proved that I put in the work, even if it didn't happen *here*?"

"It's more than that," Ned says, staring into his mug as though he finds the contents fascinating.

"More?"

"The truth is," Perry says, "she feels threatened by you. She's worried about her position at the top."

"The top of what? What position?" Perry and Gemma look at me like I'm stupid. Even Ned lifts his gaze. "Oh, wait, you mean the *rankings*? Why in all fae would *I* be a threat to her?"

I receive another are-you-really-that-slow look from Perry. "You're Ryn Larkenwood's sister. Everyone know he's one of the best guardians around. And not only are you related to him, but he's been training you."

"A month," I say. "He trained me for a month. The rest of my training happened with—someone else."

"Oh." Perry shovels a fork-full of banana pancake into his mouth. "Well we could spread that bit of information around for you, if you'd like," he says with his mouth half full. "It would definitely make you seem less threatening."

"And it helps that you're hanging out with us," Gemma adds. "People don't exactly find us intimidating."

"Really?" I say with a straight face. "I thought Ned was *terrifying* when I met him yesterday."

Ned's cheeks turn pink, and he stares deeper into his mug. Perry laughs and points his fork at me. "See, Gemma? That's what's called a joke. I'm not the only one who makes them. Calla's gonna fit right in here." He raises his mug and taps it against my cinnamon twist. "Welcome to Club Outcast, Calla."

"Welcome," Gemma says, raising her smoothie glass, then sipping the brownish-green liquid. "I mean, not that you're an outcast," she adds after swallowing. "You definitely look like you could be one of the cool people, so I didn't mean to imply that you're—"

"Oh, no, I'm an outcast. Attending seven different schools by the age of fourteen will do that to a person."

"*Seven?*" Gemma says, pulling her head back in surprise.

"Uh … yeah." I guess that story hasn't reached the Guild yet. "Um, four different junior schools, then healer school, then cooking school, then art school …" I trail off as I realize I probably shouldn't have shared all that. Now they'll want to know *why* I went to so many schools. "Anyway," I rush on, "why do you guys qualify as outcasts?" I pick up the cinnamon twist and take a large bite before anyone can ask me a question.

"Oh, well Ned's scared of girls," Perry says, "and I'm a super nerd. So that counts us out of the cool crowd."

"Thanks a lot, man," Ned mutters.

"What? Calla's part of our group now. She needs to know these things."

"And what about you?" I say to Gemma, hoping to draw attention away from Ned so he can have a chance to recover from his embarrassment.

Gemma finishes the last of her smoothie and says, "My mom's an admin and my dad's a florist. So, you know, I don't have the cool guardian heritage that almost everyone else here has. And I often get accused of being a halfling because apparently I'm not two-toned. Hello." She points at her head. "Brown plus black equals two colors, and the brown matches my eyes, so I'm *all faerie*, thank you very much." She hesitates, then rushes to add, "Not that there's anything wrong with being a halfling."

Perry shakes his head, then looks at me. "My sister's a halfling. Half-faerie, half-human. Gem likes to make fun of her."

"I do not!"

"A halfling? Does ..." I look around, then lower my voice. "Does the Guild know?"

"Oh, yeah. She's on their registry. No point, though, since she doesn't have any magic. She lives in the human realm with her mom. I visit her sometimes. It's cool to hang out there with all the human tech instead of using magic all the time."

"When he says 'human tech,' he means movies," Gemma tells me. "All he ever talks about when he comes back from visits is what movies he watched."

"Movies are amazing," Perry says. "The fae world doesn't know what it's missing out on."

The light in the dining hall dims for a moment, then brightens again. "Does that mean something?" I ask, licking cinnamon and powdered sugar off my fingers.

"Time for class," Ned says with a sigh.

"My mentor's taking today's lesson," Gemma says. She taps her tray twice with her stylus, and it vanishes. Perry and Ned do the same. "Potions are her specialty," Gemma adds. "I think we're doing sleeping potions today."

"Oh, that's great," I say as we stand. "I know all about those."

Perry raises an eyebrow. "Drugging your boyfriends?"

Gemma smacks his arm while I laugh. "No, my mom has sleeping issues. She's been concocting sleeping potions for as long as I can remember. She'd flip her lid if I got a tattoo or started dating a fifty-year-old, but she's totally fine with me learning the art of illicit potion-making in our kitchen."

"Ah, she likes the strong stuff, does she?" Perry says, nodding as if he knows all about strong potions.

"She won't let you get a tattoo?" Gemma asks before I can laugh at Perry. "But you were with that tattoo artist last night. I thought you guys must be friends since he was helping you fight off that other guy. Unless ... was it the other way around?"

"Oh, is he a tattoo artist?" I picture the guy whose house I broke into. I wonder if the dark shapes marking his arms are his own work. "No, I don't know him. I only met him last—"

"Excuse me." Saskia steps in front of me. "You've got something that belongs to me. My tracker band."

The tracker band hiding next to the bangle in my drawer. The tracker band I plan to burn when I get home this afternoon. "Yeah, I'm really sorry about that," I say in my best I-don't-give-a-pixie's-ass tone of voice. "I lost it."

CHAPTER ELEVEN

"SWORD! SCIMITAR! BOW AND ARROW!" OLIVE BARKS OUT, snapping her fingers between each command. "Calla, you're not keeping up. Dagger!" Finger snap. "Chakram!" Finger snap. "Whip!" Finger snap. "I don't see a whip, Calla."

I try to block out her harsh voice and impatient glare and concentrate instead on the feel of the whip in my hand. Eventually, it appears within my grip. I bring it swiftly through the air, watch the end wrap around a low-hanging branch, and tug it hard. The branch cracks and breaks and sails through the air. The whip vanishes as I let go, but the branch keeps coming. I dodge so I don't get myself knocked out.

We're outside at the old Guild ruins, an area that's apparently used quite often for training. It's large enough to accommodate plenty of trainees and their mentors without anyone having to interfere with anyone else. I'm here with Olive and her other fifth-year trainee, a petite girl named Ling who hasn't said a word to me. We used part of the ruins as an obstacle course to warm up, then practiced a few single combat moves Olive decided we needed to perfect—most of which ended with, "Not good enough. Do it again."—before moving on to weapons control. It's a simple exercise in which we have to make the required weapon appear instantly before moving to the next. It's an exercise I suck at.

"Ridiculous," Olive says after the broken branch lands somewhere behind me. "How exactly did you make it through four years of training if you can't even control your own weapons? Oh, that's right. You didn't get through four years of training."

The afternoon has been full of gibes like that one, and I've held my tongue every time. But we've been out here for almost three hours now, and I'm tired of being mocked. "You're right," I say to her. "This *is* ridiculous. When am I ever going to be in a situation where my opponent recites a list of weapons for me to produce instantly, one after the other?"

Olive marches across the overgrown ruins and stops with her face inches from mine. "I have ninety-three years of guardian experience, so you'd damn well better believe me when I tell you that this exercise is crucial. When you're in a combat situation and forces are coming at you from all sides, you need to be able to adapt in a second." She snaps her fingers once more, right beside my ear. "Now you are *not* leaving here until I'm satisfied with your performance. Ling, you can go home. Calla, start again."

The weapon names keep flying at me, and I keep trying to match Olive's pace. I don't seem to be getting better, though. If anything, I'm getting worse. "Useless," she says after a further half hour. "Useless! I give up. I've got more important things to do than waste my time on this, Calla."

She heads back to the Guild through a faerie paths doorway as angry tears blot out my vision. I blink them away before they can fall. I press my lips together and stare at the ground, wondering for the first time if Olive and Saskia and all the other people who think I should have started at the bottom might have been right. I thought I was good enough for this level of training, but I haven't managed to get a single thing right this afternoon, and it's only my third day at the Guild. Things will only get tougher from here onwards.

"You're trying too hard," a male voice says behind me.

I spin around, surprised to find a glittering knife in each of my hands by the time I'm facing him.

"See?" the tattoo artist says. "It happens easily when you're not thinking about it."

My grip on the knives tightens as I watch him carefully. "What do you know? You're not a guardian."

"I know what I've seen. I know it's supposed to be effortless. Automatic. As easy for you as breathing."

As easy for me as breathing? If only. "How did you find me?" I ask. I need to keep him talking while I come up with an illusion good enough to distract him.

"I have ways of tracking people down, Calla."

"Okaaay, stalker. I hope you realize how creepy that sounds."

"Coming from the girl who broke into my house to look at my art."

"I was curious. That doesn't make me creepy. Definitely not as creepy as you, old man."

"Old man?"

"I saw your Stone Age furniture. If you were alive when that stuff was made, then you definitely qualify for the 'old man' label."

"Oh, the furniture," he says with a nod. "That isn't mine."

"Did you steal it? Like you stole the bangle?"

He sighs. "Fine. Yes, I stole the bangle, but not from the Guild. I stole it from the man you saw in the tunnel last night. He's dangerous, and I need to keep the bangle's power away from him."

"Well, he won't be getting it from me, so you can relax."

The artist frowns and takes a step toward me. "Please tell me you haven't given it back to the Guild yet."

Instead of answering, I release the barriers around my mind and picture an ogre stomping across the ruins. It stops in front of the tattoo artist, balls its fists, and lets out a bellow.

"Don't bother with your mind tricks," the tattoo artist says, staring straight through the ogre. "They won't work on me. I wasn't aware last night that I needed to shield my mind from you, but I am now." He starts moving toward me, walking right through the ogre.

He can't see it. *He can't see it.*

Shocked, I stumble backward, abandoning the ogre illusion. "How—how do you know I'm doing it if you can't see—"

"I can see your concentration."

My concentration? No one's ever noticed that before. The artist quickens his steps, and I throw up a shield between us before he can reach me.

"Really?" he says. "We went through this last night. Your shields mean nothing to me."

"Do all the guardians nearby mean anything to you?"

His eyes dart across the ruins, and I take advantage of his momentary distraction. I throw sparks into the air, as bright as I can make them, and in the blinding flash that follows, I release the knives, grab my stylus from my belt, and write a doorway beside my feet. A gust of power blows my hair back and knocks me onto my side. He's broken through my shield. I roll into the opening darkness of the faerie paths, but something snaps around my wrist and yanks hard. I hang there, half in darkness, looking up at the vine wrapped around my arm and the artist at the other end, raising me from the faerie paths with a sweep of his hand through the air.

I slice wildly across the vine with my stylus. It breaks. I fall.

And the darkness closes above me.

* * *

The faerie paths dump me in the spare room at Ryn's house, because that must have been the first place I thought of. I immediately open another doorway and hurry through it to my bedroom at home. I sit on the edge of the bed and breathe slowly as I run through what just happened. The tattoo artist couldn't see my illusion. That's *never* happened before. Does that mean he's far more powerful than the average faerie, or is it simply that other people have never been aware of the need to protect their minds from me?

I shake my head and cross the room to the chest of drawers. It doesn't matter what the reason is. The important thing now is to return the bangle to the Guild before anyone else gets hold of it. I open my sock drawer and stare at the dangerous piece of jewelry. Aside from the continually shifting shades of green in the stones, there's no hint of the power it contains. I pick it up carefully, afraid I might vanish in an instant and reappear somewhere in the past. Nothing happens, though. As far as I know, it only works when I put it on, and I certainly won't be doing that again.

"Cal, is that you?" Dad calls from downstairs. He must have heard me exit the faerie paths.

"Yes," I shout back. I lean out of my doorway and add, "I'm just going back to the Guild quickly. I forgot some stuff there." It isn't a lie. I *did* forget to return to the Guild to fetch my books in my haste to get away from the tattoo artist.

"Okay, but could you come down here for a moment?"

I run down the stairs and find Dad sitting at the dining room table surrounded by papers. Dad used to save lives for a living. Now he manages the business side of a private security company so that other people can save lives and Mom doesn't have to worry about him getting hurt. I think he probably wishes he was still a guardian. He probably wishes many things. Not having a daughter with a Griffin Ability is no doubt near the top of the list.

The words I heard him say to Ryn replay in my mind as I

cross the room toward him. *All I'm asking is that you make sure there's no record of the bribes anywhere.* It's a shock to know that my father would even consider something like that, let alone carry it out. But I have to remind myself to be grateful for whatever he's done rather than morally indignant. After all, his actions have kept me off the Griffin List.

I wonder if Mom knows what he's done. Probably not. She's so fragile, I'm sure Dad would want to protect her from this like he protects her from everything else.

Dad stands as I reach the table and lean against it. "I came across this in a cupboard earlier today," he says, lifting a knife from a box. The wooden handle is beautifully carved with elaborate patterns and looks just the right size to fit comfortably in my hand. "It was the tokehari my mother left for me," Dad says. "Something special I could always remember her by." He holds it out to me, along with a leather sheath. "I'd like you to have it. I know you have guardian weapons now, but there may come a time when you don't have access to those. A guardian should always be prepared."

"Thank you, Dad." I take the knife and test the weight and feel of it in my hand. I run my finger along the patterns in the handle. "It's beautiful."

"The sheath can be secured to the inside of one of your boots. That way you won't have to remember to pack it every time you have an assignment or training."

"Cool." I slide the knife into its slim leather covering. "I'll do that tonight. Then I can start practicing with it tomorrow."

With a smile and a nod, Dad sits and returns to his work. I head for the stairs.

All I'm asking is that you make sure there's no record of the bribes anywhere.

I stop and look back over my shoulder. "Dad?" He looks up. "I'm sorry for … being the way I am. I'm sorry for whatever you've had to do to keep me off the Griffin List."

He frowns, then stands and comes toward me. He pulls me into a tight embrace. "I'm not sorry," he says. "Anything I've had to do to keep you safe, I would gladly do again. One day when you're a parent you'll understand that."

I nod against his chest. He steps back, pats my cheek, then returns to the table. I climb the stairs and reach my bedroom as music begins playing from the direction of my desk. I walk over to it and pick up my hand mirror. Zed's face appears on the shiny surface, but I don't touch it to accept the call. There's a traitorous part of my heart that wants to hear his voice, but I'm still annoyed and hurt. Besides, I have something more important to do right now. I can speak to him later when I've returned the bangle. I toss the mirror onto my bed and turn back to my drawer.

The room vibrates.

"No, no, no," I whisper, raising my hands to steady myself. The world ripples and jolts, and suddenly I'm standing in an entirely different place. "What?" I cry out. "How?" There is no bangle on my arm. I wasn't even touching it.

A woman pushes a trolley through the right side of my body and continues walking. I jump away from her and look around. I'm standing in a large shopping mall somewhere in the human realm. I don't recognize anything until I spot the music-themed cafe. I see a younger version of myself nestled in a couch beneath a guitar on the wall, and I remember this day instantly. It was my first day at Ellinhart, and I was still furious that Mom had once again refused to let me join the Guild. I left school as soon as my last lesson ended, defied my mother's rules and fae laws, and sat down in a human coffee shop in full view of every human who walked by. Of course, none of them knew what I was, so I probably wouldn't have been in much trouble if anyone found out, but I still felt like a rebel.

"Ugh, what am I *doing* here?" I jump up and down and shake my arms around, hoping to jolt myself back to the present. It doesn't work. Maybe I'm stuck here forever because I don't have the bangle with me. But then ... how did I get here in the first place?

"Don't panic, don't panic," I murmur to myself. I managed to return to the present last time this happened, so I have to trust I can return again. I walk into the cafe and hover near the couch where thirteen-year-old me is sipping a mug of coffee. I know what's coming next, and a crazy, stupid part of me wants to relive the moment. I look around and find him sitting at the piano-painted counter.

Zed. He's looking this way with a frown on his face. He abandons his drink, crosses the room, and sits beside younger me on the couch. She almost spills her coffee in fright, but then she recognizes him. She knows who he is before he speaks. "This is going to sound really odd," he says, "but I think I know you. From ... well, do you remember me?"

Of course I remembered him. How could I forget the guy who was locked in the hanging cage next to mine? He did his best to distract me from my fears. The terrifying Unseelie

119

prince, the wails and cries of the other prisoners, the creatures that swam in the dark water below us, the blood of the man I tried to get away from—

The world tips and shudders and jolts me back to the present.

I stumble across my bedroom and catch myself against the desk. Nausea attacks me. I double over, clutching my stomach. Breathing deeply, I manage to get to my bathing room without throwing up. I kneel beside the enchanted pool, pressing my fingers into the small white pebbles that cover the bathing room floor and watching my rippling reflection in the water. After a minute or so of deep breathing, the nausea passes.

I have to get rid of this bangle.

CHAPTER TWELVE

I WRAP THE BANGLE IN A T-SHIRT AND PUT IT INSIDE ONE of my painted tote bags before heading to the Guild. "Back for some extra training?" the guard asks as he scans my pendant.

"No, I just left my homework in my locker," I tell him with a smile and an eye-roll.

The moment I step through the doorway into the foyer, I remember the extra layer of magic that exists there. My smile slips. I freeze for a moment, expecting an alarm to go off as the protective charms detect the bangle. But nothing happens. Relieved, I keep walking. I guess the bangle's magic isn't seen as a threat. Or perhaps, I think to myself as I head for the staircase, it's an unknown kind of magic, like the magic that allows me to create illusions. The protective doorway has never seen *me* as a threat—even though it probably should.

Instead of climbing the stairs, I walk behind them toward the elevator. I didn't know it was here until the last week of summer break. Ryn never seems to use it, and neither do most other members of the Guild. I'm usually happy to climb the stairs, but I don't want to be seen this afternoon. I wave my hand in front of the ornate elevator door, then step back and wait. After several moments—during which I keep my head down and hope no one joins me—the door ripples and vanishes. I step inside the elevator and turn to the brass clock face on the left wall. There are far more than twelve numbers around its edge. With my finger, I move the pointer from zero to five. The door reappears, and the elevator moves up. When it opens once more, I step out near the library.

I considered giving the bangle to a Council member, but then I'd have to answer questions about how and where I got it. I could give it to Ryn and ask him to keep my name out of it, but then *he'd* be under the spotlight. Better just to keep everyone out of trouble and leave the bangle where a Guild member can find it.

I walk into the library and head down one of the aisles, scanning the shelves as if looking for a particular book. I reach the other end, look around to make sure no one is watching, then remove the wrapped bangle from my bag. I place it on the floor before pulling the T-shirt off. Without pausing a moment longer, I straighten and walk back down the aisle. Now I just need to get my books and training bag out of my locker, and I can—

"Oh!" I jump back as I reach the end of the shelves and almost walk into someone.

"Oops, I'm sorry," Gemma says, bringing her hand up to her mouth. "Oh, Calla, hey." She gives me an apologetic smile. "I'm sorry, that was totally my fault. I was rushing in here to get my stuff. I've just been upstairs with, um …" She reaches up to touch her neck in a self-conscious gesture. "Well, there's this guy. He's a Seer trainee. You know the top three floors are for the Seers, right?"

I nod, hoping I don't look as guilty as I feel.

"Yeah, so we don't see them often because our training is completely separate from theirs, but I ran into him a few times when I started here because his mom is also an admin. I've kinda had a crush on him for, like, a year." She rolls her eyes as pink appears in her cheeks. "We hang out sometimes. As friends. Because he's awesome and I'm too shy to tell him I like him. Anyway," she rushes on, "what are you doing here? I saw Olive just now, so I figured you were done for the day."

"Yes, I just … forgot my books." In my locker. Which is downstairs. Nowhere near the library. "And I was looking up something I didn't quite understand in one of the lessons earlier," I add quickly.

"Oh, cool," Gemma says, without a hint of suspicion. "I'm walking home now. Do you want to join me?"

"Walking?" I follow her to a table where she retrieves her bag from a chair. "Don't you use the faerie paths?"

"I do. Don't worry, I'm not one of those extremists who hasn't used the paths since Draven's reign. I just like to take the Tip-Top Path when it isn't winter because it's so pretty. Have you been on it before?"

"Uh, no." We walk out of the library and aim for the stairs.

"I don't actually live in Creepy Hollow, so if I were to walk home it would take a very long time. Faerie paths are my only option."

"Oh, but you're missing out. It's so pretty up there. A little dangerous, obviously," she adds as we descend the stairs, "but it's a little dangerous everywhere in Creepy Hollow."

"I guess I could walk with you for a bit and then take the faerie paths home," I say.

After stopping by the lockers so I can fetch my things, we leave the Guild through the entrance room and come out of the faerie paths near the start of the Tip-Top Path. It begins at the base of a tree where large gnarled roots twist around each other to form uneven steps. Higher up, where the roots end, low branches bend around and over and under each other to form more steps. The uneven stairway continues in an easy gradient from tree to tree until it reaches the forest canopy. While the stairway isn't steep, the bark is slippery in places where it's been worn smooth over the centuries. I almost lose my footing several times, but it's easy enough to catch hold of nearby branches.

The Tip-Top Path continues on for miles through the canopy, constructed from the topmost branches of adjacent trees. At intervals here and there, an uneven stairway like the one we climbed at the start leads down to the ground—which is so far down I can barely make it out between the tangled branches and leaves. The twilight sky is perfectly visible from up here, though. A pinky purple haze like watercolor paints bleeding into one another. In the fading light I notice minuscule glow-bugs far smaller than those that appear closer to the ground sitting on the autumn leaves. Umbrella sprites race each other along the smaller side branches, jumping and then opening the tiny umbrella-like appendages attached to the backs of their necks so they can glide from one branch to the next. Asterpearls, small white perennial flowers, grow here and there amongst the moss on the path. Their faint scent lingers in the air.

"You're right," I say to Gemma. "It's really beautiful up—"

My words are cut off as a miniature sphinx jumps from the shadows onto the path in front of us and bares its teeth. Gemma clutches my hand. We both freeze. It's the size of a large house cat but looks ferocious enough to do some damage. We've both been taught not to fight anything unless we're first attacked, though, so we wait, motionless. After more growling, the sphinx bends its front legs and leaps away from us into the shadows on the other side of the path.

"Whew," Gemma says, letting go of my hand and continuing along the path. "I think I've seen that one before. It always gets a bit aggressive, but it doesn't attack as long as you don't make any threatening moves."

"Do you know this from experience?"

"Unfortunately, yes. I was with Perry. He did this weird arm-flapping dance thing, and the sphinx jumped and clawed his chest. He wanted to go after it when it flapped away, but I managed to get him to sit still while his wounds healed."

I smile and step carefully around a small furry creature that decided the middle of the path was a good spot to have a nap. "Have you guys been friends a long time?"

"Since first year at the Guild."

"Okay." I nod. And then I nod some more because I've never been fantastic at making conversation with new people.

"So, um …" Gemma swings her arms at her side. "What do your parents do? Hopefully something more exciting than my parents."

"Not really," I say with a laugh. "My mom's a librarian at that enormous library attached to Wilfred Healer School, and my dad works for a private security company. He used to be a guardian, but he stopped working after his first son died and his first union fell apart. After he met my mom, he quit being a guardian altogether. Deactivated his marks and everything."

"Seriously? Wow. I don't know anyone who's had their marks deactivated."

"Yeah, I guess it's not common. The Guild reactivated his marks after the Destruction because they needed all the help they could get, and Dad didn't want to hide in the shadows, even though my mom would have been happy with that. She was terrified every single day that she'd get a letter saying he died or had been captured and marked. Anyway, that didn't happen, and after Draven's reign was over, he left the Guild again."

Gemma's expression turns thoughtful. "I can't imagine ever leaving."

"Me neither." I duck so I don't walk into a procession of silver spiders crossing the path on a single silver thread. "Anyway, parents are boring. Tell me about this Seer you have a crush on."

"Oh." Gemma grins down at her feet. "His name is Rick. He's good-looking and smart and funny and kind and just generally all-around perfect. He's been girlfriend-less for four whole months, and I don't know why because *all* the Seer girls want to be with him."

"Well, maybe he's Seen *you* in his future," I say, nudging her arm with my elbow and wondering how many Seers have used that pick-up line.

She groans. "I doubt it. That's not what he's trained to See. I mean, sure, Seers are born with the ability to See pretty much anything in the future, but that's why those who work for the Guild have so much training. They have to learn to hone their skills so they See the dangerous stuff that's coming, not the frivolous stuff. That's their focus, and all their magic goes into that. He probably doesn't have much magic left to See visions of his relationship future."

"Maybe he's powerful enough to—Oh!" I grab a hanging vine as my boots skid sideways, almost sending me off the edge of the uneven path.

"Careful, that part's slippery," Gemma says, turning back and catching my hand.

"Uh huh." I step over the smooth, shiny patch of bark and aim for the rough parts that provide a better grip for my shoes. "Anyway. I was saying maybe he's powerful enough to See both the dangerous stuff and the frivolous stuff like his love life."

"I don't know. I'm not sure I'd *want* to know that kind of thing ahead of time, if it were me. Takes the thrill out of it, you know? And Rick's just a regular Seer, not super powerful or anything, so I'm sure all his magic goes into Seeing for the Guild." She plucks one of the few remaining green leaves from a branch and twirls it between her fingers. "Did you know that the more powerful a Seer is, the further into the future he or she can See? Rick said his great-grandfather once Saw an attack fifty years before it happened. Guardians found the faerie who was going to do it. He was still a little kid, and it turned out his parents were abusive. The Guild got involved, the kid ended up with a new family, and fifty years later, the attack never happened."

"That's amazing. I wonder how many other events changed because the Guild intervened in that boy's life."

"Countless events, I'm sure. The future is always changing. You know how it is with some of our assignments. We'll show up after being given the brief about what's supposed to happen, and then it never does."

"Really? That's happened to you?"

"Yes. It means something else has changed, which in turn affected the event I was supposed to be changing." She looks at me and frowns. "I think. It's all rather complicated. Sometimes I glaze over when Rick tries to explain stuff."

"That's because you're probably staring at his perfect eyes or his perfect lips or some other perfect feature of his."

She attempts to look affronted, but then dissolves into giggles. "Yeah, that's probably true."

As our laughter subsides, I remember a question I've always had when thinking about the Seeing ability. "Sometimes I wonder why the Seers never saw the Destruction coming."

"Ugh, yeah, you and everyone else. Rick and I almost had a fight over that issue because apparently *everyone* asks the Seers that, and they're tired of it. It's the only time he's ever been upset with me."

"But did he have an answer for you? Does he know why they didn't See it coming?"

"Apparently someone from Draven's special army, one of the first people who ended up on the Griffin List after Draven's reign ended, was a woman who could block visions. The Seers always say that Draven was using her to block their vision of what was coming."

"Oh, okay. Uh, what's your opinion on the Griffin List?" I ask casually.

Gemma lets out a long sigh and drops the leaf off the edge of the path. "The Griffin List is stupid. I mean, think about it. These people and their special magic have existed for centuries and they've never bothered anyone before. It wasn't their fault Prince Marzell rounded them up into an almost unstoppable army. They were under his and Draven's control just as much as any other magical being. But then the Guild comes along and has to give labels to everything—Griffin abilities, Gifted people—and order everything on a registry the way they do for halflings, most of whom are also harmless. It's just ridiculous."

"I agree," I say, "but on the other hand, you can kinda see the point of the list, can't you? Some of these Griffin Abilities are really dangerous."

"Well, yes, there are some dangerous ones, but that doesn't mean the people who own them are dangerous. It's just …" She hesitates, gathering her thoughts. "Criminals come in all shapes and sizes and races, from all kinds of backgrounds, and with all kinds of magic. *Anyone* could be a criminal, not just one of the Gifted. So why treat them differently?"

I'm liking this girl more and more. "That makes complete sense to me. If only the rest of the world saw it that way."

"I know. But you can't argue too much about it otherwise people start to think *you're* Gifted."

"Yeah." I start thinking this is probably a good time to head home. It's great that Gemma and I are in agreement about the Griffin List, but if we continue talking about it for much longer, I might end up giving something away. "I think I should probably get home."

"Me too," she says. "This is around about where I usually go into the faerie paths. My house is nearby, but it's easier to take the paths than climb down all those stairs."

We say goodbye and exchange a semi-awkward hug. Then I open up a doorway and walk into it. Instead of taking the faerie paths straight into my bedroom, I come out by one of the waterfalls near my home. We live in Carnelian Valley now. It isn't a natural forested area like Creepy Hollow or Woodsinger Grove. The trees were planted specifically to be used as faerie homes. They're arranged in concentric circles around a system of eight interlinked lakes at the base of the valley. It's supposedly an expensive and highly sought-after area. Ryn said Dad must have pulled some serious strings to get a house here so quickly after Mom chose this area.

I stand with my hands on my hips and survey the area, comparing it to the forest I just walked though. The lakes and cascading waterfalls are beautiful, but there's nothing appealing to me about the perfect circles of trees rising up the sides of the valley. I'd far rather have a home in the tangled forest of Creepy Hollow.

I head away from the water. As I near our tree, I notice someone sitting on the ground beside it. I stop and take a closer look. The moment I recognize him, I feel that familiar jolt in my stomach. Not as strong as it used to be, though. I think I'm getting over my silly crush.

"What are you doing here, Zed?" I ask as I stride toward him.

"You've been ignoring me," he says as he stands. "I wanted to check on you."

"So you decided to lurk outside my home? I'm surprised my dad hasn't come out here to find out who you are and what you want."

"Oh, I've met your parents already. I told them I'm one of the training instructors at the Guild and that I came by to organize a schedule for the extra training you requested. They said you weren't home yet, so I told them I'd wait outside."

I blink, then drop my bag on the ground and cross my arms. "So you didn't come by to explain why you were hanging out with the drakoni who wanted to kill me?"

"Look, I didn't realize he was such a guardian hater. I only just met the guy. He's part of a group of people with ... well, similar interests."

"Similar interests?"

"Yes, it's ..." Zed scratches his head. "We're all survivors who were locked up in Prince Zell's dungeon back before the Destruction. It's like ... a support group."

"A support group? Now you're just making things up."

"I'm not, Calla. There really is a group. I don't know how these guys found each other, but they did, and now they've found me."

"Well … that's great."

"What happened last night when you vanished?" Zed asks, stepping closer to me. "That was really weird."

"Oh, that was nothing. Not a big deal." I step past him and write a doorway onto the wide tree that conceals my home.

"Are you sure? Because you looked seriously—"

"I'm sure. It was just one of my illusions. I made everyone think I had disappeared. But then I couldn't hold onto it because, um …" A jolt passes through me. Ripples radiate away from me. "Oh no." I spin around and reach for Zed, but everything vanishes.

I find myself standing in the same scene I was in earlier. Zed is sitting beside younger me on the couch in the cafe, and younger me is saying, "… so glad you got out of there. I always wondered what happened to you. My brother said the Guild would rescue everyone, but I never knew for sure that they did."

"No!" I shout. I'm not supposed to be traveling through time anymore. I'm nowhere near that stupid bangle. Why is it still affecting me?

"They didn't rescue us," Zed tells younger me.

"What? But then how did you get out? Did you … oh my goodness, did you have to fight for Draven? Did he brainwash you?"

I slide my fingers through my hair and tug at it. *Take me*

back to the present. Back to the present. BACK TO THE PRESENT, DAMMIT!

"No," Zed says. "They had to take us out of our cages to mark us, and that's when some of us got away. It was ... well, I won't tell you how we did it because it was pretty gruesome. We were desperate. We knew by then that the Guild was never coming."

"It wasn't the Guild's fault, okay?" I shout at Zed as he continues telling my younger self how he decided never to return to the Guild. "It's complicated with the Seelie and Unseelie Courts. The Guild can't just go charging in wherever they like. They probably would have started a war a whole lot sooner if they'd ignored all the laws, and you *know* that."

The scene vanishes along with that sudden rushing sound I'm becoming accustomed to. The nausea and dizziness hit me the moment I'm jolted back into Carnelian Valley. I try to steady myself against the tree and find the doorway into my home still open.

"What was that?" Zed demands. "What just happened?"

"H-how long was I gone?" I ask between deep gasps of air.

"I don't know. Two or three seconds, like last night. What's going on?"

"Nothing, I'm fine." I push him away and drag myself and my bag inside. The doorway closes, and I drop into the nearest armchair. I lean forward and place my head between my knees. *Don't be sick, don't be sick, don't be sick.*

"Hey, sweetie," Mom calls from the kitchen. "Did you see that instructor outside?"

I take another deep breath and say, "Yeah, I spoke to him."

"Good. I'm glad you're home. Dinner will be ready soon, and you need plenty of food to keep your strength up for all this extra training."

"Terrific," I murmur, tilting my head back and closing my eyes. I only need one thing right now, and food isn't it.

I need the tattoo artist.

CHAPTER THIRTEEN

AFTER MOM AND DAD HAVE GONE TO BED, I GET DRESSED and open a doorway. I know exactly what the inside of the tattoo artist's living room looks like, so I focus on that as I walk into the darkness. As light appears, I hurry forward, but I've barely left the faerie paths when I feel myself falling, spinning, twisting. I grasp desperately at the air as my body is flung about by an invisible force and a banshee screech wails in my ears. When my surroundings have finally become a slowly swaying landscape rather than a topsy-turvy jumble, I realize I'm hanging upside down.

"What … what the freak?" I gasp.

The screeching stops, and a voice behind me says, "Well, I'm glad to see my intruder alarm is working." An invisible force swings me the right way up and deposits me on top of the couch. "I should probably thank you for alerting me to the small flaw in my security system," the tattoo artist says. He leans on the back on an armchair and surveys me. The tips of his fingers are smudged with black. Ink? Paint? Charcoal? I can't tell from here. "So, Calla. I'm assuming you've had a change of heart since this afternoon?" he says.

"Actually," I say carefully, "I need your help. The time travel thing … it's happening even when I'm not wearing the bangle."

He closes his eyes and sighs. "I told you not to put it on."

"No. You found me *after* I'd put it on and then asked what was wrong with me. Now there really *is* something wrong with me, and I have no idea how to make it stop."

"And you think I can help you."

"Well, you seemed to know what it was going to do to me."

He nods slowly. "I did."

I wait for him to tell me whether he knows how to fix me or not, but he says nothing. "Okay, how about this," I say. "If you can help me, I'll give you back the bangle." That might not be possible anymore, but he doesn't need to know that. Yet.

The artist raises an eyebrow. "I don't think you're in any position to bargain with me."

"But I have something you want. Isn't that how bargaining works?"

He straightens, walks around the chair, and sits. "How about this," he says. "You give me the bangle, and I agree not to tell the Guild about your Griffin Ability."

"W-what?" I press my fingers into the soft cushion as my insides freeze.

"The Griffin List?" the artist says. "I assume you've heard of it. I also assume you're not on it. If you were, the Guild wouldn't allow you to be one of their guardians."

His words hang in the air between us. Words that threaten to steal away everything I've ever dreamed of having. I take a deep breath and place my hands carefully in my lap. "What's your name?" I ask.

"My name is Chase."

"Well, Chase," I say slowly. "I don't actually have the bangle anymore."

His expression barely changes, but his lips press tighter together. When he speaks, his voice is quieter than before. "Did you return it to the Guild?"

"I did."

He stares at me a moment longer, then drops his head into his hands. He groans and rubs his temples. "You don't know what you've done."

He sounds so despondent that I wonder for the first time if I may, in fact, have made a mistake in returning the bangle to the Guild. "Is ... is something bad going to happen because I did that?"

"Probably." Chase rubs his chin and stares at the waterfall painting on his right. "If he stole it before, he'll steal it again."

"He?" I ask, sitting forward.

"Saber. The man who found us in the tunnel last night. Ever since he began meeting with one of the prisoners at Velazar, he's been hunting down the bangle. I assume it's because he's been told to go back in time and find some important piece of information. And this prisoner ... well, he's extremely dangerous. Whatever information he's after, I'd rather he didn't get it."

I tilt my head to the side, eyeing him with suspicion. "How do you know all this? Are you working for the Guild? The Seelie Court?"

He chuckles quietly and shakes his head. "Guardians aren't the only ones trying to rid the world of evil."

"So you're—what—some kind of vigilante?"

He laughs again, then turns his bright gaze on me. "Do I look like a vigilante?"

"I don't know. I can't say I've met many vigilantes, so I'm not sure what they look like. I do know they act outside the law, though, and should probably be reported to the Guild."

With amusement, Chase says, "You're threatening me? You, the one with the dangerous secret you're trying to keep from the Guild, are threatening to report me, the person who knows your secret." He shakes his head. "You don't have a clue how this bargaining thing works, do you."

"I know exactly how it works," I say as I stand. "I was just hoping you'd want to keep your secret as badly as I want to keep mine." I drop to one knee and write a doorway on the worn rug.

"Hey, wait a minute." Chase jumps to his feet, but I'm already falling through the darkness.

I drop onto the old Guild ruins, then immediately open another doorway and come out closer to the new Guild. Ryn's warned me before that it's possible to be followed through the faerie paths, and I'd rather not have Chase coming after me. I need to think.

I stand amidst a clump of giant mushrooms and bite my lip.

I know what I should do now. I should go to the Guild Council and tell them everything I know. The bangle, the artist vigilante, this guy called Saber and how he's been meeting with someone at Velazar Prison, home to the most dangerous criminals in our world. But if I do that, I'll be sacrificing my future as a guardian. I'll be sacrificing my freedom. Chase will tell them what I can do, and my name will end up on the Griffin List, available for anyone who chooses to look it up. The Guild will keep tabs on me for the rest of my life. They'll track everything I do and everywhere I go. They might even find out about … that *incident*. The one I like to pretend never happened.

No. I have to get that bangle back. Besides, if Chase is right and Saber gets hold of it again because I returned it to the Guild, then I'm actually doing the *right* thing by stealing it back. And, now that I think of it, who am I to judge Chase for working outside the law when I've spent the past few years doing the same thing? The Guild had nothing to do with any of those 'assignments' Zed gave me.

Decision made, I head for the Guild's interior entrance through the faerie paths. Fortunately, my trainee pendant is still around my neck, so I don't have to go home for it. I expect the night guard to question me when I show up in the entrance room, but he doesn't say a thing. I suppose it's normal for trainees to show up at odd hours if they've had late night assignments. And people like Saskia who are obsessed with the rankings probably come here to train in the middle of the night.

I hurry up to the library, hoping this will be as easy as

returning to the spot I left the bangle and picking it up. It isn't, of course. The bangle is gone. "Obviously," I mutter to myself. Life is never that easy. I walk to the front desk. After making sure no one is around, I search, carefully lifting books and scrolls and opening drawers.

I don't find the bangle.

Shoot. It's probably been returned to the artifacts level already. The highly secure artifacts level. Can I come up with an illusion good enough to get myself in and out of there without getting caught? I suppose I'll have to if I—

Hang on. As I walk past the librarian's office, I see something sitting on his desk. Something with clockwork pieces and green jewels. "Yes!" I whisper. I look around once more, but I still don't see anyone here. If the office door is open, does that mean the librarian is around somewhere? Probably not. He can't work all day and all night.

I slip inside and grab the bangle—and hear a thump from the library's front desk.

Of course. Because life is never that easy.

I drop down and crawl behind the desk just as someone walks into the office humming quietly. I peek beneath the desk and see the pink high-heeled shoes of the assistant librarian. She places something heavy on the desk, then moves around the side.

Think, think, think! I let down my mind's defenses and project an image of one of the messenger dwarves knocking on the door. And he says ... Crap, what would a messenger say at this time of night?

"Evening, ma'am," I imagine the dwarf saying. "I just saw a

trainee attempting to vandalize one of the plaques in the Hall of Honor. I couldn't find any other offices open, and since I knew you were here this evening, I thought you could perhaps deal with it."

"Oh, thank you for telling me. That's very strange, but I'll be sure to deal with it."

I make the dwarf move out of the way as the assistant librarian hurries from the office. When I'm sure she's gone, I jump up and leave. I push the bangle into my jacket pocket and take the elevator down to the foyer. A minute later, I'm hanging upside down in Chase's living room with that horrible screeching threatening to deafen me once again.

"Ugh! Get me down from here!" I shout. A moment later, I drop clumsily onto the couch as the noise stops. I scramble into a sitting position and point a finger at him. "You could have stopped your intruder charm from flinging me around a second time."

He shrugs. "Perhaps."

I pull the bangle out of my pocket and slam it down on the coffee table. "There. Now you have no reason to tell the Guild what I can do."

Incredulous, Chase says, "You *touched* it again?"

"I didn't have time to make another plan. Besides, it's already affected me, hasn't it? How much worse can it get? Now tell me what I have to do so you'll help me with this time traveling problem."

He sighs and picks up a paint-stained cloth from a box beside the desk. "You don't have to *do* anything, Calla. Of course I'll help you."

"You—you will?"

"Yes." Using the cloth, he picks up the enchanted bangle. "Despite what you're probably thinking, I'm not the bad guy in this situation."

"But ... you threatened to expose my ability to the Guild."

"I wasn't actually going to follow through on that. I was just trying to get the bangle back. And hoping to stop you from running off to the Guild with crazy stories about me being a vigilante." He removes a small wooden box from a draw and places the bangle inside. "I happen to be strongly opposed to the Griffin List, as it happens. I understand why it exists, of course, but I believe everyone has a right to privacy. I wouldn't want to be responsible for putting anyone's name on that list." He locks the box and holds the key up in front of his face. He blows gently on it, and it disappears. "I probably should have locked it up the first time," he says, looking over at me. "Then you wouldn't be in this mess."

I sit on the arm of the couch and stare at the wooden box. "How does it work? I mean, it seems random—I don't know when it will happen, and I don't know what time it will send me back to—but I assume it's something that can be controlled if I know how."

Chase nods and leans against the edge of the desk. "There is someone who knows how to control this power. Unfortunately, I'm not that person."

My shoulders slump. "Terrific."

"But here's what I do know," he continues. "The magic was supposed to stay inside the bangle and only work when someone wears it, but it turns out it's kind of ... clingy. It likes to stick to people. It seems that spikes in emotion are what trigger the magic to jolt out of this time and into another one. It can only send you back, not forward, and you can't do anything to influence the scene it sends you back to. You can only observe. You can't use any magic when you're back there, and none of your communication devices will work. When you return to the present, you feel sick. The further back you travel, the worse you feel when you return."

"I'm familiar with that delightful side effect," I say with a nod. "I assume you know all this from experience?"

"Yes."

"But you're better now, right? Which means you can help me."

"I can't, but I can take you to someone who can."

"Thank goodness." I stand. "Can we go now?"

"Sorry, I have some other business to deal with tonight." He pushes away from the desk and walks to the door. "Come back tomorrow night."

"Um, okay. No, wait, I have my first assignment tomorrow night."

"Well, the next night then." He opens the door.

I look at the open doorway, then back at him. "I can't wait that long."

"It would appear you don't have a choice."

"But what if it happens while I'm in class? Or in the training center? Or, I don't know, while I'm standing in the middle of the dining hall with half the Guild watching?"

A ripple slides away from me, distorting the room for a moment.

"Crud."

"Stay calm," Chase instructs. He leaps over a small side table and moves toward me.

The vibration intensifies. I throw my hands out as the rushing sound begins.

"Stop!" Chase shouts, grabbing my hand firmly.

Everything stops—and I remain exactly where I am, in the present, in Chase's living room. "How—how did you do that?"

"You can't take anyone with you." He drops my hand. "So I guess it helps if you've got someone strong enough to anchor you in the present." He looks away, then walks back to the door.

Strong enough.

He's strong enough to knock down a shield of magic in one blow, strong enough to block my projections, and strong enough to root me in the present when a magical force wants to tear me away from this timeline. Instinct tells me it's dangerous to get involved with someone with so much more power than the average faerie. But what choice do I have? He's the only one who can help me.

CHAPTER FOURTEEN

I SPEND MY FOURTH DAY AT THE GUILD FOCUSING ON CALM thoughts like gentle streams and snowflakes dusting quiet winter landscapes. I make it through the day without traveling to a different time, but I almost project an image of a sunset on Ned as the two of us walk into the Fish Bowl to fight each other. I watch him frown, blink, then shake his head while I mentally reinforce the barrier around my mind. Ned then proceeds to kick my butt because, as it turns out, he's far better at fighting than he is at talking to people.

After dinner, I return to the Guild to meet Olive so she can give me my first assignment. She doesn't greet me when I enter her office, but I'm quickly becoming used to that. Annoyed With Life seems to be her default setting.

"Sit," she says after I've hovered near her desk for several uncomfortable moments. "I've got things to do, so let's get this over with."

Let's get this over with? Fantastic. That's exactly what I want to hear right before my first assignment as a real trainee. *Calm thoughts, Calla. Calm thoughts.*

"It's a fairly straightforward assignment," Olive says as she scans through the paper in her hand. "Normally I'd be happy for you to handle it on your own, but since I've never observed you in action before, I feel it would be irresponsible of me not to be present. Depending on how you do tonight, I'll decide whether I need to babysit any more of your assignments."

Be calm, be calm, be calm.

"So. We're going to a home in the human realm, and we're expecting a harpy to show up and try to take a four-year-old boy. You should know the assignment rules already, but since your training has been severely lacking, and things have changed since your brother's day, you probably don't."

"I'm aware of the—"

"You can't do anything to the harpy unless she first makes a move against a human. Once she does, you should protect the human first, then restrain her so she can be brought to the Guild. If she gets away, you're unable to do anything else, and your assignment will end once you've laid protective spells around the area. If she fights back and you have no way of resolving the situation without killing her, then you have to do that. There will be an inquiry to determine whether you were justified in killing her. If you were, you'll continue with life as normal. If you weren't, you'll be suspended. And there's counseling, of course." She appears to shudder slightly, probably at the thought of having to counsel me. Hopefully that never has to happen, since I don't plan on killing anyone. "Here's your tracker band." She hands me a narrow strip of leather. "Put it on, and don't take it off until the assignment is over."

"Oh, is it still necessary for me to wear it if you're with me?"

"Yes. All assignments are recorded via a replay device and kept for three years, after which they're disposed of. If there's an inquiry, it will be used for evidence. Didn't anyone record the assignments you did during your summer break crash course?"

"Uh, no. I didn't have a tracker band then."

Olive makes an annoyed *tsk* sound and shakes her head. "How are we supposed to run things properly when people simply disregard policies? This is how things went wrong the first time. This is how the Guild fell."

"Actually, I think the Guild fell because a lunatic named Draven somehow got an explosive device inside the old Creepy Hollow Guild, where most of the Council members, who were *following policies* by meeting to deal with an impending threat, were then killed."

Olive's lips form a tight, straight line, and her jaw tenses.

"At least, that's what my textbook says," I add before she can explode. "Anyway, we should probably get this assignment started."

"We should. And you should keep your smart mouth shut if you're hoping to make it to the end of this year without failing."

I consider adding a 'Yes, ma'am,' but decide to follow the keep-your-smart-mouth-shut advice instead.

We arrive in the kitchen of the house where my assignment

is to take place. Olive walks out of the paths behind me and hovers nearby while I try to pretend she isn't there. The kitchen is empty, but a doorbell rings moments after we arrive, so I leave the room and search for a front door. I walk into a large living area and see a woman letting a teenage girl inside. "Thank you, Lizzie. I know it was short notice," she says. "He's already had dinner, so you don't have to worry about that. He's in the playroom now. You can let him play for another—" she checks her watch "—half hour or so, but then he must go to bed. Anyway, you know the drill." She hurries to the foot of a staircase and shouts, "Simon, we need to go." Then she disappears into another room.

I follow her there and find her hugging a little boy goodbye and reminding him to be good. I assume this is the boy I'm here to protect.

"Come on, Mary, let's go," a male voice calls. The woman hurries away, and Olive walks in behind Lizzie.

"Hey there, Jamie," Lizzie says. She sits on the floor and joins in playing with the cars. I stand with my arms at my sides, waiting for something to happen. In my left hand, I gather magic from my core so I can stun the harpy as soon as she appears and makes her move. My right hand is ready to grasp a weapon if needed. Olive stands in a corner, looking bored.

After a few minutes, Lizzie moves to the couch, finds the TV remote, and flicks through channels while the boy pushes his cars around the floor. Another minute goes by. I step over the various toys scattered across the carpet and peer outside through the blinds. No movement in the garden.

Then I hear the rush of flapping wings.

I spin around. The harpy swoops down toward the boy, her feathered wings beating the air and her great bird talons reaching out for him. Her human-like face is twisted into an angry expression. I throw my stunner magic, but she wrenches her wings out of the way, and the magic strikes the wall behind her, leaving a hole. *Dammit.* I lunge toward her, realizing as I go that there's already a sword in my grip. I'm vaguely aware that Chase was right—*it happens easily when you're not thinking about it*—as I slash at the harpy. She backs off with a screech that sounds unnatural coming from a human mouth. Her black eyes stare hatred at me. Then she dives again.

I raise my weapon to slice at her, but she moves at remarkable speed and wraps her talons around my arm before I can swing the sword. She shakes me vigorously, yanking me off my feet before dropping me back down. I stumble, then duck down as she swoops once more. As she swerves in the small space and comes back for me, I release the sword and throw myself at her. We drop to the floor in a confusion of clawing, flapping, and scratching. Toys are kicked to the side, and the boy is screaming, and Lizzie is screaming, and I just ... can't ... pin her ... down.

"This is none of your damn business!" the harpy screeches as her wings flap heavily around me, almost knocking me out. With a great thrust of her talons, she kicks me off her. I fall onto my back, then roll to the side and jump up. I'm standing against a wall—and the harpy is coming straight at me.

I have nowhere to go.

I whip my hand up. A dagger materializes in my grip,

pointing straight at her. It's too late for her to slow down. She's going to fly right into it. The blade will pierce her heart, and she'll die. This fight will over.

But I can't do it.

At the last second, I move my arm out the way. She crashes into me, flattening me against the wall, squeezing all the air from my lungs, and knocking my head back so hard I feel the crack of pain throughout my entire body. I blink and groan and try to suck in air. The knife is still in my hand, and I slash blindly at her wing. I feel it sinking into flesh and feathers. She shrieks in pain and pulls away from me. Flapping clumsily, she rises to the ceiling. I stagger over to the boy and place myself in front of him. Despite the intense throbbing pain that makes me want to drop to the ground and clutch my head, I raise my eyes and give the harpy a defiant look that says, *You'll have to go through me to get to him.* She flaps some more, her dark eyes sizing me up, then drops toward the whimpering girl on the couch.

"No!" I shout as the harpy grabs Lizzie's arm and yanks her into the air. She plunges past me, aiming for the door along with the screaming girl who can't see any of what's happening. I dive after them and manage to catch Lizzie's ankles. I pull hard, dragging her closer to the ground. With one last furious cry, the harpy lets go and vanishes.

Lizzie and I hit the floor. She's still screaming, and I'm still trying to catch my breath after being flattened against a wall. But no one's dead, and the little boy wasn't taken, so hopefully that means I've managed to earn some—

"Get up," Olive hisses, grabbing my arm and tugging me

away from Lizzie. She kneels beside the girl and holds a small vial to her lips for a moment. Then she moves to the boy and does the same thing. She opens a doorway to the faerie paths and pulls me into it. Seconds later, we appear in the garden. "Don't move," she snaps. She walks to the outer wall of the house, holds her hand against it, and mutters some kind of protection spell. Then she opens another doorway, grips my arm roughly, and pulls me after her. We come out in Creepy Hollow somewhere near the Guild entrance.

"Absolute disaster," Olive says.

"What? But I managed to—"

"Do you know what this costs?" she demands, shoving the tiny vial in my face. I manage to make out the word *Forget* on the label before she snatches it away. "A lot. And I wouldn't have had to use any of it if you had done your job properly."

"Done my—but I did. I stopped the harpy from taking the—"

"What is *wrong* with you? You had the knife pointed at her. She was going to ram herself into it. That would have been it. The end. No need to worry that she'll probably attempt to come back."

"But that would have meant killing her."

"Yes," Olive says, nodding slowly and looking at me as if I'm stupid. "Because she was trying to kill you. You were *defending* yourself."

"That wasn't the only way to end the situation."

"No, but it was better than almost getting yourself killed, having both humans way more involved in the mess than they should have been, *and* letting the harpy get away."

"I didn't want to *kill* her, okay? I just wanted to stop her. I was trying to come up with another way to—"

"Sometimes there is no other way!" Olive shouts. "This is the job you're training for. What did you think was going to happen? That you'd be able to save the world without anyone ever dying?"

Yes. That's exactly what I want, and I shouldn't be ridiculed for it. My voice is quietly defiant as I say, "It should be possible to do that."

"It should be. And in a perfect world, it would be. But we're not in a perfect world." Olive shakes her head. "If you're too scared to kill someone, then you're not cut out for this life."

"I'm not scared, I just don't want to."

"Nobody *wants* to. But the rest of us suck it up and do it if we have to."

"Well," I say quietly, "I happen to believe that's not the only option."

"Then you're going to wind up dead a whole lot sooner than I thought." Without waiting for a response, she turns and walks away through the forest, leaving me wondering if perhaps she's right.

CHAPTER FIFTEEN

"CHECK THIS OUT," PERRY SAYS, SLIDING INTO THE CHAIR across from Gemma and me at breakfast the next morning. He pushes a slim rectangle of amber toward us. "It's epic. Everything in one. Amber on one side, glass on the other. So you've got your mirror calls, social spells, latest news, everything. And a quick X like this—" he draws an X across the screen with his stylus "—and it shrinks to fit easily in your pocket."

Gemma and I watch the device shrink down to about a quarter of its size. "Pretty cool," I say. "I guess this means my amber is no longer the latest thing." I remove my amber from my jacket pocket and place it on the table beside Perry's.

"Ha!" Perry points at it and laughs. "That amber is so last month."

"Moron," Gemma mutters, but she's smiling into her smoothie glass.

"Well, my so-last-month amber serves me just fine." I return it to my pocket while Perry carefully slides his new amber into his bag.

"Are you having breakfast?" Gemma asks him.

"Nah, I ate at home today. Mom made waffles."

"Lucky you," I say. Gemma convinced me to try the health smoothie today, and I can't say I'm impressed.

"Do you have space for half a smoothie?" Gemma pushes her glass toward him. "I also ate something at home, so I'm kinda full now."

"No thanks. You know I'm not into the earthy vibe. Leaves and squirrel poop aren't my thing."

"Oh my goodness, it's not squirrel poop! How many times do I have to tell you that? It's a mixture of various kinds of nuts and—"

"She's so easy to wind up," Perry says to me with a wide grin stretched across his face. "Ow!" He glares at Gemma. "Seriously? Did you just kick me under the table?"

"Really, guys?" Ned places a tray on the table and sits beside Perry. "You're not six years old anymore."

"Well, I know I'm not," Gemma says. "I don't know about Perry."

"Hey, Ned," I say to him, hoping he'll be more relaxed around me after our time in the Fish Bowl yesterday.

"Oh, uh, hi." He meets my gaze briefly before staring intently at his food. I guess he needs a little more time. "Um, Calla, I think there's a note stuck on the back of your jacket,"

Ned adds before shoveling some food into his mouth.

Gemma leans behind me and removes something from my back. "Guild Traitor Family," she reads. "What does that even mean?"

"So stupid," I mutter, taking the paper from her and crumpling it up. "It's referring to my brother's wife." I let out some of my annoyance by attempting to flatten the crumpled paper against the table surface. At the raised eyebrows of my friends, I add, "She was very much in favor of the reptiscillas joining the Guild, and when the petitions were denied, she was one of the first who went along with the plan for them to start their own guardian training program."

"Oh, yeah, I remember when all that was going on," Gemma says. "We were in junior school then. My mom would come home and tell us about all the arguing going on at the Guild. How stupid it was that everyone was so divided over this issue when we'd all fought together so well after the Destruction."

"Yes, so after the Council voted and decided the Guild should support the reptiscilla training institute, some guardians volunteered to go work there instead. You know, help them get their whole system set up and develop training and all that."

"Nothing wrong with that," Perry says as he pokes at the leftover contents of Gemma's smoothie with a spoon.

"Exactly. But there were obviously people at the Guild who weren't happy with that. Vi and everyone else who volunteered were called Guild traitors. It's actually kind of a joke in our family now, but, if you think about it, it's completely unfair. They're trying to make our world a safer place by training

155

more people to protect it, and they get told they're traitors for doing that?"

"Not cool," Ned says quietly, shaking his head.

"Who should we throw it at?" Perry asks, taking the crumpled, flattened paper from me and shaping it into a ball. He looks around. "We could probably reach Blaze from here. Or … oh, your mentor's here this morning, Calla. How about we bounce this off the back of her head?"

"No!" I grab the paper back from him. "She'll use it as a reason to get me suspended. She'd love to see me—"

A shrill siren rings out, cutting off the rest of my words. "Ah, man," Ned says above the noise. "I just started eating."

"What does that mean?" I ask. All around the dining hall, people are tapping their trays and standing up.

"Emergency drill," Gemma says. "They make us practice at least three times a year. We have to report to lesson room four."

"Five," Perry corrects as we join the crowd moving toward the door. "We're in fifth year now, remember?"

"Oh yes."

"Wait, listen." I grab Gemma's arm as I hear a female voice speaking over the siren.

"This is not a drill. This is not a drill. This is not a—"

"Oh crap," Gemma says.

The crowd moves faster as people become aware of the message. Raised voices and fearful expressions surround us as everyone jostles to get out of the dining hall. We eventually make it to lesson room five, where we have to listen to our classmates' theories on what's gone wrong while we wait for a mentor to show up. After about ten minutes, Olive strides in.

"Okay, here's what's going on," she says, crossing her arms. "An enchanted storm has been detected over the Bordeon Mountains not too far from the edge of Creepy Hollow."

Silence greets her statement, then someone murmurs, "Draven?"

"No way," Blaze says. "He's gone."

"There must be other people who can do spells that influence the weather," Ling says. "Draven can't have been the only one."

"Whatever the cause of the storm," Olive says, "it is large enough and close enough to be considered a threat. All trainees are being sent home until further notice."

"Yes!" Perry whispers beside me. "Holiday!"

"Why can't we stay here?" Saskia asks. "What if there's some kind of attack and you need us to help?"

"We won't," Olive says firmly. "The only guardians allowed to fight for the Guild are those who've graduated. Trainees are to be sent home. That's the protocol in this situation."

"Stupid protocol," Saskia mutters.

"Please proceed to the foyer and line up in two straight lines," Olive says. "The faerie paths blocking charm will be lifted from the foyer walls for the next few minutes so we can send you all home as quickly as possible."

Amidst plenty of muttering, everyone starts filing out of the room. I walk over to Olive, trying not to think of my disastrous assignment last night and the unpleasant exchange we had afterwards. "You don't really think Draven is back, do you?"

"It certainly looks like he might be," she says, her sharp eyes pointed over my shoulder as she watches the trainees leaving.

"That isn't possible, though. Draven is dead." I've heard the story first-hand from the person who killed him: Violet.

Olive turns her gaze to me. "Is he? There was no body. And I'm never satisfied unless I see a body."

Well, that's mildly disturbing. "A dead body proves nothing," I tell her. "That can be faked."

Her brow furrows in suspicion, then smoothes as understanding comes to her eyes. "Of course. You've obviously heard Kale Fairdale's story because of your brother."

"His story isn't a secret anymore, is it?" I say, somewhat defensively.

"No. But we didn't spread it around either."

"We?" Was Olive involved in Vi's dad's faked death?

Olive makes her signature you're-wasting-my-time noise. "Those of us who were around when Kale 'died' and then discovered after the Destruction that his death was a ruse. But that has no relevance now. There is no proof that Draven was actually killed, which means it's possible he survived."

"How about the fact that he completely vanished along with the enchanted winter that covered almost the entire fae world. Isn't that proof enough?"

"No. My guess is that he was weakened, and it's taken him this long to regain his former power. Now, you need to join your fellow trainees in the foyer." She points to the door, and I realize I'm the only one left in the room.

I hurry down the corridor toward the foyer. When I get there, I see a number of faerie paths doorways opening and closing as trainees step into them one after the other. A mentor stands at each doorway, ticking names off a scroll. I join Gemma, Perry and Ned.

"Oh, there you are," Gemma says. "Do you want to hang out with us for the rest of the day?"

"Uh, I've got some stuff to do actually." I lean closer to her and say, "You know that tattoo artist I met when I was Underground the other night? Do you know where I can find him during the day?"

"That's the 'stuff' you have to get done?" she says with raised eyebrows. "A tattoo?"

"No, I just need to talk to him about … something."

"Okay, I'm going to try pretend I'm not super curious about whatever's going on with you and the tattoo guy—"

"There's nothing going on."

"—and instead tell you that you can find him Underground at a place called Wickedly Inked."

"Okay, thanks. Have you been there?" Gemma doesn't seem like the tattoo type, but I don't want to offend her by saying so.

"A few times. My brother has a bit of a tattoo addiction, and Chase is his favorite artist. Sometimes I go with when he gets a new one."

I nod as we shuffle forwards in the queue. When it's my turn to walk into the darkened paths, I don't think of my home in Carnelian Valley. Instead, I think of the Underground tunnels and hold the words Wickedly Inked in my mind.

* * *

I walk into Wickedly Inked and find a spiky-haired elf girl sitting behind the counter writing on her amber. After looking around at the many framed artworks hanging on the walls, I walk over and say, "Hi, is Chase here?"

She spends another few moments writing on her amber, then looks up. She takes in my appearance before saying, "You don't have an appointment."

Wow. Friendly girl. "I know that. Is Chase here?"

"Yeah, but he's busy."

"Well, I'll wait then."

"For what? You don't have an appointment."

A flicker of anger burns to life inside me, but I smother it, reminding myself to remain as emotionless as possible if I don't want to find myself flung into the past. "Okay, then I'd like to make an appointment."

"For what time?"

"For whatever time you have available."

"I don't think we have any—"

The door behind the counter opens and a man walks out ahead of Chase. He has the same bald head and slitted eyes as the drakoni club owner, which causes panic to clutch my insides. But he's taller and leaner and can't possibly be the same man.

Be calm, be calm, be calm, I remind myself.

"… all settle down in no time," the drakoni man is saying. "Then we can get back to business as usual."

"Yeah, just keep me updated." Chase shakes the man's hand and says goodbye before looking my way. If he's surprised to see me here, he doesn't show it. "Miss Goldilocks," he says. "Skipping school today?"

"Miss Goldilocks?"

"Yes. A little girl with golden locks who features in a well-known human nursery story you've probably never heard of."

Fantastic. So now I'm a little girl. "Yes, I'm skipping school," I say as I cross my arms. "I decided I'd rather get a tattoo than a guardian education. I was thinking a dragon. A big one. Right across my back."

I was hoping to shock them, but the girl gives me an unimpressed I-don't-think-so look while Chase appears amused.

"Fine. I'm not skipping school. The Guild's freaking out because of an enchanted storm, so they sent us home for the day. I figured I'd come see you now."

"An enchanted storm," the elf girl says, her voice devoid of emotion. "That sounds terrifying. Don't you think that sounds terrifying, Chase?" She isn't looking him, though. She's still looking at me, and I'm about ninety-eight percent sure she's making fun of me.

"Anyway." I turn to Chase. "Is there somewhere we can talk?"

Still looking amused, Chase steps to the side and gestures to the open door behind the counter. Ignoring the girl, I walk past him into a room where the adjustable reclining chair in the center takes up most of the space. A smaller, wheeled chair is pushed against the wall beneath shelves of ink containers, tattoo styluses, and what I assume are other tattoo-related supplies.

"So," Chase says as he closes the door. "Time to get rid of that annoying time travel ability you recently acquired."

"Yes. I mean, if you're not busy right now."

"Not at all. Let me just cancel that appointment with the princess of the Seelie Court, and I'm all yours."

I roll my eyes. "You expect me to believe you have clients in the royal family?"

"Does Unseelie royalty count?" he asks innocently.

I cross my arms. "Is that supposed to intimidate me? Because it doesn't. I happen to have met my own share of Unseelie royalty." And it was intimidating as hell, but he doesn't need to know that.

"Right," Chase says with a laugh. "Of course you have. Anyway, as it happens, my schedule is clear today."

"Great. Let's get going then. Where are we—Wait, what happened to your phoenix?" I ask, suddenly noticing the dark shape on his upper right arm. I'm almost certain I saw a phoenix there the other night, but it looks like the bottom half of a horse now.

"Oh, the phoenix is gone for now," Chase says, lifting his T-shirt sleeve so I can see the rest of the tattoo. "I drew this pegasus a little while ago, and a friend of mine did it yesterday."

"But … I thought tattoos were permanent."

"Not the way humans do them." He pulls his sleeve down and reaches for a black coat. At my questioning gaze, he adds, "Human tattoos obviously involve no magic. They're just ink under the skin. For humans, the ink stays there, but for magical beings, the body's healing magic acts on the ink. The tattoo fades within a few days."

"So if I wanted a permanent tattoo …"

"Your tattoo artist would use enchanted ink." He pulls on his coat. "Make sure to check that before you get your giant dragon done."

I walk over to one of the shelves where a collection of different colored bottles are standing. I lift one. "Is this enchanted ink?"

"Yes."

"Okay, then I've checked."

"Well then," Chase says as he opens a doorway against a bare space of wall. "I'll get my friendly assistant to make you an appointment when we get back."

"Good luck with that."

I take hold of his outstretched hand and walk into the faerie paths with him. As light forms at the other end, an icy wind blows my hair back. We step out onto frost-covered ground. Shivering, I look around. No trees, no bushes, no signs of life. The clouds are puffs of grey and white above us, and spread out before us is a vast lake, its dark surface marred only by the faintest of ripples. In the distance, beyond the water, the ground rises steeply into a snow-capped mountain.

"Where are we?" I ask.

"Far from home."

"Yeah, I guessed that part. The sudden change in seasons was a bit of a giveaway." I rub my hands up and down my arms. My thin summer jacket won't do much for me here.

"You'll be warm once we get inside."

"Inside where?"

He points across the lake toward the mountain peak. "There."

"I see. And you didn't perhaps want to bring us out of the paths a little bit closer?"

"Not possible. Everything from the lake onwards is protected. We'll be flying up there." He brings his fingers to his lips and lets out a piercing whistle.

Seconds tick by, and nothing happens. "Are you sure your whistle worked?" I asked.

"Patience," Chase says. "He's coming."

I follow his gaze and see a grey shape in the air above the lake. It grows larger as it moves toward us. Soon I can make out wings, four limbs, and a tail, but it isn't until the creature swoops down and lands beside Chase that I realize what it is.

Its head is demon-like, with ridged horns curving backward and fangs protruding from its wide mouth. Its muscular limbs end in large, taloned claws. Wrinkles course across its grey, leathery hide, making it appear almost as if the creature is covered in cracked stone.

"That's ... that's a gargoyle," I gasp, stepping hastily backward.

"It is."

"And you want me to *ride* one? Are you crazy? It's illegal enough to *have* one, let alone ride it."

"Mm, illegal? Or just not encouraged?"

"Illegal. Definitely illegal. They're bound to protect the Unseelie Court. They don't answer to anyone else."

"Well, Jarvis answers to me."

"Jarvis? You *named* it?"

The gargoyle lets out a low growl.

"Him," Chase says. "Not it. And yes, I named him. It's a reference to … well, never mind. I doubt you'd get it. Now hurry up and get over here. If we spend any more time in this cold we'll have to waste magic to heat ourselves up."

"No." I take another few steps backward, shaking my head. "No. You know what? This is crazy. This is just … this is too far. I barely know you, I've followed you to who knows where, and now you're trying to get me onto a highly dangerous, illegal creature so you can whisk me off to a distant mountain where I'll probably never be heard from again."

Chase gives me a quizzical look. "What exactly do you think I plan to do with you?"

"I don't know, but—"

A vibration shudders through the ground. Everything blurs as a ripple races away from me. "No, not again," I moan. *Be calm, be calm, be calm.*

A second later, Chase is standing in front of me, his hands gripping my shoulders tightly. "Don't," he says, his voice ringing loudly above the whooshing in my ears. And, just like the other night, the jolt never comes. We stand like that for several moments, frozen in place, until it becomes clear that I'm not going anywhere. Chase's hands slide away from me, leaving my shoulders colder than before. He steps back. "I haven't forced you into anything, Calla. All I'm trying to do is help. You came here of your own free will, remember? And you're welcome to leave right now if that's what you want."

I hug my arms around my middle and frown at my feet. "But then I'll keep finding myself thrown into the past."

"Exactly."

I close my eyes and resign myself to the fact that there's no other way to fix this. "Okay. Let's do this."

CHAPTER SIXTEEN

GARGOYLE RIDING IS A TERRIFYING EXPERIENCE. JARVIS'S wings flap and heave, making for an exceptionally bumpy flight, and I constantly feel as though I'm clinging to the side of something rather than sitting *on* it. Chase hangs onto a harness fixed to the gargoyle's back, and I keep my arms wrapped tightly around him and my head buried behind his back. He complains several times about having trouble breathing, but I don't loosen my grip for a second. I could probably slow my fall if I tumbled off Jarvis, but I'd still have to hit the water at some point, and who knows what could be lurking beneath its dark surface.

After what feels like an excruciatingly long time, Jarvis drops through the air and lands clumsily on a ledge far above the base of the mountain. I let go of Chase and slide off Jarvis's back. My shaky legs almost deposit me flat on my backside, but I manage to remain standing. Chase climbs off the gargoyle and pats its back. "Wasn't that fun?" he asks.

"That was horrible. There's got to be an easier way to get up here. We live in a world of magic, for goodness' sake. Riding on the back of a gargoyle can't be our only option."

"Well, I'm sorry my pegasus and magic carpet were unavailable today. I'll make sure they're around next time. Or perhaps you'd prefer a dragon? You seem to have a certain fondness for those."

"Your sarcasm isn't helping."

"Neither is your brattiness."

My mouth drops open.

"Yeah, you heard me. Now come inside before we both freeze. You can apologize to Jarvis on the journey home."

I try to come up with a snappy response, but part of me recognizes that Chase has a point. He's going out of his way to help me, so I should probably stop complaining about the unorthodox means of transportation.

Chase puts a hand inside his jacket and pulls out a slim square of metal with patterns etched into it. He walks across the ledge and presses the metal against the rock face. When he steps back, an arch-shaped outline glows for a moment before disappearing, leaving an open archway in the side of the mountain. "After you," Chase says.

I walk into an entrance hall with wooden floors and walls painted cream. A clear glass orb containing a collection of glow-bugs is attached to the center of the ceiling, lighting the room. The aroma of a hearty meal hangs in the air. "What exactly is this place?" I ask, turning to look at Chase.

"Uh, a friend of mine lives here," he says as he uses the metal square to close the archway. "This is his home."

"He must be a good friend if he gave you a key to the front door."

Chase smiles and walks past me toward the staircase. "Come. He'll be up here." I follow Chase up the stairs as he calls, "Gaius? It's me."

On the next floor, we walk down a carpeted passage and, after a brief knock on an open door, we enter a study. It's far more chaotic than any I've seen before, and it isn't just because of the books, scrolls and bits of machinery piled everywhere. It's because of the plants. Plants on every surface, spilling out of glass bowls, draped over bookshelves, and twisting around the desk legs. Amidst the chaos is a skinny man with unkempt hair, flipping through the pages of a book as he paces.

"Gaius?" Chase says.

The man looks up. "Chase, dear chap! Well done for finally wrapping up the—" Chase interrupts him with a loud cough, then looks at me. Gaius follows his gaze. "Ah. I see. Well done for the, uh, that tattoo business."

I want to roll my eyes. It's so obvious they're not referring to anything tattoo-related.

"And this is?" Gaius asks, crossing the room with a wide smile. "The young lady with the time traveling problem?"

With an uncertain smile, I say, "That sounds like me."

"Gaius, this is Calla," Chase says. "The Guild girl I mentioned to you. Calla, this is Gaius. He's—well, as you can probably tell—a botanist. He actually worked for a Guild once, about two centuries ago."

"Yes. London Guild." Gaius nods. "I was there for four years before they, uh, restructured my department. Seems they restructured my job too. Gave it to someone else."

"Oh. I'm sorry about that."

"Not to worry. It was a long time ago." He snaps the book shut. "So, young lad. Shall we get this girl fixed up, and then you can both be on your way?"

"Young lad?" I smother a laugh.

"Yes, he's—what?" Gaius turns to Chase. "Thirty-something?"

"Twenty-something."

"*Twenty*-something?" I repeat, turning to Chase. "And here you are calling me 'Miss Goldilocks' as if you're somebody's grandfather."

Gaius chuckles. "I think I'm the only grandfather in this room. Now, let me just clear a space for you to sit." He leaves the book on his desk before moving things off an armchair and piling them on the floor.

"So, Gaius, do you ever leave the mountain?" I ask.

"Well, most of the time I'm happy to stay here—I've got plenty to keep me occupied—but I do leave occasionally."

"And how do you enjoy gargoyle riding?"

"Gargoyle riding?" Gaius laughs as he gathers some papers from the armchair and crumples them up. "No, no, the gargoyle is Chase's. I use the faerie paths."

"Is that so." I cross my arms and turn to Chase, who's regarding me with an innocent expression.

"Yes, well, one of those faerie doors," Gaius continues.

"You know them? Where there's a set destination on each side."

Anger rises inside me as I glare at Chase. "So you made me ride that thing when we could have walked straight out of your tattoo studio and into this mountain?"

"It's not a thing. It's Jarvis."

"Why would you do that?"

"Hmm. For fun?"

"Chase!"

"You're right. It really wasn't that fun." He puts his hand into his back pocket and pulls out a twisted gold key. "Gaius, I may have accidentally melted my key for the faerie door—" he gives me a pointed look "—leaving Jarvis as my only travel option. Could you possibly make me another one?"

It happens quickly this time. The vibrations, the blurring, the shockwave rippling away from me. Fear grips me. I throw my hands out toward him. "Chase—"

But I'm gone.

I'm jolted into a familiar Underground living room. Chase stands nearby, his hands pushed into the pockets of his hoodie, the hood pulled over his head. "What do you think?" he asks. He can't be talking to me, so there must be someone else here. Still breathless and dizzy from the time-travel shock, I take a moment to pause and breathe before looking over my shoulder. A woman stands there, dark-haired and dressed for winter: elegant coat, thick scarf, high-heeled fur boots.

"It isn't really my style," she says, running her gloved fingers through the tassels of the old lampshade, "but it's a vast improvement on the hovel you were living in before."

"I wouldn't quite call that 'living,'" Chase says quietly. He picks up a decorative, lacy cushion from the desk chair. "This isn't exactly my style either, but ... well, it was a gift. I'm grateful."

This is fine, I tell myself. *This is fine. This is fine.* I've landed in the past several times now, and I always manage to get back to the present after a few minutes. I just need to remain calm and wait for—No. Hang on. I'm supposed to remain calm if I *don't* want to time travel. So I need to ... make myself emotional?

"I didn't know you could draw," the woman says, walking to the desk and lifting a sketch from its surface.

"Oh, that's nothing." Chase plucks the paper from her hand and slides it into a drawer. "Just a ... recent hobby."

My mind turns to Zed and his girlfriend. That's usually a pretty upsetting thought. I purposefully imagine him making out with someone else—and find that it doesn't elicit much reaction from me. "Darn," I murmur. It seems I've finally managed to get over the crush I've had for the past two years. And at the most inconvenient time.

"But, darling, it's so good," the woman says to Chase. "Don't hide it away."

Darling? My attention reverts to the scene I'm standing in. I walk closer as the woman snakes her arms around Chase's neck. Something seems different about his face, but I can't figure out what. Perhaps it's the shadow cast by his hood, or the fact that he's most likely younger here than the Chase I know in the present. "Fine, don't show me your pretty pictures," the woman says. "But can I convince you to come with me tonight? We can go dancing like we used to. It'll be fun."

He leans closer to her. For a moment I wonder if he's going to kiss her—a thought that makes my insides squirm with awkwardness—but then his lips stretch into a grim smile. "Sorry," he says. "Not working."

She gives him a quick kiss on the cheek, then steps away from him with a laugh. "It's always worth a try." She sashays across the room to the door and pulls it open. "I need to go. Keep well, darling." She walks out, then looks back over her shoulder. "And ... I'm glad to see you're doing so much better than last time. Try to stay focused on the good things, okay? Everything will be all right."

He nods, and she closes the door. The moment she's gone, he lowers himself onto the desk chair and places his head in his hands. With his shoulders stooped and his face covered, he breathes out a slow, shaky breath. "Nothing will ever be all right," he murmurs.

My heart aches for him. Even from behind this weird green-tinged veil that separates the two of us, I can feel his pain. How could I not? Only the hardest of hearts could fail to empathize with the despair and—

Vibrations and ripples. A whoosh. The jolt slams nausea into me with such force that I almost throw up the moment the plant-filled office reappears. Dizzy, dizzy, spinning. Reeling and swimming and why can't the room keep *still*, dammit?

"Calla?" I feel hands on me.

"Sick ... gonna be sick, gonna be sick." I feel the floor beneath my knees. A bin is thrust in front of me. I grab hold of it as my stomach heaves and loses its contents. I wipe my mouth with the back of my hand, and then there's more spinning and tossing until I'm finally lying down on something.

I close my eyes and wait it out.

When the world has stopped spinning and the nausea is gone, I blink and find myself lying on a four-poster bed.

"Feeling okay?" Chase asks.

"That was so gross," I mumble. "I'm sorry."

"There's a bathing room through there," he says, pointing to a door. "If you want to clean up."

"I do." I'm a little shaky still, but I need to get rid of the awful taste in my mouth.

When I've cleaned my hands, rinsed my mouth, and splashed water on my face, I walk back into the room and sit on the bed.

"I'm sorry," Chase says quietly. He pushes away from the wall and comes to stand by the bed. "That one was my fault. I was ... provoking you. And I should have been able to hold you back, but I didn't reach you in time."

I pull my legs up and wrap my arms around my knees. "I saw you," I tell him. "In the past. In your home."

"What?" His hand tenses around the bedpost. "What did you see?"

"Don't worry, it wasn't anything *inappropriate*. You must have just moved in. There was a woman there. She said the furniture wasn't really her style, and you said it wasn't yours either."

"Oh, that home." Chase sounds relieved, but his grip on the bedpost hasn't changed. "What else did you see?"

"Nothing. That was it." I can't tell him what else I heard, what I saw. It's too personal. He wouldn't like the fact that I witnessed a moment of such despair.

"That was eight or nine years ago. No wonder you felt so sick when you got back." He swings around the bedpost and sits beside me. "When I was experimenting, trying to figure out if I could control this power, I ended up watching the moment my parents met each other. That was almost thirty years ago."

"Wow. That must have made you really sick."

"I was in bed for a full day. The world wouldn't stop moving."

I look up at the sound of footsteps and see Gaius in the doorway. "All better?" he asks. "I'm sure you're ready to get rid of that ability now."

"Definitely." I stand. "So how does this work? Do you have some special plant concoction for me to take?"

"No, no." He waves the idea away as if it's a ridiculous one. "Nothing nearly as complicated as that." He holds his hand out to me. I eye it, then look at Chase.

"Don't worry, he won't bite," Chase says.

"Okaaay." I raise my hand and grasp Gaius's.

He closes his eyes, then opens them a moment later. "Oh. I didn't expect that."

"Expect what?"

"Two Griffin Abilities. One is your own, I assume?"

I snatch my hand away from his as a chill crawls up my spine. "How do you know that?"

"Because, my dear," he says gently, "that is my Griffin Ability. I can sense, absorb, and transfer other abilities."

I look from Gaius to Chase. Chase nods. "So you're also one of the Gifted," I say to Gaius. "Does that mean that the time traveling ability in the bangle once belonged to another Gifted person?"

"It belonged to Saber," Chase says. "The man who's been trying to steal it back."

"But then—"

"I know, I know. What right do we have to take his own ability away from him? Well, after he kept using his power to learn important secrets that ended up getting a lot of people hurt, we decided everyone would be better off if he couldn't visit the past anymore."

"But that isn't your decision to make. The Guild should arrest him."

"They did. They've arrested him twice over the past year. Nothing short of drugging him will contain him."

"So then—"

"Then what? Drug the man for the rest of his life? How is that any better than killing him?"

I place my hands on my hips. "This is the part where I should probably ask how you know all this, but I doubt you'd answer me."

"You doubt correctly," Chase says.

I shake my head and turn back to Gaius. "When you absorb the time traveling ability, will that affect my own ability in any way?"

"No," he says. "I won't touch what's yours."

"Okay." I hold my hand out. "Then please take this time

traveling problem away from me before I wind up in the past again."

He takes my hand and closes his eyes. I feel rather stupid as I stand there, waiting for something to happen, wondering if it will hurt when it does. I find Chase watching me, and I manage to hold his gaze for several moments before looking away. Doesn't he know it's rude to stare?

Gaius releases my hand and says, "All done."

Surprised, I ask, "Are you sure? I didn't feel a thing."

He chuckles. "Yes, I'm sure."

Chase puts his hand into his coat pocket and removes a shape wrapped in cloth. The bronze bangle. "You can put the power back in here," he says to Gaius, handing him the enchanted jewelry. "Then I'll destroy it. I should have done that the first time around instead of experimenting with it." He crosses his arms and looks at me. "It's been on quite a journey since then. Someone was waiting for a tattoo and overheard me talking about it. She stole it after coming in for a second tattoo. The Guild got wind of it after that, which is how it wound up in their artifacts collection. It was there for several months before Saber got hold of it. I stole it from him, and then you stole it from me."

"And now you're going to destroy it."

"Yes."

There's something that doesn't feel entirely right about snuffing out another person's magic. But I have to admit that Chase is right. If this guy is dangerous and the only other option is for the Guild to keep him drugged for the rest of his life, then he's better off without this ability. "Is it straight-forward to destroy this bangle? No long, complicated ritual that will provide the bad guy with plenty of opportunity to steal it back?"

"We don't have to journey to Mount Doom, if that's what you mean."

"Mount Doom?"

"Never mind," he says with a sigh. "Let's go. We can use the faerie door this time. I know how fond you are of Jarvis, but it'll be faster this way."

I follow Chase and Gaius along the corridor and downstairs to the entrance hall. He stops in front of one of the doors, and I notice that it's slightly different from the others leading off this room. The patterns covering its surface are more intricate. Gaius produces a gold key similar to the one Chase handed him earlier—although this one doesn't appear to have been twisted into an odd shape—and unlocks the door. It melts apart and vanishes, leaving darkness beyond. "You can take my key," Gaius says, handing it to Chase. "I'll make another one."

"Thanks." Chase gestures for me to go ahead of him.

"Am I supposed to hold your hand?" I ask. I've never used a faerie door before; I don't know if they work the same way faerie paths do.

"No. This path has only one destination on the other side. It isn't possible for you to end up anywhere else. But," he adds with a smirk, "you can hold my hand, if that's what you want."

I swat his raised hand out of the way and walk ahead of him. I keep walking, through the weightlessness and through the utter darkness pressing against my eyes. A rectangular outline of light appears up ahead of me. I walk toward it—then smack right into a hard surface.

"It's a door, Calla," Chase says. "You have to open it."

"Thanks for the warning," I mutter as I feel for a doorknob. I twist it, push the door open, and walk into the back room of Chase's tattoo studio. Convenient. Clearly Chase visits Gaius quite often. I'd love to ask him what that's all about—if only he'd give me a straight answer.

"Well," I say, turning to him, "thank you for helping me, Chase. I appreciate it."

He inclines his head. "It's been a pleasure meeting both you and your illusion magic." He slides his hand into an inside pocket of his coat and pulls out his amber. He holds it toward me. "In case you need help again."

Right. Because sending him an amber message will be a lot simpler than showing up unannounced inside his home and dangling upside down. I pull my own amber from my pocket, reach forward, and brush it against his. The two rectangular devices glow briefly as their amber IDs connect. Now, when I write a message and think of Chase, the message will show up on his amber. I return mine to my pocket and clear my throat. "I guess I'll be heading home then."

"Okay." He opens a cupboard on the other side of the room and removes a stone urn. He lowers it to the floor with some effort. "You'll be back for your tattoo, of course."

"Of course," I say absently, curiosity distracting me from coming up with a smart reply. Chase lifts the urn lid, and I lean forward so I can see the contents. An orange glow eman-ates from the opening. Taking a step closer, I see flames burning. I feel their heat.

Chase looks up. "I thought you were going home."

"Um, yes." I hesitate before turning away. I place my hand on his arm. "Remember. As long as my secret stays secret, so does yours. I'm just a regular faerie, and you're nothing more than a tattoo artist."

He considers me with bright eyes I wish I could paint. I wonder if I could ever get the color right. The perfect mix of storm grey, palest green, and moonlight. As I watch him, his expression changes. He frowns, his eyes taking me in as if for the first time.

"Is something wrong?" I ask tentatively.

"No," he says slowly. "I just ... remembered something I was told a long time ago." He blinks, shakes his head, then extends his hand toward me. I grasp it. "Agreed," he says.

I walk away from him. I open the door, wondering if I might possibly be brave enough to make a real appointment for a real tattoo. I'm saved from having to make that decision, though, because on the other side of the door, leaning against the counter with a crossbow in one hand, is Saber.

"Ah, you're back," he says. "It's about time."

CHAPTER SEVENTEEN

AFTER A GLANCE AT THE MOTIONLESS ELF LYING ON THE floor, I back up slowly, raising my hands. Shield magic hangs in the air in front of me, but it won't last long if attacked repeatedly with a crossbow. "Chase?" I say as I place one foot behind the other. "Looks like I'm not going home just yet."

Saber crosses the threshold into the room, and I cast a quick glance over my shoulder at Chase. He's standing over the urn with the bangle held in a cloth. "Ah, look who decided to join us for the festivities," he says. "You're just in time, Mr. Saber."

"That's mine," Saber growls. "I want it back."

"You did just fine without it all those months it was at the Guild."

"Things change."

I edge further back until I'm next to Chase. I sense his

shield magic joining mine. "By 'things change,'" Chase says, "do you mean someone at Velazar Prison told you to get it back?"

Sparks fly from Saber's tongue as he speaks. "What I do at Velazar Prison is no business of yours. Now give me the bangle before I shoot your girlfriend through the head."

"Anything to do with that particular prisoner *is* my business, Saber. What information does he want you to find?"

"You won't know until it's too late."

"Then I suppose we have no reason to delay this any longer." Chase drops the bangle into the urn and places the lid on top.

"No!" Saber takes a few steps forward, then stops as the sound of an explosion rips through the still air. The urn rocks, but remains intact. "NO!" Saber raises his crossbow and fires. Again and again, bolts strike our combined shield.

"Now would be a good time to do your thing," Chase says between gritted teeth.

"But I'm pouring all my energy into the shield. I can't—"

"I'll hold the shield. You distract him."

I breathe out slowly, releasing both my shield and the control around my mind. I close my eyes and focus on what I need Saber to see. I imagine a second explosion within the stone urn. This time, it cracks. It shatters. It sends stone and flame and heat flying across the room. When I open my eyes, I see the scene I'm imagining. I feel the searing heat. Saber is on the other side of the room, his arm raised to protect his face against the imaginary burning debris that just flew past him.

Chase kicks the reclining chair across the room, knocking Saber to the ground. The crossbow clatters onto the floor, and Chase forces a gust of wind from his hand strong enough to sweep the weapon out the door. Saber rolls away from the broken chair, jumps to his feet, and runs at Chase. Chase bends and uses the man's momentum to flip him over his shoulder. Saber lands on his side and kicks at Chase, but the tattoo artist leaps out of the way. As Saber scrambles up and flings sparks at his opponent, Chase ducks. Then he jumps and kicks, striking Saber in the chest with his solid combat boot. Saber goes down with a crash, and Chase raises a spinning, crackling ball of magic above his hand and slams it down onto Saber. The green man collapses, his head dropping back to the floor and his limbs going floppy.

The flames, smoke and heat of my projection fade away. "You can fight," is the first thing I say, followed quickly by, "Was that stunner magic?"

Chase nods as he looks down at the knocked-out man.

"How did you draw so much power so quickly? It takes me minutes of concentration to gather enough to stun someone."

Without meeting my eyes, Chase says, "I suppose you need to practice. The more important question, though, is this: What did Saber do with my lovely assistant?"

"Oh no." I jump over Saber and run to the doorway. "I saw her lying here when I opened the door, but ..." I look around the room. "She's gone."

Chase walks to my side. "She must have gone for help."

"Hopefully that means she's—"

I fall backward with a cry as something grabs my arm and pulls. I tumble into darkness. Chase flails at my side, shouting angry words, and the grip on my wrist never loosens.

Until we hit the ground.

I gasp in a breath or two before being able to move. Then I pull my knees up, roll my weight back onto my shoulders, and kick directly up into the air. The force of my kick pulls the rest of my body up. I snap my legs down and land in a squat. I straighten and spin around, attempting to get my bearings. "You can stay down here until he decides what to do with you," Saber snarls. I see him a few feet away, a bright white ball of magic hovering above each hand. I reach for a throwing star, aim for his shoulder, and let it loose. "Personally," he adds as the glittering weapon whizzes over his shoulder and disappears into the faerie paths, "I hope you die a horrible death first."

I hold my hands up as a bow and arrow form in my grasp. I let the arrow go—just as Saber jumps backward into the void. The arrow flies into the narrowing gap as the edges of the doorway grow toward each other. A second later, the doorway and the faerie paths are gone. And so is the light.

"Chase?" I ask tentatively. A groan is my only response. I gather magic into a ball of yellow light and send it into the air above me. Looking around, I find we're in a tunnel. Narrower and lower than I'm comfortable with—*don't panic, don't panic*—and completely bare. On the ground nearby lies Chase. "Crap." I drop to my knees beside him. "What happened? Are you okay? Are you hurt?"

He lifts his hand to the back of his head. "Feels like I cracked my skull open. Doesn't seem like anything's bleeding, though. Must have just dazed me for a bit."

"Let me check." I raise my hands as he sits up, but he brushes them away.

"Don't worry, I'm fine. What happened?"

"Saber brought us here through the faerie paths."

"An impressive stunt for an unconscious man."

"Yes. Apparently there was something wrong with your stunner spell."

"There wasn't." Chase carefully rubs the back of his head. "He must have thrown a shield up at the last moment. That would have absorbed most of the stunner spell."

"Maybe." I stand, reach for his arm, and pull him to his feet.

"So he threw a little tantrum and brought us to another Underground tunnel," Chase says as he looks around. "Seems like a waste of everyone's time."

"Perhaps he's busy trashing your tattoo studio." I slip my stylus out of my boot. "We should probably check on that." I write a doorway spell against the dusty tunnel wall. The words glow and fade—and nothing happens. "That's weird."

"Honestly, do I have to do everything myself?" Chase produces his stylus and writes on the tunnel floor. The result is the same: no doorway.

"You were saying?"

"Damn. This isn't good. I think I know where we are." He pushes his hand through his hair as he stares down the tunnel. "This must be the labyrinth."

My heart rate bumps up a level at the thought of being trapped in a tunnel known as The Labyrinth. "You're right.

That doesn't sound good." *Don't panic. DON'T. PANIC.*

"You haven't heard of it?"

I shake my head.

"It's become something of a legend. They say there are dangerous creatures who roam these passages and enchantments that confuse and muddle the brain, making it even harder to find a way out. It's connected to the Underground tunnels, and, as far as I know, that's the only way out."

"Dangerous creatures, huh?" I squint into the darkness beyond my light and remind myself that I'm trained to fight creatures of all kinds. The thought of facing one down here shouldn't bother me.

"Yes, but I've heard these tunnels were abandoned after the Destruction, so hopefully we won't come across any."

"Okay, so no creatures, but we're still lost in a labyrinth of tunnels." I swallow. "We need to start walking."

"Don't bother." Chase removes his amber from his coat pocket. "We'll never find our way out."

Despite my best efforts to remain calm, my breathing is definitely becoming faster. "Well then, Mr. Optimistic. What do you plan to do?"

"I'm not above asking for help." He writes quickly across the surface of his amber. After putting both amber and stylus away, he looks at me. "I've asked Gaius to send tracking owls to the labyrinth entrance. It shouldn't be too hard for him to call in a favor or two and find out where it is. Once the owls are in the tunnels, they'll easily track us down."

"And they'll be able to find their way back to the entrance?"

"Of course. They're tracking owls."

"Right." I send heat to my hands before running them over my arms a few times. "And until then?"

Chase lowers himself to the ground and leans back against the tunnel wall. "We wait."

Wait. In a confined space. That might run out of air. "If it's all right with you," I say, "I'd prefer to keep moving."

Chase peers up at me. "Uh, okay."

I pick a direction and Chase follows me. My conjured ball of light comes with us. I increase its glow, hoping that by lighting more of the tunnel, the space will feel bigger. It doesn't. What does grow, though, is the silence. I say nothing, Chase says nothing, and soon enough it feels as if it's too late, too obvious, to attempt to begin a conversation. Besides, the thought of the tunnel walls narrowing until they crush us to death is occupying too much of my brain. There isn't space left to come up with anything to say.

Focus on something else.

It's the logical thing to do. After all, you can't stop thinking a thought by telling yourself not to think it. You have to think a different thought instead. Such a simple piece of advice, yet so difficult to execute. The first time I tried it, I was at my third junior school and wanted to go down the blue twisty tunnel slide all the other kids loved so much. I focused on the thought of flying. It worked until I got to one of the bends and stopped moving. I thought I was stuck. I panicked. That was also the day Incident Number Two happened. It wasn't—

"Calla." Chase puts a hand out and stops me. I look up and, in the moment before it disappears, I see a playground scene with a shattered blue slide and children running away in terror. Then it's gone, leaving nothing but the empty tunnel ahead of us.

"Ugh, I'm sorry. That was me." I rub my temples while mentally reinforcing my mind's brick wall. "I'm not sure how that image slipped out. Maybe I'm not being as careful as I usually am because you already know what I can do." I drop my hands to my sides. "But how did you see that? I thought you could shield your mind from me."

"I can," he says as we begin walking again, "but I haven't since you returned the bangle to me. I wasn't expecting any more mental attacks from you. What I have been wondering, though, is how you've managed to keep your ability a secret from the Guild all this time."

"Probably because I've only been there one week."

"What?" He leans away as he examines me. "It's possible I could be wrong, but you don't look like a thirteen-year-old first-year trainee."

"I'm not. Thanks for noticing." I explain my lifelong desperation to be a guardian, Mom's determination to keep me away from the Guild, how it all blew up when she discovered I'd been training behind her back, and then her sudden, strange change of heart. Which reminds me that I need to ask Ryn if he's discovered anything else about the person named Tamaria. I file the thought away for later. "Yeah, so after proving to the Guild that my skills were up to scratch, they let me begin in fifth year instead of starting at the bottom."

"And why, Miss Goldilocks, do you want to be a guardian so badly?"

Ignoring the nickname, I say, "I want to help people. I want to fight the bad guys and rid the world of evil. All that honorable stuff."

"You know you can do all that without being a guardian, right? You don't need guardian weapons. You don't even need magic."

"I know, but that's the way *I* want to do it."

"Fair enough. So if you've only just joined the Guild, what school were you at before?"

With a humorless laugh, I say, "Where should I start?"

Chase eyes me. "That many, huh?"

I pull a loose thread off my jacket and slowly twist it around my finger. "That's what happens when you have an overactive imagination and keep accidentally sharing it with everyone else." I unwind the thread, then wind it again, tighter this time. "I left my first junior school because I projected an image of a troll in a tutu after the two girls I was with decided a dancing troll would be the funniest thing ever. I left my second junior school because I imagined a boy's hair was on fire after he pushed me into a door, and three people saw the imaginary fire. At my third junior school, all the kids on the playground saw an exploding slide. It was the twisting tunnel type, and I got stuck inside it and freaked out. In my head I kept wishing I was strong enough to break my way out. I guess I ended up projecting an illusion of me smashing the slide apart and climbing out. That was the, uh, projection you saw back there." I wave awkwardly over my shoulder.

What the hell are you doing, Calla?

I don't know. I don't know why I'm telling him everything.

No. That isn't true. I do know the reason. I'm telling Chase

189

everything because he's the only person it's safe to tell. I've had to keep quiet my whole life, but I've finally found someone I don't have to be quiet around. He already knows what I can do, and he won't tell the Guild.

"I got through my fourth junior school without any *incidents*, as my mother calls them. I wanted to join the Guild, but Mom said no. She suggested a healer school, so, like a good girl, I agreed. There was a boy in my class who'd heard about all the schools I'd left. He'd heard the rumors about how I was ... abnormal. Even dangerous. He made sure everyone knew what a freak I was. Soon after I started there, I'd had enough of his taunting. He just wouldn't stop. On day ten, he arrived at school on one of those winged bicycles just as I got there. He swooped right by me, knocked me over, and shouted out, 'Score! Ben: one, Freak: zero.' So I let the wall down and showed him exactly what I wanted him to see: He was inside a maze being chased by a harpy. She'd already eaten the wings off his bicycle so he couldn't fly away. He had to keep riding or she'd eat him too."

Chase snorts, then covers it with a cough. "It, uh, sounds like he got what he deserved."

"Yes. As it happens, that's exactly what everyone said about me when I was asked to leave."

Chase's smirk vanishes. "I'm sorry, Calla."

I shrug and drop the loose thread. I've wound it so many times around my left forefinger that the skin is covered in fine lines. "That's life, right?" I say, trying to keep my voice light. "Everyone has difficulties they have to deal with. My difficulty just happens to be one I'm not supposed to tell anyone about."

Chase nods slowly, not looking at me. "So then Mom suggested I become a chef," I tell him. "I wasn't too excited about that idea, but the Guild still wasn't an option, so I said okay. I was there for two months, and then …"

And then …

No. Don't think of it. Just keep pretending that one didn't happen.

"Wait, why did we take this tunnel?" I ask. I vaguely remember turning left at a fork just now, and I've suddenly noticed how low the ceiling has become.

"No particular reason," Chase says. "It doesn't matter which way we go. I thought we were just walking because you can't sit still."

"I can sit still. Just not … here. Let's go back and take the other tunnel."

"What's wrong with this one?"

"It, um, smells weird."

Chase gives me a bemused look, but says nothing.

"Uh, so then I decided I wasn't interested in cooking or baking. Mom still wouldn't let me anywhere near the Guild, and the only other thing I could think of was art. So I joined Ellinhart Academy of the Arts. Visual, literary and performing arts. I picked visual."

Chase stops walking. "You're an artist too?"

"Yes. Well, sort of. Not in the same league as you."

"So when you broke into my house, you actually were admiring my art?"

"Yes." Then I add, "Along with looking for something to steal for a stupid initiation thing."

An amused smile turns his lips up. "Of all the villains I thought might find a way into my home one day, an art-appreciating, guardian trainee thief is the one I least expected."

I tuck my hair behind my ears and smile at him. "Glad I could keep your life interesting."

We begin walking again, and he asks, "Did you enjoy Ellinhart?"

"It was ... okay. Just like with the healer school and the chef school, I didn't entirely want to be there. But I enjoyed drawing and painting, so I decided if I couldn't have my first choice, then I'd have to make the art thing work. The rumors followed me there, of course, but I managed to make a few friends. They said they weren't the kind to pay any attention to rumors. In the end, though, everyone listens to rumors. How can they not when they've all seen things around me that can't be explained."

And with that, the story of all my schools and incidents comes to an end. In the silence that follows, our footsteps sound overly loud. I swing my arms at my sides, suddenly feeling insanely awkward that I've spilled all this information to someone I barely know. "Anyway," I continue, "that's me. What's your story?"

Instead of answering me, Chase says, "I'm amazed the Guild didn't hear about any of your ... what did you call them? Incidents?"

I nod. The tunnel makes a hairpin bend to the left, and we continue following it. "My parents always explained things away somehow. Or, as I've recently discovered, they bribed people to keep quiet."

"Bribes? That's always an interesting conversation to have with one's parents."

"Oh, they don't know that I know. It's something I overheard my dad saying during one of my time traveling trips. I'm not sure my mom even knows. He might have kept it from her too."

"Well, everyone has their secrets."

I nod slowly, chewing on my lip as I consider Dad and his secrets. I wonder if he has others. Maybe he doesn't simply take care of the business side of the private security company he works for. Maybe he's actually one of their bodyguards.

"Can you hear that?" Chase says, stopping suddenly.

I halt my steps and listen. "Trickling water?"

"Sounds like it."

"Maybe we should turn back. I would normally assume that a trickle of water is harmless, but that's probably not the case down here."

"Probably not."

We turn around and walk in the opposite direction. I push my hands into my jacket pockets to keep from swinging them around or plucking more threads from my clothing. "So," I say, "now that I've spilled all my childhood dramas, why don't you spill yours?"

"My childhood didn't have any drama."

"Come on. Everyone's childhood has some kind of drama in it, even if it's just your parents refusing to buy you that toy everyone else has or that kid who calls you unicorn poop."

He looks at me. "Someone called you unicorn poop?"

"The Destruction!" I say. "If that doesn't qualify as drama, I don't know what does. Where were you when that happened?"

He looks away. "At home. At least, it wasn't exactly my *home* but it's where I lived back then."

"Wait. Listen." Instead of getting quieter the further we move away from it, the sound of trickling water is getting louder.

"How strange," Chase says after a pause. He starts walking again, and I hurry to catch up to him. We reach the hairpin bend and keep going. Around the other side, we find the source of the noise.

Water, sparkling as if every drop contains a different colored gem, runs in tiny streams from the center of the tunnel ceiling, down both sides, and meets in the center of the tunnel floor, where I assume it seeps into the ground.

"This definitely wasn't here a minute ago," Chase says.

"I'm aware of that. I was walking right next to you." It's beautiful, though, this rainbow colored water. I move a step or two closer to examine it. Perhaps if I splashed every color paint I have onto a canvas and left it in the rain, I'd achieve a similar effect. And for the twinkling sparkles where the water catches the light, I'd capture sunlight and sprinkle droplets of it onto the canvas. I'd need a charm to keep the paint and sunlight moving, to mimic the effect of—

"Are you kidding me?" Chase grabs my arm and pulls me back. "Don't they teach you at guardian school not to go around touching random stuff? You could get yourself killed."

I pull my arm out of his grasp. "I wasn't going to touch it." But I realize that my hand was raised, and it seems I was standing far closer to the water than I thought.

"Oh really?" he asks. "Is that what you told yourself before you picked up a stranger's enchanted jewelry and *put it on*?"

I cross my arms, keeping my hands pinned beneath them so they can't betray me again. "Yes, that was my mistake. But this …" I nod toward the water. "This is something else. Let's keep going the other way."

We turn back—and the hairpin bend is gone. Instead, the tunnel stretches straight ahead and the ground appears to be covered in moss.

"Now I'm freaked out," I whisper.

Chase says nothing. He looks over his shoulder, then forward again. "Someone or something is messing with us." He slips a hand inside his coat and produces a knife with a curved blade. "Whoever it is, they'd better hope we don't run into them."

Fear tingles at my fingertips. "I thought you said these tunnels were abandoned."

"I did. It would appear I was wrong, though. This labyrinth is definitely in use again."

"Fabulous." I wrap my hand around the air and think of my dagger. It appears in my grasp a moment later. "Well, my friendly mentor keeps telling me to practice, and there's no time like the present, right? So. Shall we brave the water or the moss?"

"Neither." Chase raises his free hand, squeezes it into a fist, then opens it. A single flame burns above his palm. He leans forward and blows the flame toward the mossy side of the tunnel. Fire streaks through the air and lands on the moss. It ignites immediately, growing quickly into a blaze of light and heat. As the roaring of flames rises to a level that threatens to deafen us, Chase raises his arm as if to shield his face. The temperature drops immediately, as does the noise, and I know he's placed a shield between us and the fire.

The inferno explodes, sending flames rolling toward us with alarming speed. I jump back with a yelp, but the flames slam against Chase's invisible shield and go no further. Then, as if the explosion is happening in reverse, the flames are sucked backward in one quick rush. A moment later, they're gone, leaving no evidence of moss, flames or smoke. The tunnel is completely bare.

Chase lowers his arm. "Okay. The way's clear. Let's go."

I hurry after him, never letting go of my dagger or the strand of concentration that keeps my ball of light glowing above us. "That was an impressive fire."

"Thank you. I've acquired a number of useful pyro spells over the years."

"I see. Tattoo art must be a dangerous business."

His eyes remain trained ahead, but I see the hint of a smile on his lips. I shake my head and smile to myself. I wonder if I'll ever find out what he really does. Probably not, since I doubt I'll see him again after we get out of here. Well, unless I get a tattoo. Or several. Mom would hate that. She wouldn't be too keen on me spending time with someone like Chase, either. The thought makes me pleased. Or perhaps it's the thought of not saying goodbye to Chase just yet.

"You're doing it again," he says without breaking his stride.

I raise my eyes and see the image that just played through my mind: the moment Chase shook my hand in his tattoo studio. That moment before I opened the door and found Saber there.

"Dammit," I mutter as the image vanishes. The tunnel curves sharply to the left. We keep walking, and I smack my fist against my forehead a few times, as if that could help keep the projections inside. "Sorry."

"Why? You didn't do anything wrong."

"I did. I'm supposed to have this perfectly under control, and now I'm slipping up. That can't ever happen at the Guild, which means I need to make sure it doesn't happen in private either. I—" A vibration shudders through the ground and up into my feet. My first thought is that I'm about to be whisked into the past, but then the ground trembles again, and again, like the heavy footfalls of a giant. "What now?" I murmur.

"Now," Chase says, turning to face the sound, "it's time to play."

The shuddering footsteps grow louder and closer. Part of me wants to run, but the rest of me feels the shot of anticipatory excitement that always brings life to my veins in the moments before I'm about to face a foe. I let go of my dagger and feel for my bow and arrow instead. Arrows first, then throwing stars, then blades. That's my plan.

The footsteps reach the curve in the tunnel, my hands tense around my weapon, and into my line of vision steps an enormous beast. A ferocious bull-like head sits atop an upright muscled body. Its legs end in large hooves, and in one clawed hand it holds a double headed battle axe.

"Minotaur," I whisper, half in horror and half in awe.

The minotaur opens his mouth to reveal sharpened teeth.

He lets out a deep, gravelly laugh I swear I can feel vibrating in my own chest. His glowing eyes settle on Chase and, in earthy, rumbling tones, he says, "So. We meet again."

Wait, what? Meet again?

I tear my eyes from the minotaur long enough to glance at Chase. For the first time since I met him, he looks afraid. Which means I should be afraid too. I train my eyes on the minotaur once more, aiming my arrow at his chest and swallowing against the dryness in my throat. Olive's words are a whispered memory inside my head: *You're going to wind up dead a whole lot sooner than I thought.*

From the corner of my eye, I see Chase backing away. "What are you doing?" I whisper. "We can take this guy down. With my illusions and your strength, we can—"

"No," he says. "We run."

"But—"

"RUN!"

I release my weapons. Chase pushes me ahead of him. We hurtle along the tunnel with the minotaur's angry cries and pounding footsteps following us. The tunnel splits and twists and straightens once more. My heart pumps adrenaline through my body. Fear lends me speed. We run and run and run and still the minotaur is behind us. We run and run and run—

And then we fall.

I didn't see it coming. I didn't see the abyss until we ran right off the edge. And now we're falling, falling, falling, flailing limbs and screaming, darkness all around, and a pale blue light far below.

"Slow yourself!" Chase yells.

I know I'm supposed to be able to do that. Send magic out, push against the ground, slow myself to a halt. And I'm trying, but I can't see the ground, and I can't direct my magic because it's whipped away as air streams past us, and all I know is that I'm *plummeting to my death*.

A hand catches hold of mine. Chase tugs me closer, pulling me into an embrace. We spin through the air together as a whirlwind surrounds us, slowing us. Slowing, slowing, slowing—

And then we strike the ground.

CHAPTER EIGHTEEN

THE SMELL OF SAND AND WATER FILL MY NOSE. A HARD, uneven surface presses against my back. I'm aware that I've been asleep, but I don't know for how long. A low groan escapes me as I stretch my limbs and try to remember where I was before I fell asleep.

The labyrinth.

The minotaur.

The fall.

Adrenaline shoots through me, aiding my efforts to pull myself to the surface of consciousness. I blink. After focusing in the dim blue light, my eyes manage to make out a rock wall somewhere above and behind me. With a great effort, I sit up. The action causes my head to throb, and I raise my hand to the source of the pain. I feel something wet on the back of my head. I pull my hands away and find a dark substance on my fingers. Blood. I feel my head again but can't find an open wound. It's obviously had time to heal since we hit the ground.

We.

Chase.

I look down and find him beside me. "Chase?" He doesn't respond. I can barely see anything in the pale light, so I gather magic into a ball of warm light above my palm and leave it hovering near Chase. With tentative fingers, I examine him. An alarming amount of blood is pooled beneath his head, but when I tilt it to the side, I find only a surface wound. Thank goodness for our superior healing abilities. If we were lesser magical beings, that fall would definitely have ended us.

I rest my hand on his arm as I look around. We're at the bottom of a gorge with rocky walls rising steeply around us. A few paces away, a shallow stream runs past us, tripping over and around sharp-edged rocks. The source of the pale light is somewhere on the right. I wonder if it's a way out. If I follow the stream, I'll find out, but I don't want to leave Chase in his current state. Some creature might appear and drag him off to its lair.

I return my attention to him as his arm twitches. He breathes in deeply, then lets out a long groan.

"Are you okay?" I ask.

"You landed on top of me," he mumbles, his eyes still closed.

"I did?"

"I think I broke every bone in my body."

"I think you may be exaggerating. But I am sorry. I wasn't

planning to land on you. And thank you. For slowing us both down."

He peels one eyelid open. "Clearly not enough."

"Well, enough to keep us from splattering across the rocks down here."

He opens the other eyelid and frowns at me. "Not the nicest image, Calla."

"Sorry."

He moves as if to push himself up into a sitting position, then collapses back with a groan. "Damn ribs," he says between shallow breaths. "Say what you will about exaggerations, but I'm pretty sure I fractured a few of those."

"Well, keep still until they finish healing." I return my hand to his arm so I can push him down if need be.

"How long have I been out for?" he asks.

"I don't know. I just woke up. Hopefully not more than a few hours." I remove my amber from my jacket and touch the screen, realizing belatedly that I've now put blood all over it. My heart sinks when I see the time. "Ugh. Twenty-two minutes to five. We're not likely to be home in the next twenty-two minutes, are we?"

"Why, what happens at five o'clock? Got a hot date?"

"No, that's when my mom gets home from work. The Guild would have notified her about sending all trainees home early today, so she'll expect to see me there."

"So tell her you're with a friend. That isn't a lie."

"Oh, we're friends now?"

"Yes. I think it's a nicer label than 'that thief who broke into my house.'"

"True." I find my stylus, which is fortunately still intact, and write a message to my mother telling her I'm hanging out with a new friend and will be back later tonight. "Okay," I say as I put the amber away. "That buys us another few hours. Now we've got until 11 pm. If I'm not home by then, my mother will go into full on panic mode at precisely one minute past eleven."

Chase attempts to laugh, but his face crumples into a grimace of pain. When he's recovered, he says, "You have a curfew?"

"Shut up. Of course I have a curfew. And I'm sure it wasn't that long ago that you had a curfew too."

He tilts his head away from me and closes his eyes. "Feels like a lifetime ago."

I watch his chest rising and falling as he breathes through his pain. "Do you need some healing magic?" I ask eventually.

He opens his eyes just a crack. "I thought you only lasted ten days at healer school."

"Yes, but my guardian training this summer included a crash course in basic healing magic."

His eyes slide shut. "Forgive me if I don't find that entirely reassuring."

"Why not? It's simple stuff. Just transferring magic through your skin to aid your body's own healing process."

"Don't worry about it. My body's pretty good with healing itself. I'll be fine in a few minutes."

"Are you sure?"

"Yes. And if this is your way of asking if you can rip my

shirt open and feel my chest, you're not exactly being subtle about it."

After a split second hesitation, I say, "Yes. That's exactly what I'm asking. Can I start now?"

His eyes widen. His lips part, but no sound comes out.

"What?" I ask. "You can dish out comments designed to make others feel awkward, but you can't take them?"

"I'm ... just ... surprised."

"Because you were hoping I'd wind up spluttering defensively about how I have no interest in touching your bare chest?"

"I was just joking."

I lean closer and say, "So was I." It wasn't my first reaction, but in that split second before responding, I decided not to be the stuttering, embarrassed school girl. My face didn't seem to get the message, though, and I'm glad there isn't enough light down here for Chase to see the heat in my cheeks.

He lifts his arm and places his hand over mine. "I like you, Calla. If I had to fall into another chasm with someone, I think I might choose you."

Aware that he's most likely making fun of me again, I place my other hand over his and say, "Well, now, that is just the sweetest thing anyone has ever said to me."

He laughs, which is a good indication that he's almost fully healed. I laugh too, although it isn't quite genuine, because of all the things that have ever been said to me, it probably is one of the nicest. And that's kind of a sad thought.

The sound of falling rocks brings our laughter to a sudden end. I extinguish my ball of light and look further down the gorge. In the dim light, I see a skinny shape moving upstream, splashing as it goes, kicking rocks here and there.

"Here we go again," Chase mutters as he sits up. He peers through the semi-darkness. "At least it isn't a towering mino-taur. Whatever it is, we should be able to get rid of it easily."

"Perhaps it doesn't mean us any harm. It looks quite preoccupied with its own business."

"You," Chase says, "are so naive. Everything here is harmful. It probably wants to strangle us and eat our brains for dinner."

"How graphic," I comment. "And cynical."

"I have reason to be." He moves to stand up, but I put my hand on his arm.

"Don't. Let me project a simple illusion. The creature won't even know we're here."

Chase relaxes and nods. "Sounds sensible."

I'm tired from my body's efforts to heal itself, so a simple illusion is all I've got energy for. Thankfully, in this situation, it's all that's needed. I imagine the area we're sitting on and the rock behind us. I picture the scene as it would be if we weren't here. I hold the image in my mind as the creature passes us. It's about half my height and appears lizard-like, walking on its hind legs instead of crawling. It makes an odd humming sound as it splashes through the water. It keeps moving, and Chase and I remain silent until we can no longer see it.

"Look at that, Mr. Cynic," I say to him, nudging his arm. "Off it goes on its own merry way."

"That doesn't prove it isn't harmful, Miss Naiveté. It might still have eaten us if it knew we were here."

"Miss Naiveté?" I shake my head and stare down at my lap. "I'm not nearly as naive as you think I am. I just like to assume someone is innocent until they prove to be otherwise."

"And almost everyone *does* prove to be otherwise." Chase tilts his head down, trying to meet my gaze. "Don't you know what the world is like?"

I lock down the barriers of my mind as images of a dungeon filled with hanging cages and wailing prisoners surface from the depths of my memory. "I know exactly what the world is like," I say quietly. "I know the evil that exists. I know the terrible things people do to each other. I've lived it. I've *survived* it. But just because I've seen the palette of dark colors doesn't mean I have to paint the rest of my world that way. I can choose the bright colors instead. I can see them, paint them, draw them, surround myself with them like a loud, glorious song drowning out all the darkness in the world." I look up at him. "You know?"

He shakes his head. "No. I don't know. But I wish I did."

His words make no sense to me. "But … you do. I've seen your paintings. They're life and light and joy. You can't possibly create masterpieces like that and tell me you know nothing of the beauty in the world."

"That isn't what I mean. What I mean is …" He rubs a hand across his brow. "There is too much darkness, and no matter how much life and light and joy I paint, I can never drown it out."

The way he sounds—so somber, so despondent—reminds me of the Chase I saw when I traveled back in time. The Chase who said nothing would ever be all right again. "Why do you—"

"We should get moving," Chase says, standing suddenly. "I feel fine now. Told you my body was great at healing itself."

"Uh, okay." I climb to my feet as Chase examines his amber.

"Damn, I should have checked this earlier. Gaius released the owls into the labyrinth two hours ago. An hour ago he sent another message saying the owls returned with nothing."

"That's weird."

"It is. Those owls have never failed me before."

"Perhaps we fell too far down for them to detect us."

"Or perhaps," Chase says, "we're not inside the labyrinth anymore." He pulls out his stylus and writes a doorway spell against the rock wall. The surface melts away to reveal a doorway into the faerie paths.

"Yes!" I clap my hands.

"We can stop by your home first," Chase says, grasping my wrist loosely as we walk into the darkness. "That way your mother has no reason to panic."

"No, we need to check your tattoo studio, remember? Besides, Mom thinks I'm out until later. I don't need to get back immediately."

"Okay. But if she somehow missed your message and *is* expecting you, don't blame me."

"Yeah, yeah."

We walk out of the faerie paths into the back room of Wickedly Inked to find it in the same state we left it in: not much damage aside from the broken chair. Saber obviously didn't come back here after dumping us in the labyrinth. In the bright light, I'm far more aware of the blood dried on my hands and streaked across my clothing. I touch the back of my head and feel strands of hair crusted together.

"You look terrible," Chase says.

"Thanks. You don't look so great yourself." The back of his head, neck and coat are covered in half-dried blood.

He leans against a counter and gestures toward me. "Are you planning to go home looking like that?"

"You know, that kinda sounds like the reverse of what my mother says when I want to go out wearing something she doesn't approve of."

He smiles at his feet. "Sorry, I just don't want you getting in trouble. If I had ever arrived home looking like that, my parents wouldn't have let me out the house again."

"Yeah, you're right. This definitely qualifies for panic mode in my mother's eyes."

Chase slides his hands into his coat pockets. "You can clean up at my place if you want."

"Thanks. I think I'll take you up on that offer." My only other option is Ryn's house, and, while Ryn wouldn't panic like Mom, he would definitely ask questions.

"Great." Chase pulls out his amber. "Let me just tell Gaius we're both fine. Then we can go."

* * *

I soak in the pool in Chase's bathing room while my dirty clothes, laid out flat on the grass-enchanted floor beside me, are slowly cleaned and dried by a laundry spell. It isn't a spell I'm particularly proficient at, since Mom's the one who does most of the laundry at home, but I think it'll remove most of the blood I somehow managed to wipe all over my clothing.

"Stop hogging the pool," Chase calls from outside the door, startling me. "You're not the only one who needs to clean up."

"Sorry!" I shout. "Almost done."

He uses the bathing room when I'm finished, and I discover more of his paintings and sketches while he's busy. He has a small home—living room, kitchen, bedroom, bathing room— and every room is filled with his work. I'm sitting at the desk in the living room examining a rough sketch of a minotaur— which I assume he did while I was in the pool—when he walks into the room.

"Oh, you're still here. I thought you might have gone home by now."

I stand. "It would be rude to leave without saying goodbye, wouldn't it?"

"I suppose it would."

"Well, anyway, thanks again. For—well, for a number of things now." Like earlier, I shake his hand.

"Happy to help," he says with a shrug. "If you need my assistance with anything in the future …"

"I'll know where to find you," I say with a smile. I realize our hands are still clasped, and I step away before the moment becomes awkward. I check the barrier around my mind so I don't project anything embarrassing, like the unsettling wish that I could hug him goodbye instead of simply shaking hands. Then I open a doorway and send myself home.

There's still a smile on my lips as I walk out of the faerie paths and into the kitchen at home. A smile that vanishes the moment I see the upturned table and smashed dinner plates. For a frozen moment, I stand there, my eyes darting around as fear and adrenaline course through me. I grab a throwing star in one hand and a knife in the other.

I step silently over the debris. The kitchen door is half open. In the visible slice of living room, I see ripped cushions, dark soil spilling from a fallen flowerpot—and a slender arm stretched out across the floor.

"Mom!"

I abandon all efforts at stealth and rush into the living room. Amidst the wreckage of overturned furniture and shattered belongings, lying motionless and silent, are my parents.

CHAPTER NINETEEN

CHAOS.

"Of course they're connected! Why would two unrelated criminals attack the same household in the space of a month?"

"She's still breathing, but I can't wake her up."

"Maroon, yes. And a scar on his left cheek. See if anyone knows anything Underground."

Ryn is arguing with several guardians while three healers kneel on the floor attending to Mom and Dad. Violet has her arm around me as she speaks quietly into a mirror to one of her reptiscillan contacts.

I wish they'd all shut up. I wish they'd let me near my parents. I wish I could *do* something. Instead I'm sitting on the edge of an upside-down couch as that image—that image I will *never be rid of*—torments me: Mom and Dad lying with limbs bent at uncomfortable angles, a knife within Dad's limp grasp, the stuffing from a cushion forming a puffy halo above Mom's head, and a small glass bottle lying between them.

"Excuse me." I blink and find one of the healers standing in front of me. She looks over her shoulder and adds, "Mr. Larkenwood?"

Ryn abandons his argument and hurries to my side. "Yes? What did you find? Will they be okay?"

"Your father appears to have been stunned. He should be awake and fine within a few hours. Your mother ..." The healer turns her gaze to me. "We can't find anything wrong with her, but we can't wake her. She needs to be taken to a healing institute so—"

"There's a healing wing attached to the Guild in Creepy Hollow," Ryn says. "Can you take her there?"

"Certainly.

"And my father as well, in case he requires further healing when he wakes."

The healer woman nods before returning to Mom and Dad.

"Cal, you can stay with us tonight," Ryn says.

I nod numbly. Ryn steps away, but I catch his arm. "What if ... what if she doesn't get better?" Guilt fills me as all the negative words I've ever applied to my mother rise to the surface of my mind—crazy, weak, overprotective, silly, narrow-minded. What if I never get to say anything nice to her ever again? What if I can never tell her how much I actually love her?

Ryn turns back and catches my hand in his. His gaze is determined, unblinking. "She will be."

* * *

I sit on Ryn and Vi's couch with a blanket over my knees and a sketch pad on my lap. I doodle absently as my mind wanders from random thought to random thought. It was so warm only a few days ago, but now a slight chill in the air attests to autumn's arrival. *Summer doesn't last forever*, I tell myself as my pencil scratches an image of a sun falling from the sky. I wonder if the enchanted storm is over. Everyone at the Guild was so worried about it. Swirling clouds, thrashing rain, a sky painted in shades of anger. Ryn hasn't said a word about it, so I assume it isn't a real threat. Black droplets of rain along the edge of my page morph into a vine of thorns. I forgot to ask Chase if that was a permanent tattoo or if it will disappear like the pegasus on his other arm. What is he doing right now? He needn't have worried about me getting in trouble with my mother. I might never be in trouble with her again—

Stop. Don't think like that. She's going to be—

Mom.

Lying on the floor.

Her chest barely moving.

I push the sketch pad aside and stand up. The blanket falls to the floor, but I ignore it. I pace the living room, because I can't think of anything else to do. I've tried to distract my mind over and over, and it never lasts for long. Ryn and Vi are in the kitchen, discussing who knows what. They have each other, and I have no one. No friends to call. No one who knows me well enough to care about this. No one I want to sit and talk to.

Well, except perhaps for—

A loud knocking interrupts my pacing. Ryn strides into the living room a moment later. He opens a section of the wall, and in walks my father. I run into his arms, and he hugs me tightly. "What happened, Dad?" I ask when I step back. "Was it the same guy as before? Is Mom going to be okay? Do they know what's wrong with her yet?"

"It was the same man," Dad says. He moves further into the room but doesn't sit down. "I don't understand how he got in. That home is protected by every defense I could get access to. I fought him off for a while—told Mom to run—but then he stunned me. I wasn't aware of anything else until the moment I woke up."

"And Mom? Do the healers know anything more?"

Dad crosses his arms. "Those geniuses can tell me only one thing: she's sleeping."

Vi makes a frustrated sound. "That isn't very helpful."

"The bottle," I say, remembering suddenly. "There was an empty glass bottle on the floor near Mom. A small one, like the ones she puts her sleeping potions in."

Furrows form across Dad's brow. "Why would the man drug her to sleep? That doesn't make sense."

"No," Ryn says. "It would make more sense if she drugged herself."

"If she wanted to hide information," Vi adds.

"What information could Mom possibly need to hide?" I ask. "She's a librarian at a healer school. It isn't exactly a top-secret organization."

"I don't care what the reason is," Dad says. "I care that someone is threatening my family. I'm going to find this man and make sure he's locked up where he can't threaten anyone else ever again." He places a hand on my shoulder. "Cal, you need to stay here for … I don't know. A little while."

"Where are you going?" I ask in disbelief. "You can't just take off on your own mission. You don't work for the Guild anymore."

"No, but I have a friend who does."

"My dad," Vi says quietly. "So you're going to finally talk to him, then?"

"I suppose I'll have to if I need his help." Dad was good friends with Vi's father Kale for many years. After Draven's reign ended and he discovered that Kale's death had been an elaborate trick, he was furious. The two of them don't speak anymore, so Dad must be desperate if he's willing to ask Kale for help.

"You are aware that he works at the Seelie Court, aren't you?" Ryn says. "He won't know anything about this."

"Probably not, but he has more connections than anyone else I know. He'll be able to point me to someone who can help."

"Dad, this isn't the right way to go about—"

"I know what I'm doing, Ryn." Dad hugs me briefly, then turns to leave.

"Wait." Ryn's voice is loud enough to stop Dad in his tracks. I watch my brother as he appears to debate his next words before finally saying, "You need to tell Calla."

When no one moves or makes a sound, I say, "Tell me what?" Apprehension stirs up a sick feeling in my stomach. "Dad?"

Dad's shoulders stoop slightly. Ryn walks to his side and says, "No one paid much attention to this case when it was just a break-in. I'm the only one who followed up on the info Calla gave us. But now that there's been an assault and you've confirmed it was the same man who broke in before, they'll look up all records of the name Tamaria. They'll find what I found, and it won't be long before Calla knows."

"Knows what?" I demand. "Dad? Tell me what Ryn's talking about."

Dad turns slowly and says, "It isn't my secret to share."

"Then who's secret is it?" When he doesn't answer, I shift my gaze to Ryn. "Can you please tell me what's going on?"

With a final look at Dad, Ryn crosses the room and sits on the edge of an armchair. "After the scarred man broke into your home several weeks ago, I looked up every Tamaria I could find a record of at the Guild. One was a mentor more than a century ago, one was a Fish Bowl setting designer, and one was a Seer. She trained at the Estra Guild a few decades ago. And guess who was in her class."

"No way."

"Your mother."

I shake my head. "That isn't possible. If my mother were a Seer, I'd know."

"Your mother is a Seer, Calla," Dad says. He leans against the back of the couch. "She was born with the Seeing ability. She's always hated it. She went to the Guild because that is what good, law-abiding Seers are supposed to do: use their abilities to help the rest of fae kind. She was nearing the end of her first year when she had a ... major vision. Something terrible. Something the Guild tried to force her to tell them about. She was traumatized by it and by whatever the Guild did to try and get her to talk. She left and hasn't set foot inside a Guild since."

"Okaaay," I say, slowly lowering myself onto a seat.

"She has visions almost every day, while she's awake and while she's sleeping. She takes strong sleeping potions every night so she won't remember the visions when she wakes, and during the day ... well, you've seen the way she turns. Instead of embracing the visions, letting them pull her in, she's found that if she physically turns away from them, she can resist them."

The crazy circles Mom does sometimes. She's stopping a *vision* every time that happens? "I don't understand," I say. "Why is this a secret? Why don't I know this about her?"

"Because she doesn't like this side of herself. She'd rather people didn't know about it."

"People? I'm her *daughter*! This is an integral part of who she is. How could she keep it from me?"

"Calla, you really don't need to be this upset," Dad says in the kind of patronizing tone he used to use when I was little. "It isn't a big deal that she's a Seer."

"No. It isn't." My right hand tightens around the nearest scatter cushion. "It's a big deal that you've both been lying to me: Mom has sleeping problems; Mom only ever went to Hellenway Business School; no one in Mom's family has ever had anything to do with the Guild. *All of that is a lie.*"

"Calla—"

"How would you feel if you only found out *now* that I can project illusions into people's minds? How would you feel knowing that I kept a major part of who I am a secret from you for all these years?"

Dad pushes away from the couch, shaking his head. "That isn't the same thing."

I stand up, clutching the small cushion tightly to my chest. "Of course it's the same thing!"

"I didn't want you to have to lie about something else!" Dad shouts. "You already have to keep your own ability a secret. Isn't that enough responsibility?"

"But ... being a Seer isn't a bad thing. Why would I have to keep it a secret?"

"Being a Seer isn't bad. But when a Seer breaks the contract she signed by refusing to reveal a vision that she's been specifically trained to see and then flees with her family so the Guild can never find her—that is a bad thing."

"She ... what?" My disbelieving voice is little more than a whisper. "You're telling me Mom is a Guild fugitive?"

"Essentially, yes. It's one of the reasons I left the Guild. It's the reason she wouldn't hear of you joining the guardian training program for so long. She doesn't trust anyone who works there, and she never wants her family to have anything to do with them again. So the fact that she decided you'd be safer there than anywhere else must mean there's something she's *very* afraid of."

"She—that's—I can't believe you never told me any of this."

"We decided you were too young to keep this a secret—"

"Too young? How long have I kept my Griffin Ability a secret, Dad? My entire life!"

"—and *then* we decided there was no point in bringing it up at all. Mom doesn't like to talk about it, so …"

"So basically you were never going to tell me. That sounds like a *brilliant* plan, Dad. What did you think would happen when the Guild finds out?"

"They were never going to find out—until some lunatic showed up and brought her past to light."

Dread coats my veins with ice. I look at Ryn. "Do they know already?"

"No. Like I said to Dad, the guardians who were assigned this case had far more important things to deal with than following up on a break-in, but now that there's been an attack and someone is unconscious, the case will be bumped up. They'll find out who your mother is within a day or two. They'll certainly know by Monday."

"And then what?" I squeeze the cushion tighter as I start to feel sick.

"Well they can't do anything as long as your mother's asleep. I'm not sure what the protocol will be once she wakes up. I'll need to speak to the Seer representative on the Council."

"And me? They won't believe that I didn't know about this. They'll think I kept this from them."

"You don't know what they'll think," Dad says.

"I know they won't want someone they can't trust working for them. And my position at the Guild is already precarious with so many people thinking I shouldn't have been allowed in. They'll probably ..." My voice wobbles as I consider the consequences once the Council finds out who my mother is. "They'll probably ask me to leave."

No, no, please, this is everything *I've always wanted.*

"Stop being so self-centered, Calla," Dad snaps. "Your mother is in an enchanted sleep after being attacked, and all you're thinking of is yourself and your own future?"

"*I'm* the one who's being self-centered? If everything you've told me is true, then Mom is the one who's self-centered. And a coward. Her visions could be used to save thousands of people over the course of her lifetime, and instead she drugs herself so she doesn't have to see them. And yes, it's *her choice* to do that, but don't tell me it isn't a selfish one."

Dad strides across the room and stops right in front of me. "Don't you dare speak about your mother that way," he says, his voice thick with emotion. "You have no idea what she's been through with this supposed *gift* of hers—"

"What about what *I've* been through?" I demand, hot tears coalescing along my lower eyelids. "Living for years with a desperate fear of my own magic. My private thoughts splashed across other people's minds. All the teasing and the meanness and the lies to cover up what I've done. *I didn't want any of that either!* So don't tell me I have no idea what Mom's been through. I UNDERSTAND. I know what it's like when you just want to be normal, but it'll never be an option." Heavy drops spill their way down my cheeks, and I hate that I can't control the wobble in my voice. "But I'm not the one who's hiding from what I can do. I'm the one who wants to *help* people, and if I can use my illusions to do that, then I will."

"It was her choice not to tell you, Calla, and she had every right to—"

"*Why?*" I wail. "Why did she choose that? Why did she choose to lie when this is the one thing that could have brought us closer together and helped me to understand her—"

"Stop it," Ryn says, loud enough to cut me off. "Both of you. This isn't helping."

"It certainly isn't," Dad says, looking angrier than I've seen him in a long time. "Not when the man who attacked my family is still out there. So thank you, Oryn, for your impeccable timing. Perhaps you'll think twice next time before deciding when to reveal private information that has nothing to do with you." Dad scribbles onto the wall and storms out of the resulting doorway. The wall seals up, and I fling my cushion furiously at it. It drops to the floor with a barely audible and highly unsatisfying thump.

I press my fists against my eyes, as if I could force the tears back. Without looking up, I ask, "How long have you known?"

Ryn is silent for several moments, which is how I know I'm not going to like his answer. "For about a month."

"A month?" I look up, blinking away my tears so I can see him more clearly. "You've known about this for a month and you didn't say anything?"

Vi steps closer. "Calla, we—"

"You knew too and you didn't say a word."

"You were doing all that training and studying," Vi says.

"We didn't want to—"

"I don't care!" I shout. "I don't ... I just ..."

I don't want to be here.

I don't want to be mature.

I don't want to *understand*.

I want to be angry and not have to feel guilty about it. Mom lied. Dad lied. Ryn and Vi found out, and they didn't say anything until they had to. Don't I get to be *angry* about any of that?

Not after what you've done. Hypocrite.

I beat the insidious voice down where I don't have to listen to it. "I'm leaving," I announce. I stride across the room, grab my jacket from a hook on the wall, and push my arms into the sleeves.

"Calla," Ryn says. "This isn't the best time for—"

"Goodbye."

A doorway melts into existence in front of me, and I step through it.

PART III

CHAPTER TWENTY

I WALK OUT OF THE FAERIE PATHS INTO CHASE'S HOME—
and nothing happens. No screeching alarm, no tumbling
through the air, no dangling upside down. It's late, but the
tasseled lamp in the corner is on, and I can hear movement
coming from his bedroom. I decide immediately that this was a
mistake. He won't want to see me. He's probably glad he got
rid of me after the time traveling mess was over. My stylus is
still in my hand, so I look around for the nearest surface on
which to write a doorway spell.

"Calla?" I look toward the bedroom. Chase walks out,
securing a harness around his torso. Diagonal strips of leather
house two knives on each side his chest. A belt of smaller
weapons is slung around his waist. "I realized someone was
here," he says, "but I didn't expect it to be you."

I take in his appearance. "On your way out?"

"Yes, I have some … business to attend to. But it can wait a little longer."

"Business? Are you telling me someone is in urgent need of a tattoo? In the middle of the night? And you need to arm yourself with knives and various other bladed weapons in order to take care of it?"

"No." Chase pulls the final strap tight. "I wasn't planning to tell you anything. I'd rather not lie."

A humorless laugh escapes me. "Well, that makes one person in my life."

He crosses the room and stops in front of me. "Bitter cynicism. I thought that was my role."

I shake my head and stare past him. "I guess Miss Naiveté has left the building."

"What happened?"

I step backward and lower myself onto the edge of the couch. Chase sits beside me. "I got home earlier and found … I saw …" I stand suddenly. "I'm sorry. I don't know what I'm doing here." I back away from the couch. "We barely know each other, and you shouldn't have to listen to my silly problems. You've got things to do, and you're probably thinking, 'Why won't this girl just *leave*—'"

"Calla." He catches my hand and pulls me back. "You stole from me, you fought me, you rode a gargoyle with me, you traveled into my past, we got lost in a labyrinth, we fell into an abyss, you know I'm not just a tattoo artist, and I know you're hiding a Griffin Ability from the Guild. I'd say we've gone beyond the barely-know-you stage."

"I … I guess." I return slowly to the couch. I realize my hand is still in his, so I slide it out and wrap it tightly around my other hand in my lap. Then I tell Chase what I found when I returned home hours ago. I tell him of the secret my brother revealed about my mother. The secret everyone in the Guild will soon know. By the time I'm telling him all the things Dad and I shouted at each other, I'm blinking back tears once more. "I know I'm being selfish. I know I'm being childish. But I just want to be *angry.*"

Chase leans forward on his knees. "Anger isn't childish. It's a natural response to discovering information you feel you should have been told sooner. And you can tell yourself you shouldn't be feeling it, but if that's what you feel, that's what you feel."

I bury my head in my hands. "That isn't what I feel, though. All I feel is guilt."

"Why?"

"Because," I whisper, "I have a secret too. Everyone thinks they know me, but they don't. They don't know what I've done." Unable to sit any longer, I push myself up. I pace in irregular patterns around and between the furniture. "You know the dark things in the world?" I say, because now that I've started, I can't stop. I have to keep going. I have to *say this out loud.* "The dark things we were talking about earlier? The things we do our best to drown out?" I stop pacing and stare at his feet, not wanting to meet his eyes as I whisper, "I think I'm one of those dark things."

"What?" Chase lets out an uncomfortable laugh. "That makes no sense at all, Calla. You're the one who chooses the bright colors in life. There's nothing about you that's dark or evil."

I force myself to sit. "But there is. I … I did something terrible." I pull my knees up and start rocking back and forth. "Really terrible. This is my secret. My true secret. Worse than being born with a Griffin Ability. Because if the Guild knew about it, they wouldn't just put me on a list. They'd lock me up for good."

Chase rests a hand on my shoulder. "Whatever it is, it can't be as terrible as the things I've done."

I hesitate, knowing I can still turn back. I can leave without saying another word. I can keep my secret until the day I die. But I don't want to carry it for that long. I don't want to carry it another minute. "At the chef school I attended briefly," I say, "there was a boy in the year above me who … who killed himself. No one ever knew that I was there when it happened. No one ever suspected me. No one ever found out that—" I take in the shuddering breath I've been waiting years to breathe and finally, *finally* release it "—I was the one who made him do it." I plunge ahead, my words coming easily now that I've confessed the worst part. "He was moody and manipulative. Friendly and flattering one day, then nasty the next, telling me I was only born beautiful so I could lure people close enough to make them go crazy. He always apologized when he was having a good day, but he'd go right back to being vindictive when his mood changed. I stayed away from him whenever possible, and when it wasn't possible, I ignored him, no matter his mood.

"One day he showed up in Woodsinger Grove, where I used to live. I was out getting some exercise, and I came across him near my home on my way back. He surprised me and pulled me into the faerie paths. We came out on top of the school. It wasn't a hidden place like the Guilds. It was out in the open, a grand building with many floors. There was a flat section of roof where people—couples—used to go so they could be alone without teachers stumbling upon them.

"I knew what he planned to do with me the moment we got there. After he struck me down and stood on my arm so I couldn't squirm away, he told me he didn't believe any of that nonsense about me having powerful dark magic. If I did, I'd easily be able to stop what was about to happen. 'And you know what's about to happen, don't you,' he said to me as he began unbuttoning his clothes.

"I hated him then. I hated him like I've never hated anyone before or since. And in that moment, I remembered a girl warning me to say away from him. With fear, she'd said, 'You don't want to be the object of his attention.' I realized he'd done this before, and he would probably do it again. And that hatred inside me boiled into a deep desire to hurt him. To stop him. For good.

"I imagined a great black serpent slithering past me across the rooftop. It backed the boy into a corner until he had nowhere to go but up onto the wall that enclosed the area. He searched in desperation for an escape, and that's when I showed him a bridge. A bridge from the wall leading into the nearby treetops. He didn't question it. He stepped onto it— and he fell.

"He was a faerie, but it was high, and the ground was solid, and his head was injured beyond anything his body could hope to heal, and I looked down and *I didn't care*. Later I tried to wash the blackness from my soul, the horrifying guilt at having ended a life, but it's a stain I'll never be rid of. It's always there, at the core of my being, along with that dark voice that whispers, 'He got what he deserved.'" I look at Chase for the first time since beginning my confession. "So I am one of the dark things in the world," I tell him, "because deep down inside me, there's something that craves death and darkness. And no matter what my mentor says about all guardians having to kill at some stage, *I won't do that*. I refuse to give in to that side of me. If I do, I'm afraid it will consume me, and everything I wish so desperately to be—a strong protector, a good person—will be gone."

"Calla," Chase says, covering both my hands with his. "I wish I could explain to you how wrong you are. Trust me on this: I have seen the dark things of the world, and you are not one of them. The very fact that you long to protect and save others—even your enemies—shows that you aren't evil."

"But I *killed* that boy! And it wasn't just self-defense. I could have projected something different. I could have got away without killing him. But I *wanted* him to die. That says there's something evil inside me."

"And later you were overcome by immense guilt. That says you have a *conscience*."

"But … that doesn't change the fact that I killed him."

"No. It doesn't." He shifts closer to me, peering more intently into my eyes. "Calla, this is part of life. Sometimes people do terrible things that, later on, they wish they had never done. But no amount of remorse can change the past.

Believe me, I am horribly aware of that fact. The only thing you have control over now is your future. If you want to protect people, then do that. If you want to saves lives without ever killing an enemy, then do that too. I know from experience that it's a whole lot more challenging to go about it that way, but I can also tell you it's possible."

I blink through my tears at him, realizing this is the closest he's come to telling me what he really does during his non-tattoo hours. I look down at our joined hands and bite my lip. I'm partly horrified that I just shared my greatest secret with someone, but mainly I'm immensely relieved. I thought Chase would be shocked to hear what I've done, but it seems he understands better than I expected. "If I asked," I say carefully, "would you tell me what it is you're so remorseful about?"

I look up and find him giving me a wry smile. "You wouldn't like me nearly as much if you knew."

Mustering my own smile, I say, "What makes you think I like you now?"

"You're here, aren't you? I imagine you'd have gone somewhere else if you didn't like me."

I nod slowly, then keep my eyes on his as I ask, "Is it ... something to do with what you said earlier? About there being too much darkness to drown it all out?"

Chase's smile fades, but his eyes never leave mine as he says, "Yes. It is." He looks away then and lifts his hands off mine. "And I hope you'll forgive me for saying nothing more than that. The past is ... well, it's the past."

"That's fine," I say, rubbing my hands along the tops of my legs. "Rather say nothing than lie, right?"

"Right." He raises his hand toward his coat hanging over the back of the desk chair and curls his fingers in a come-here motion. His amber slides out of an inside pocket and flies through the air. He reads a message quickly, then stands. "I'm so sorry, but I can't stay any longer. I need to be somewhere."

"Oh, that's completely understandable. It's not as though I—"

"You can stay, though," he adds hurriedly as I stand. "I mean, if you don't want to go home. Nothing improper, just … you hanging out here if you don't have anywhere else to go right now." He frowns. "That sounded a lot less awkward inside my head."

I laugh and wipe away the last of the moisture beneath my eyes. "Thank you. I think I will. Just for a bit."

"Okay."

"Oh, your horrible alarm didn't go off when I arrived. Did you deactivate it?"

"I was playing around with some modifications." Chase slides his coat on, concealing the weapons secured to his body. "I'll cast the charm again when I'm outside. You won't need to worry about any surprise visitors showing up."

"Is that something that happens often?"

"No, actually, you were the first." He regards me with a thoughtful expression. "And you were of the pleasant variety rather than the kill-him-now variety."

"I see." My skin warms at the thought that he considers my abrupt arrival in his life 'pleasant,' but I doubt he means anything by it. "Acquired a few enemies over the years, have you?"

"A few." He pockets his amber and stylus and heads for the door. "Which you can probably figure out means 'a lot.'"

He heads out with a final goodbye, and I return my backside to the couch. After staring sleepily at the paintings for a while—I can't decide if the leaves in the forest scene are actually moving, or if it's my imagination—I look at my amber and find a message from a few minutes ago.

I know you're Underground. Don't worry, I'm not coming to get you. I know you're angry. I understand why. Just tell me you're okay (otherwise I will have to come and find you). V

Darn my family and their annoying Griffin Abilities. I can't hide anywhere without Violet finding me. Puffing out a frustrated breath, I write two words: *I'm fine.*

After a jaw-achingly wide yawn, I get up and search the room for a blanket. I find one in the wardrobe beside the door and wrap it around myself before returning to the couch. I'm exhausted from the labyrinth ordeal, anxiety over the attack on Mom and Dad, and the emotional upheaval since then. I'll just rest here for a bit before returning to Ryn's house.

I snuggle against the cushions, letting my mind wander back over my confrontation with Dad. With my mind relaxed, flashes of the scene play out against the backdrop of Chase's living room. Dad getting in my face, Ryn trying to stop the two of us fighting, me throwing a cushion at the wall.

A Seer. Mom is a *Seer*. The sleeping potions and the weird turning in circles and the dazed looks and her paranoia about

233

the Guild. Everything makes sense now, but my brain still has trouble reconciling this new information with the picture I already have of my mother. The woman I've always thought of as delicate and, well, weak actually has magic powerful enough to show her the future.

And she planned on never telling me.

Why? And why did she run from the Guild? Why couldn't she just tell them what she saw, go through the process of officially ending her training, and live a free life?

I wonder what she saw that traumatized her so much.

Of course! My sleepy eyelids pop open as I realize something. This must be the information the scarred man is after. He wants to know what Mom saw in her vision all those years ago. But how would he know about it in the first place? Tamaria. He must have heard it from her. She was in Mom's class, so she must know something about what Mom Saw. But not enough, obviously, or the scarred man wouldn't have come after Mom.

My mind keeps cycling through possibilities and theories as my body grows closer to sleep. The last clear thought I have before drifting into unconsciousness is what Dad said before we began yelling at one another: *She doesn't trust anyone who works at the Guild, and she never wants her family to have anything to do with them again. The fact that she decided you'd be safer there than anywhere else must mean there's something she's very afraid of.*

CHAPTER
TWENTY-ONE

"HOW ABOUT THAT ONE?" I POINT TO THE HALF-FINISHED sketch of a wing that might belong to a phoenix.

"No, I think that's more feathery than the look she's going for," Chase says. "I've got this one, which is based on sprite and sylph wings, very long and wispy. That one over there has just a bit of a feathery influence, so she might be open to it. And this one ... well, it's a bit different."

We're sitting on Chase's living room floor with some of the furniture pushed aside so there's space for the sketches we've spread out around us. Despite my intention to return to Ryn's house last night, I never woke up from my brief rest—which turned out to be not so brief, as I discovered when Chase woke me some time this morning. I was highly confused for at least five seconds before I remembered where I was and why.

Now, after ten minutes in the bathing room, I'm helping Chase decide which drawings to present to his most high-maintenance client, who decided she wants a pair of wings tattooed across her shoulders—and she wants it done now. "Oh, I really like that one." I point to the sketch in Chase's hand. "It looks like ink is dripping off the ends of the wings. Definitely show her that one." I look around and add, "These are all incredible, though. I wish I'd been born with your kind of skill."

With a short laugh, Chase says, "Sometimes I wish I'd been born with this skill too."

"What do you mean?"

He runs a hand through his hair as he surveys the drawings spread across the floor. "This isn't something I've always been able to do. It was a gift. From … a friend. She was the real artist. Before she died, she gave me this skill."

I try to remember if I've heard of anything like that before, but my brain comes up with nothing. "I didn't know that was possible."

"I didn't either, but apparently it is. She was an elf. Maybe it's a type of magic we don't know about."

"Maybe," I say. "So … stick figures one day, fine art the next?"

"Something like that. I never had the desire to draw or paint anything when I was younger. Not even stick figures. I certainly wasn't the creative type."

"I doodled on everything," I say, smiling as I picture the myriad ink drawings covering every school notebook I've ever owned. Well, except for my most recent ones. I've barely had any time for daydreams and doodles amidst my efforts to catch up—and then keep up—with all my guardian studies. "Hey, have you ever used fire paint?"

"No, I've only ever used regular paint. None of that fancy stuff with flames or sparkles or water or smoke or ... whatever else you get."

"They had the fancy stuff at Ellinhart, but it's expensive so we only got to use it once. The fire paint was definitely the most exciting painting experience I've ever had. I mean, you're painting with flames. Just imagine it."

"I am. I'm imagining a charred canvas."

"No! You'd think that would happen, but it doesn't. It's incredible. The flames continue burning wherever you place your brush, as if the paint is made of burning magma. I ended up with burns all over my hand and Mom freaked out about it, but it was so worth it."

"Perhaps I should try it."

"You should. And the water one as well. It's beautiful."

"Okay then."

I smile back at him and hold his gaze for a moment too long. Feeling suddenly awkward, I look down and search for something else to say. "So, um, I know you're talented, but you didn't draw all of these this morning, did you?"

"No, most of these are old," Chase says as he gathers the drawings into two separate piles. "I only had time to do three more based on my client's vague brief after I got back this morning."

"This morning? You mean you haven't slept yet?"

"Who needs sleep?"

"Um … me?" I say in a small voice.

He smiles. "I do sleep, just not much. Which is fortunate, since my non-tattoo work takes up many of my nighttime hours."

"Seriously?" I say to him. "Your *non-tattoo work*? Just come out and admit what it is you really do. You know I know."

"I will admit to nothing," he says with a superior grin. "And you don't know nearly as much as you think you do." He stands and carries both piles of drawings to the desk. "Okay, I need to get to work, and you need to do what people do when they have a family member in a hospital." He gives me a pointed look.

"Hospital? That sounds a whole lot like a word humans use to describe their healing institutes."

"You should visit her."

"Does that mean you've spent a lot of time in the human realm?"

"It means I've decided it's quicker to say 'hospital' than 'healing institute.' And don't think I haven't noticed you're doing your best to avoid the subject."

I release an overly dramatic groan and say, "Firstly, what point is there in visiting someone who's asleep and can't hear a thing I say? Secondly, I'm still angry with her and my dad, and, as childish as it sounds, I'm not ready to let go of that anger yet. And thirdly, why do you even care if I visit my mother?"

"Firstly—" Chase ticks off one finger "—it doesn't matter if she can't hear you. Secondly, visiting her doesn't mean you have to stop being angry. And thirdly … what kind of a question is that? I'm not a stranger, and I'm not a heartless

238

monster, so of course I care."

"Um … okay." I instruct myself not to dwell on the part where he said he cares—*he would care about anyone in this situation, Calla. You're no one special*—and focus instead on points number one and two. "I suppose I could think about the possibility of visiting her."

"That sounds like a start." Chase rolls up the chosen artwork and opens a doorway near his desk. "Ladies first," he says.

"Right." I need to go to Ryn's now, where he'll probably want to know where I've been all night—and I doubt he'll settle for the vague answer Vi will already have given him: Underground. His protective tendencies were sweet when I was little, but I'm getting over it now. He needs to realize I'm no longer a child.

"Oh, before you go, I wanted to ask you something." Chase rubs the back of his neck and hesitates, his mouth half open as if he's about to speak. "Actually, don't worry about it."

He seems awkward suddenly, and I wonder if … maybe … *No, don't be ridiculous, Calla. The cool, tattooed vigilante faerie does* not *feel that way about you.* "Well, now I'm curious," I say as sprite wings flutter in my stomach. *No. You are not curious. Didn't you learn your lesson with Zed?*

"I was going to suggest something," Chase says, "but …"

"You were going to suggest what?" I ask before the logical side of my brain can take over and stop me.

"I'm fascinated by your Griffin Ability and the opportunities it presents. I'd love to work with you, but with your loyalties strictly aligned with the Guild and their way of doing things, and me being … *not* with the Guild, it probably wouldn't work out so well."

"Oh, right, yes. That's probably not a good idea." Which makes it so confusing that my first thought was actually, *That would be so much fun!* It would be fun, but I have a feeling Chase operates outside the law, and that would be a problem for me. I step through the doorway Chase has been holding open with his foot and turn around. "Thank you for listening last night. And for letting me stay." Then I walk into the darkness, try to put those intense storm-green eyes out of my mind, and think of the forest near Ryn's home.

* * *

I walk through the trees for a while before heading back to Ryn's. When I get there, Violet is out, so I have to face Ryn on my own. I tell him I spent the night with a friend. He says, "A friend who lives Underground?" I don't answer, and, with what looks like extreme difficulty, he leaves it at that. Vi probably told him to give me a break. Hopefully she reminded him that when they were my age, they were running around doing whatever the heck they pleased. He then offers to take me to the Creepy Hollow Guild's healing wing to see Mom and speak to the healers. After deciding that Chase might be right after all, I say yes.

The healing wing smells odd, like the substance Mom pours on the kitchen floor at home before reciting the cleaning spell. It's stronger, though, and mixed with the underlying sweet scent of poppinies, the flowers used to make an exceptionally strong painkiller. I rub my nose as I follow a healer into a long room and walk between two rows of beds. Some of the beds are hidden by floating curtains pulled closed around them, while other beds are visible, their occupants sitting up and talking quietly with visitors.

"She's in here," the blue-uniformed man in front of me says, stopping and pointing to a floating curtain on my right. I thank him and he leaves. After a moment's pause, I pull the curtain aside just enough to walk into the enclosed area.

I stand and look at her, a still, silent form in a neat, white bed. If not for the gentle rise and fall of her chest and the occasional flutter behind her eyelids, I wouldn't believe she's alive. I take slow, careful steps toward her. As I reach the bedside, slender branches rise from the floor and weave themselves into a stool. A cushion appears on top of it. I nudge the stool with my knee to make sure it's sturdier than it looks, then sit down.

My hand inches forward and rests on the edge of the bed next to Mom's pale arm. "Just so you know," I whisper, "I'm really mad at you. I can't believe you didn't *tell me*. Why? You made up all these stories when you could have just told me the truth." I press my fingers into the blanket. "You really need to wake up so I can shout at you properly. This whispering thing isn't working. And also ... it's just freaky seeing you lying here like this. So you have to wake up. Okay?" I lean back and watch her, waiting, hoping that somehow my voice can drag her from the depths of this enchanted sleep. It doesn't, though. Of course it doesn't.

I stand, find the gap in the floating curtain, and push my way out. I walk past the row of identical floating curtains and out to the corridor where I last saw Ryn. A woman dressed in a pale blue healer uniform is approaching him from the other side. I reach him at the same time she does. "You're Kara Larkenwood's daughter?" she says to me.

"Yes. Do you know anything more about my mother?"

"Is your father here?" she asks. "I should probably speak to both of you together."

"Um, no."

"We don't know when he'll be here," Ryn says, "so if you know something, please tell us."

The healer's eyes flick with uncertainty toward Ryn. "You are …"

"Linden Larkenwood's son."

"Please," I say. "Whatever you know, just tell us. You're starting to scare me."

Ryn puts an arm around my shoulders. The healer clasps her hands in front of her. "The bottle that was found next to your mother had several drops of liquid left inside it. Our analysis spells identified it as a sleeping potion."

I nod. "That's what I thought."

"Did you know how strong it was?"

"Well, she only took a few drops every night, so it must have been rather strong."

The healer shakes her head. "Stronger than that. One drop could send a person into a deep sleep for days. It's illegal to buy and sell potions of this strength without a permit. We don't know how much your mother ingested, but if the bottle was full, we've calculated she could be asleep for …" The healer twists her hands together, looking between the two of us, possibly weighing how best to share this final piece of information.

"For?" I prompt, not willing to wait a second longer.

"At least a year."

"*What?*"

"Probably longer."

"That's insane! How will she survive that long?"

"Potions of this sort are designed to sustain the body while—"

"Is there anything we can do other than wait?" Ryn asks. "Any potions or magic that can reverse the effects of a sleeping potion?"

"Not something this strong," the healer says, then rushes to add, "but, uh, we're working on creating an antidote. And our potion makers are very skilled. Don't you worry, I'm sure they'll come up with something."

CHAPTER TWENTY-TWO

I'M PAGING THROUGH *GRINGEL'S POTION MANUAL, Eighteenth Edition* on Saturday evening when Vi arrives home from work. After my visit to Mom, I gathered every book on potions I could find in Ryn's house and spread them over the kitchen table. I know the possibility of me coming across something that all the expert healers and potion makers don't already know about is slim, but I don't have any homework and there's no way drawing will distract me now, so this is all I've got to focus on.

I hear Vi talking to Ryn before she comes into the kitchen. She bends and hugs my shoulders and says, "Ryn told me. I'm so sorry. But at least there's nothing wrong with her other than sleep."

"A year, Vi," I say as I page through *Gringel's*. "A *year*. Or more! Imagine how much she could miss in that time?"

"It won't be that long, Calla." Unlike the false assurances of the healer, Vi's voice carries actual conviction. "We don't know how much of the potion your mother actually drank. And she's been taking sleeping potions since she was a teenager. I'm sure she's developed some form of tolerance toward them. Why else would she be in possession of one so strong?"

I tap a pencil against my chin and nod as Vi sits opposite me with a glass of her favorite energy-boosting, body-healing concoction. It's a mix of at least twenty different ingredients, all of which taste disgusting. "I suppose that makes sense. That would also explain why she makes sleeping potions so often."

"Exactly. You said she makes a new one every few weeks, right? She wouldn't need to do that if she had a potion strong enough to last a year. Or two to three years, if you take into account all the waking hours in a day when she wouldn't need it."

"Right. Okay." I sit back and close the heavy cover of *Gringel's*. "Why didn't I think of that before I spent all afternoon searching for every reference I could find of sleeping potions?"

Vi takes a big gulp of her drink, grimaces, and says, "Too anxious to think properly?"

"Maybe. So hopefully it'll only be a few weeks before she wakes up." I tilt my head to the side and add, "Do you actually like that stuff you're drinking?"

"Ugh, no. But it works." She downs the rest of the drink, shudders as she swallows, then stands and takes the glass to the sink.

"Whoa," I say as she turns. "What happened?" Her hair is secured atop her head, and across the back of her neck are three deep gashes.

"What? Oh, just some training exercises with a manticore that got a little out of hand. The wounds have been treated already, and the Drink of Supreme Grossness—" she waves the glass she just cleaned "—will help. I'll be healed in a few hours."

"Great way to end a Saturday," I mutter.

"It *was* great," she says, enthusiasm lighting up her face. "This team has made so much improvement. They're almost ready to go out there and fix up some real-life mess."

The door leading from the living room swings open and Ryn walks in. "Isn't it nice when the criminal you've been hunting down for weeks shows up unconscious on your doorstep?"

"How convenient," Vi says. "Which doorstep are you referring to, exactly?"

"The Guild's. So I need to go in for a few hours."

"Don't you guys ever get weekends off?" I ask. "Vi just got home, and now you're off to work."

"Uh, sometimes," Vi says. "Why do you think he turned himself in?" she asks Ryn.

"Not sure yet. I think perhaps one of his own turned on him."

"Sounds like the criminals are doing your job for you."

"Not complaining," he says with a grin.

"Lazy butt," Vi says. "You should come to my Guild sometime. We do real work there."

"Your *Institute* is filled with reptiscillas."

"And that's what makes it awesome," she says in a sing-song voice. "Okay, I'm going to clean up before Calla and I make something amazing for dinner."

"Hey," Ryn says as she walks past him. "What happened to your neck? I didn't see that when you came in."

"Oh, just a few scratches." Vi touches the side of her neck gingerly. "The manticore training was today, remember? It knocked me around a bit, but I'm fine."

"It *knocked you around?*" Ryn looks horrified, which is puzzling, since getting knocked around is nothing new in the guardian line of work. "This is what I'm talking about, V. This is why it isn't safe for you to work anymore."

"No, no, no," she says, turning back to him and shaking her head. "That wasn't part of the deal. We agreed I wouldn't have to stop work now."

"Well maybe we were wrong."

"Um, should I leave the room now?" I ask.

"If you're allowed to work," Vi says, completely oblivious to my question, "so am I."

"I'm not the one who's—" Ryn cuts himself off as he looks at me. "We'll talk about this later," he says to Vi, then walks out of the room.

"Yes. We will," she shouts after him. "I'll be talking, and you'll be listening to my side of things."

"I can't hear you," he shouts back. Vi looks at me and rolls her eyes. A moment later, we hear a knock coming from outside the living room, followed shortly by Ryn saying, "Tilly?"

"Tilly?" Vi says, frowning. She hurries out of the kitchen,

and I get up to follow her. "Tilly!" she shouts gleefully, and I walk into the living room in time to see her wrap her arms around someone with blond and pink hair. "I didn't know you were coming."

"I'm sorry for arriving unannounced," Tilly says, "but I suddenly had some time off, and I thought, 'Why not?' So here I am! And I brought dinner. Hi, Calla!" She waves at me over Vi's shoulder.

"Hey." I smile and wave back. As far as Vi and Ryn's friends go, wacky explorer Tilly is probably the most fun. She talks non-stop and tells amazing stories—which are made more amazing by the fact that they're all true.

"Tilly, you have awful timing," Ryn complains. "I'm on my way to work."

"Oh, bummer." Tilly looks sad for a moment, but then she grins. "Girls' night!" She throws her hands into the air and accidentally whacks Filigree in his tiny owl face. "Oh! Sorry, Fili. I didn't see you sitting there on that totally inconspicuous coat hook."

Filigree flaps his disapproval, then lands on the floor, morphs into a cat, and walks off without another glance in Tilly's direction.

"I really have to go," Ryn says. "Enjoy your girls' night."

Half an hour later, we're sitting at the kitchen table digging into the various containers Tilly picked up from The Brownie's Munch Box while mouse-formed Filigree nibbles chocolate-covered nixles. Having never eaten anything from Brownie's before—Mom has a strict home-cooked-meals-only policy—I make sure to sample something from all seven containers.

"So I'm lost in the middle of a jungle," Tilly says between mouthfuls, "my stylus has been eaten by a giant toad-rabbit thing, I've fought off two lizards in order to keep the gem safe, and now I'm faced with a whole bunch of warrior dryads who obviously think I'm threatening their home. I'm thinking this expedition is an absolute fail when, out of nowhere, Jayshu comes swinging through the trees on a vine, bellowing like an ogre. He lands in the midst of the dryads, whips out the giggle spray, and within half a minute all the dryads are doubled over, laughing hysterically."

"That did *not* happen," Vi says when she's recovered from her laughter.

"One hundred percent true story," Tilly says. "Giggle spray. Jayshu's planning to patent it. Gonna make a fortune."

"Who's going to buy that stuff?"

"The Guild. Once you guardians realize you can win every battle by making your enemies giggle."

"That's so ridiculous I don't even know where to start."

"I know. They'll never see it coming. Oh!" Tilly waves her fork excitedly in the air. "I almost forgot the best part of the meal." She reaches into the bag slung over one side of her chair and pulls out a brown glass bottle. "Galar mead. This stuff, ladies, is amazing."

"Ooh, yes, I want to try that," I say, reaching for the bottle.

"I'm not sure your mother would be too pleased if I let you do that," Vi says.

"Mom's asleep, remember? And when she wakes up she'll have far more important things to worry about than the fact that I sampled—" I examine the label "—twelve-year-old mead. Wow. That's quite old."

"And it is quite amazing," Tilly says, standing up and searching the cupboards for appropriate glassware.

"Oh, I won't have any," Vi says as Tilly returns to the table with three glasses.

"What? Don't be so boring." Tilly taps the cork with her stylus. The cork pops out, and Filigree scampers over to get a better sniff at the contents of the bottle.

"I'm not, I just don't feel like—"

"No. Not feeling like it is not an option. I went all the way to the Slievaran Mountains where the Galar dwarves make this stuff. Do you have any idea how far away that is?"

"Um ... five seconds via the faerie paths?"

With a deadpan expression, Tilly blinks and says, "Fine. Do you have any idea how hard you have to focus to wind up at precisely the right spot on the Slievaran Mountains in order to find this stuff?"

"Very hard?"

"Exactly. That's how far away this place is. So you *have* to try the mead."

Vi groans. "I'm sorry. I wish I could, but I'm just really not feeling like it."

Tilly passes me a glass with a small amount of mead, then leans back and examines Vi with a frown. "We've drunk mead together before."

"We have."

"You liked it. A lot. You said it was your new favorite drink."

"I know, but—"

"Ohmygosh." Tilly straightens suddenly, her eyes wide.

"What?" Vi and I ask at the same time.

"Ohmygosh. Oh. My. Gosh." Tilly's smile stretches wider than I would have thought possible, as if she's squealing silently. "You're having a *baby*!"

I almost drop my glass. "*What?*"

Vi's expression is frozen, her mouth half open and her cheeks rapidly turning pink. Then she slaps her hand down on the table. "How the freak do you know that?"

"Oh, it is *so* obvious."

"It is not!"

"THAT IS SO EXCITING!" I yell, jumping up and flinging my arms around her, splashing half my mead on the floor. A second later, Tilly joins us, completing our group hug with bouncing and squealing.

"No—stop—it's not exciting, it's terrifying!" Vi exclaims, attempting to swat us away.

"Well of course it's a little bit terrifying," Tilly says as she and I return to our seats, "but it's *mainly* exciting, right?

"A little, I suppose," Vi says. "But I'll be the first to admit that this wasn't part of the plan for at least the next fifty years."

"This is what you and Ryn were arguing about, right?" I ask. "This is why he doesn't want you working."

"Yes," Vi says with a sigh.

"Well, now that this baby thing is happening," Tilly says, holding up her glass and clinking it against mine, "you guys should probably get married. Make it official."

Vi rolls her eyes. "We are married, Tilly."

"Oh please. That boring-as-mud gathering we had at the

Guild where you guys signed a scroll and then went straight back to work? That was *not* a wedding."

"You're right. It wasn't a wedding because we're not human and we don't call them that. We call them union ceremonies."

"Ugh, you sound like my grandmother. Just call it a wedding. Almost everyone else does these days."

I sit back, sip my slightly dry, honey-hinted drink, and watch the argument playing out in front of me. I know Tilly's going to win, and I'm fine with that. I happen to agree with her.

"Fine. Wedding. Whatever," Vi says. "And we tried to have one *three times*, remember? It just never worked out."

"Right, because some end-of-the-world emergency always came up that one of you had to run off and deal with."

"Exactly."

"Well, not this time. This time *I'm* planning your wedding, and someone else can deal with the earthquakes and floods."

"It was a volcano."

"Whatever."

"Yay!" I lift my glass into the air again. "Wedding time!"

CHAPTER TWENTY-THREE

MONDAY MORNING COMES, AND I'M STILL RIDING THE high of knowing I'm going to be an aunt. The fact that Mom is still in a potion-induced sleep is a bit of a damper, but I'm almost certain it won't be long before she wakes. Couple that with the fact that I'm no longer furious about her lying to me—my anger is diminishing a little each day—and this looks like it could be a good Monday. Even an interrogation about my fugitive mother—which I'm pretty sure is coming—can't ruin my day, thanks to one tiny and obvious fact I remembered yesterday about Guild interrogations.

An envelope appeared on our kitchen table last night with a note from the Guild informing me that training would return to normal today. After everything that's happened since I left the Guild on Friday morning—traveling to a distant mountain, falling down a chasm, my parents' attack, Mom turning out to be a Seer, Vi and Ryn's baby—I'd completely forgotten about the enchanted storm the Guild considered a potential threat.

"So, does anyone know what that storm was actually about?" Perry asks. The four of us are sitting in a lesson room waiting for our first class of the day.

"My mentor said it was because of some silly duel two faeries were having," Gemma says. "After the storm ended, guardians found them both passed out on a mountain peak."

"Idiots," Perry mutters.

"At least your mentor tells you stuff," I say. "Olive keeps our conversations to the barest minimum."

"That's probably a good thing," Perry says as he tilts his chair back on two legs and uses magic to hold himself there, "considering how fantastically unfriendly she is."

We get through our lessons for the morning—the various procedures the Guild follows after guardians bring in law-breaking fae—and as we're about to head to the dining hall for lunch, a first-year trainee appears in the doorway of our lesson room. As my classmates file out, she raises her voice and asks, "Is Calla Larkenwood here?" I wave and hurry over to her. "Your mentor wants to see you," she says.

Here it comes.

I climb the stairs to the second floor and find Olive tapping her stylus impatiently against the surface of her desk. I sit down, she watches me for a moment, and then she says, "Why am I not surprised?"

I'm almost certain I know what she's talking about, but

since I'd rather not ask, I wait without saying anything.

"Of course you turn out to have a fugitive mother who is guilty of both breaking her contract with the Guild and creating illegal potions. So. What do you suggest we do with you now that we're aware of this? It doesn't look good at all for you that you hid this information from us."

"I didn't know until two days ago," I say, making sure my gaze never leaves hers.

She laughs. "You didn't know? You've been living with a Seer your entire life. That isn't something you can miss."

"Yes, there were signs that something was different about her, but I didn't know what they meant. Neither my mother nor my father ever said anything about her being a Seer."

"Well, isn't that a lovely story." Olive pushes her chair back and stands. "We'll have to see what the Council thinks of it. Hopefully they'll see right through it like I do, and we'll finally all agree that Calla Larkenwood shouldn't be here."

"Am I seeing the Council members now?"

"Yes. Three of them. In precisely six minutes. So I hope you've got your story straight."

"I have." I stand and walk with Olive out of her office. "I assume they'll be questioning me with a compulsion potion?"

"Of course. So no matter what story you've got planned, the potion will force the truth out of you in the end."

"Great." Compulsion potion is the tiny fact I remembered yesterday. The tiny fact that means this will all be settled soon.

* * *

Once the Council is satisfied that I haven't deceived them in any way, they come to the entirely reasonable conclusion that Mom's crimes have nothing to do with me and send me on my way. Olive is furious. She doesn't say it, and she doesn't look it, but the atmosphere between us as we leave the interrogation room feels like a brewing storm. She accompanies me down to the training center and informs me she'll be paying close attention to every maneuver I practice today. "You won't be leaving until everything is perfect," she says.

And that's how I know my Monday's not going to be so great after all.

I head to the target practice station first. Olive hovers at the edge of my vision, making me feel uncomfortable. I had planned to practice more with the knife Dad gave me, but the moment I slide it from my boot, Olive says, "No. I can't have you wasting half the afternoon walking back and forth to fetch a knife. Guardian knives disappear once they've struck the target, so you'll be using those. I want to see fifty perfect throws in a row. If you mess up, we start counting again."

"*Fifty?*" I say before I can stop myself.

Olive folds her arms over her chest, and I catch a glimpse of the underlying anger in her eyes. "Do you have a problem with that, trainee?"

I shake my head and turn back to my target without another word. I think of my invisible cache of weapons and try to pick out a knife that most closely matches the size and weight of the one dad gave me. I grasp the air, and feel the knife handle in my grip. *Ignore Olive, ignore Olive.* I pinch the handle, bring it up behind my right ear, position myself with my left leg forward, and throw.

The handle whacks the target and the knife clatters to the floor. Possibly the worst throw I've executed since Zed gave me my first lesson.

An exasperated Olive steps into my line of vision and says, "Do not tell me this is the first time you're throwing that knife."

"Of course I've thrown knives before. I—"

"*That* knife. Have you thrown *that specific knife?*"

"I've thrown lots of knives, so I'm sure at least one of them was—"

"Is it handle-heavy, blade-heavy, balanced? How far are you from your target? Is this a handle throw or a blade throw? *You should know these things!*"

"Can you just give me a chance to get the feel of it?" I've thrown plenty of knives before with Zed, and it always takes a few throws to get into the right rhythm. Adjusting my distance, changing my grip. And then once I've got it, I can hit my target almost every time.

"The *feel* of it?" Olive says. "You don't have time to get the *feel* of anything when you're in the midst of battle. In a split second, you need to be able to judge your distance from a target, choose the correct knife, and know whether to grip the blade or the handle so that when you throw it, it strikes the target. Understood?"

"Or I could use something other than a knife," I mutter.

"Or you could practice with *every single knife you have* until you know what the hell you're doing!" Olive shouts.

The other trainees in the target practice area keep their eyes averted, but I can tell that everyone's attention is on Olive and me. How could it not be when Olive's shouting loud enough for the entire training center to hear?

"New plan," Olive says, pacing behind me. "You will do this with every knife in your guardian collection. When I've seen twenty perfect throws in a row for one knife, you move onto the next."

I don't argue. I know there's no point.

When the session is up, I've only gone through half my knives. I look over at Olive, waiting for her to give me permission to move on to the next activity in my schedule—stick fighting with Perry as an opponent—but all she says is, "Why are you stopping?"

So I continue. I wonder if Perry ends up fighting himself with a stick for the duration of the second session because I only finish with the knives just as the third session begins. My arm aches from all the throwing, so it's a good thing my next activity—running—doesn't require much arm work. I head for the running rectangles, wondering how many things Olive will be able to criticize about this simple activity. I can't imagine there's much more than *too fast* and *too slow*, but I'm sure she'll find something.

"No, no, no," Olive says as she realizes we're approaching the rectangles of moving floor. "You can do this in your spare time. Right now, we need something more challenging." She looks around, surveying the various areas of the training center.

"Obstacle course," she says. "Perfect. We can have some fun with that."

Whatever Olive's idea of fun is, I don't think I'm going to like it.

"You," she says, pointing to the trainee who's already in the obstacle area examining the collection of obstacles stored in the corner. "You're doing running now. Off you go. And you—" she points at me this time "—do some stretching while I set this up."

I do as I'm told while Olive raises her hands and uses her magic to move the obstacles around, push the unwanted ones aside, and set up a course using the chosen pieces. When she's finished, I see a circle of seven obstacles: a table, six stepping stones floating above quicksand, five parallel sliding panels, a climbing net, a series of low stone walls, a flaming hoop, and a balancing bridge. Not too hard.

"Get up on the table," Olive tells me. "That's your starting block. You'll do a back tuck off the table onto the floor—landing in a crouch—then front roll under the table toward the quicksand. Three front handsprings should get you over the stepping stones. Get through the doors of the sliding panels as quickly as you can—not as easy as it looks, since the panels are continuously sliding back and forth and the doors keep changing their positions. Then climb the net and somersault off the top. You'll vault over each of the stone walls, then dive through the flaming hoop, tuck into a shoulder roll as you hit the floor, and come up on your feet. Run up the narrow beam and across the swinging bridge, somersault off the other end, and land back on the table. No wobbling."

"Okay." I climb onto the table.

"And no magic," Olive adds. "Obviously."

As Olive holds her stylus up, I tense and get ready to flip backward. She flicks the stylus, it makes a hooting sound, and I jump. I land well and go immediately into the front roll under the table. I jump up on the other side and run at the quicksand, launching into a front handspring just before I reach it. Hands, feet, hands, feet—but I've misjudged the distance, my toes catch the edge of the second-to-last stepping stone, and I fall backward into the quicksand.

Way to go, Calla.

I propel myself out of the sucking sand with magic, clean myself off with another quick spell, and head back to the table. Olive watches me with a withering expression as I climb back onto the table, wait for the starting hoot, and begin again. I almost make it to the end the second time, but after running up the beam and onto the swinging bridge, I lose my balance and tumble off the side. Third time around, I make it all the way back to the table, rising from my somersault with barely a wobble.

Sounding bored, Olive says, "Again."

Okay then.

After completing the course another five times, with Olive pointing out some minor mistake each time, she plants her hands on her hips and sighs. "Pretend you're a performer. This sequence of obstacles is your dance. You don't get to leave here until your dance is perfect."

A performance. Okay. You can do this, Calla.

The third session comes to an end, but I climb back onto my table. Ignoring all the trainees moving around to find their final station for the day, I give myself a few seconds to catch my breath. I imagine my audience, tell myself that this is an *art*, not just exercise, and leap backward. I move seamlessly into the front roll. My handsprings are perfection. I dash from side to side through the sliding panels and throw myself at the net, clawing my way up as fast as if a horde of goblins is on my tail. The rest is easy. I'm used to the way the swinging bridge moves now. I speed across it, launch myself into the air at the end, spin, and land on the table. I rise, breathing hard as I take a bow for my imaginary audience.

"Nope," Olive says. "Again."

"What? That was perfect!"

"It isn't perfect until I say it's perfect."

And so I do it again. I continue going through the remainder of the fourth session. The session ends, trainees start leaving, and still Olive doesn't let me go. "You're getting worse!" she shouts after I finish the course for what feels like the five hundredth time.

Instead of shouting back that I'm exhausted so *obviously* I'm getting worse, I sit on the edge of the table and wipe the sweat off my face while reminding myself what it feels like to breathe. Olive walks over to me with a look of disbelief. "Did I tell you to sit down? Get back up there and do it again." Behind her severe expression I see a kind of vindictive gleefulness. She's enjoying making me suffer.

I won't let her win.

I give myself another few moments to breathe, then stand

up. A number of trainees are still here, and at least half of them are watching. This really is a performance. They are my audience.

This is the one, I tell myself. *Make. It. Perfect.*

My body moves without hesitation from one obstacle to the next. Leaping, flipping, somersaulting, climbing, running, jumping—*faster, faster, faster!* It's a flawless performance. At least, that's how I feel the moment my feet hit the table and I straighten. As my chest heaves, I look at Olive.

"Well," she says. "I'm not sure that counts as perfect, but it's probably as close as you're going to get." She turns and walks away. "Oh, and make sure you move all the obstacles back against the wall," she calls without looking back.

I climb off the table on legs beginning to feel jelly-wobbly. I drag myself to the nearest mat and collapse onto it. My chest rises and falls rapidly as I attempt to get my breathing back to normal.

"That was spectacular," Gemma says. I raise my head enough to see her, Perry and Ned seat themselves on the mat beside me. "I've never seen anyone complete an obstacle course with such … *finesse*."

"Or such speed," Perry adds. "I'm pretty sure you broke a record."

"Several records," Gemma corrects.

I let my head drop back onto the mat. "That's what happens when … you have a mentor who's … insane."

"Hey, if her insanity makes you a good guardian, it's all worth it," Perry says.

"Is it?" I ask as I watch the inside of my eyelids. "I'm not sure I ... agree right now. Ask me again in ... half an hour. Or tomorrow ... when my muscles have recovered." I lie on the mat for another few minutes. By the time I sit up, my three friends have moved all the obstacles back against the wall. "Hey, thanks." I manage to stand up. "You didn't need to do that."

"I think we did," Gemma says. "Looks like you need all your magic just to keep your legs working."

"Do you think you'll have recovered by tonight?" Perry asks.

"Yes, probably. I was joking when I said 'tomorrow.' Why, do you have something exciting planned?"

"Well, *we* don't," Perry says, a grin appearing on his face, "but someone else does, and we've been invited. Sort of. I mean, I *found* an invite."

"So ... we're actually *not* invited?" I ask, struggling to make sense of what he's saying.

"It was this follow-the-clue-and-find-an-invite sort of thing. I saw it written on someone's leg when we were Underground last week looking out for you. So I followed the clue. And now we have an invitation."

"Is this an Underground party?" For some reason my first thought is, *I wonder if Chase will be there.* Stupid thought. Stupid, stupid thought.

"No, it's at the top of Estellyn Tower."

"Seriously?" I look from Perry to Gemma. Gemma nods. "That place is *super* fancy. Are you sure we're allowed to go?"

"Well, we have three entirely legitimate invitations," Perry says, "so yeah."

"I'm not going," Ned says quickly, his eyes flicking to me before looking away. "So the third invitation is yours."

"The clue led to this random old tree, and when I put my hand inside one of the knots, I was able to pull out an invitation," Perry explains. "Only one per person, though, so I got Gemma and Ned to go back with me so we could get another two."

"Because we can't let him go waltzing off to a celebrity party on his own," Gemma says. "We need to keep an eye on him. So can you come?"

"I doubt I'll ever get another chance to mix with the elite fae upper class, so yes. Definitely."

"Awesome!" Gemma loops her arm through mine as we head for the training center door. "Now what are we going to *wear?*"

CHAPTER TWENTY-FOUR

SOME TIME AFTER DINNER ON MONDAY EVENING, I WALK down the stairs in a long black evening dress, gloves, and high-heeled shoes. My hair is pinned back with a delicate gemstone clip on one side, cascading in curls over my other shoulder. The one thing Mom taught me well—aside from making sleeping potions of apparent illegal strength—was hairstyle spells. She never seems to use any herself, but she must have decided that someone born with gold hair should always keep it looking good. We used to try something different every day when I was in junior school. These days I leave it loose and unstyled most of the time, but I remember the spells Mom taught me.

I find Ryn and Vi in the living room. Ryn is draped across the couch reading some papers and Vi's sitting on the floor by the coffee table playing a card game with Filigree. He can't hold the cards in his squirrel paws, so they're resting behind the lid of a box where Vi can't see them. Her amber vibrates on the table and she picks it up. "Tilly sent a message," she says to Ryn. "'White or ivory? Lace or ribbons? Tables or picnic blankets?'"

Without looking up, Ryn says, "You're the girl. Aren't you supposed to decide these things?"

Vi pulls a face while staring at her amber. "I'm not really that kinda girl."

"Tell her to ask Raven."

I clear my throat and wait for everyone in the room to look up. The open-mouthed confusion I receive is enough to make me laugh. Even Filigree looks bewildered. When I've finished my chuckle, I say, "I decided to just be honest and avoid having to try and sneak out. I'm going to a party tonight."

Ryn frowns. "On a school night?"

"I see you're well on your way to becoming parent material," I tell him, to which he looks rather pleased. "So, do we have to argue about this, or can you just be my cool older brother who doesn't mind me going out?"

Ryn narrows his eyes. "I feel like you're trying to flatter me into giving you the answer you want."

"Where's the party?" Vi asks. "Not," she adds hurriedly, "that I'm trying to be all parental and smothering. I'm just interested. You look smarter than I'd expect for the average teen party."

"It's at Estellyn Tower. One of my friends at the Guild found an invitation after following a clue, so I'm going with him and another friend."

"Oh, I've heard about those parties," Ryn says, looking impressed. "A mix of high society and anyone else who manages to find an invitation. Your friend must be quite smart. I've heard the clues can be difficult."

"I assume you haven't heard anything bad about these parties, or you'd be telling me not to go instead of remarking on how clever my friend is."

"With the number of important fae attending those parties, I'm sure there's plenty of security. Do you know if it's at the very top of Estellyn Tower?"

"Um, I don't know. Vi, where's the best place to keep my amber and stylus when dressed like this?"

"Oh, I've got a leg strap you can use." She jumps up, crosses the room, and opens the hallway cupboard.

"I think the penthouse level is owned by that guy who makes those designer styluses," Ryn says, rolling up his papers and tapping his chin.

"Oh yes," Vi says as she rummages inside the cupboard. "Lucien de la something-or-other. I think Raven met him once. Whenever I see his name in the news he's donating obscene amounts of money to another healing institute."

"Oh, that guy with the wife who has the weird, incurable illness?" I ask.

"That's the one," Ryn says. "If the party's at his place, it will be incredible. He's got loads of money to throw around."

"Ah, here it is," Vi says, producing a black, stretchy strap with various smaller straps attached to it. "Your amber slides in here, and your stylus here. The others are for knives, but you've got guardian weapons, so you don't need anything else." She hands it to me. "Strap it on anywhere above your knee."

"Right. That's not going to look awkward at all if I need to access it in public. Hey, just excuse me while I lift up my skirt."

Vi laughs. "Yeah, it works better if you're wearing a dress with a slit, so just don't attach it too high. It'll be easy enough to access when you're sitting down."

"Or duck into another room," Ryn says, sounding distracted as he scans through his papers once more.

"Okay." I finish attaching the strap, then open a doorway to the paths before putting my stylus away. I hold it open with my arm while turning back to ask, "Ryn, you haven't heard anything from Dad yet, have you?"

"No." Ryn looks up from the pages. "He won't tell me what he's up to, probably so I can't be implicated if the Guild finds out he's gone off to do his own private investigation. They don't exactly approve of ex-guardians doing that."

I groan. "I hope he doesn't wind up in trouble because of this."

"Don't worry, he'll probably find nothing and be home in a few days."

I nod, hoping Ryn is right. "Okay. I'm going now. You guys have fun with your reading and card games. Try not to think about how you're old and boring now."

"Playing cards with Filigree is *not* boring," Vi says as she returns to her spot on the floor. "Which you obviously know, since you've played with him plenty of times yourself."

"Only when I'm feeling old and boring," I say with a laugh as I walk into the faerie paths.

"Be back by midnight," Ryn calls after me. "You've got training tomo—" The last of his words are swallowed up as the doorway closes and I'm plunged into darkness.

Estellyn Tower isn't in Creepy Hollow—"Those rich people don't want to hang out in an overgrown forest filled with scary creatures," Perry said earlier—but it isn't too far away, so I don't have to concentrate that hard to arrive at the right place. I step out of the darkness and find myself standing on a circular stone-paved driveway surrounded by a neat lawn of dark blue grass that stretches as far as I can see in every direction. In the center of the circle is an elaborate water display complete with sparks of bright magic whizzing around the various spouts of colored water. Turning away from the fountain, I see the palatial Estellyn Tower rising magnificently toward the night sky on the other side of the driveway. The outer wall of the structure is studded with millions of gems, making it sparkle in the light given off by the lamps lining the grand stairway.

I'm about to walk across the driveway toward the stairs when an enormous faerie paths doorway opens above me, and a carriage pulled by two pegasi swoops out and lands on the driveway. After trotting a short distance, the winged horses come to a halt, allowing the occupants of the carriage to climb out. Moments later, the carriage begins moving again. I watch the pegasi as they continue around the circular driveway, running faster and beating the air with their wings until they lift off the ground and disappear into a doorway that must somehow be opened remotely.

"Hey, you almost got run over," Perry shouts from somewhere behind me. I turn and find him and Gemma walking toward me. Perry laughs and points at me, and Gemma elbows him.

"You have no right to laugh," she says, "after you almost landed us in the middle of the fountain."

"That was intentional. I was practicing my stop-yourself-before-you-hit-the-water skills."

"Whatever. Calla, that dress looks great on you! My sister will be so pleased. She wore it the day she graduated from Hellenway and hasn't taken it out the cupboard since."

"Oh, thank you. You look nice too." Gemma does look lovely in her maroon evening dress and sleek, straight hair. And I'm not the only one who's noticed. Perry keeps sneaking glances at her.

Smiling to myself, I walk across the driveway with the two of them. We join other well-dressed faeries on the stairs, some of whom have also arrived via the faerie paths. At the entrance to the lobby, we're scanned from head to toe by a security guard before being allowed to enter.

"I read up about this place this afternoon," Gemma says. "There's a restaurant on the ground floor which none of us will ever eat at, unless you've got a stash of gold hiding under your bed. Then the Estellyn Grand Hotel takes up the first ten floors with rooms that cost more per night than my mom earns in an entire year. And every floor above that is the home of some rich, influential faerie."

"Man, I'm so glad I saw that clue walking past me last week," Perry says as we aim for an elevator that looks big enough to hold at least eight of the Guild's elevators inside it. He pumps his fist in the air and say, "Penthouse party, here we come."

"Don't do that!" Gemma grabs his arm and pulls it down, looking scandalized by Perry's inappropriate behavior. "You're making us look like such commoners."

"Who cares?" Perry says, but instead of looking annoyed, he seems pleased—probably because Gemma's hand is still on his arm.

"So we're going to the very top of this building?" I ask. "Where that designer Lucien de la Mer lives?"

"The one and only," Gemma says with a small squeal.

We reach the elevator. After telling the security guard which floor we want to go to, he points us to a smaller elevator past a bronze statue of a sphinx. We're asked to produce our invitations at the second elevator, and then we're each scanned again before being allowed to step inside. Five more people arrive and go through the same procedure before the elevator door reappears, sealing us all inside. A man in a blue and gold uniform with the words Estellyn Tower embroidered onto the front pocket directs the elevator to the top floor.

As we move upward, I lean toward Perry and whisper, "If you saw that clue Underground, then there must be quite a few Undergrounders coming tonight."

"Possibly. The ones who were smart enough to solve the clue and quick enough to get to the tree before all the invitations were gone."

"Where were you when you saw the clue?"

"That place you were supposed to meet Saskia and Blaze. Club Deviant."

Apprehension settles in my stomach. The drakoni man wouldn't want to come to something like this, would he? No, he's got his own club to run. Besides, I look quite different tonight. He probably wouldn't remember me.

Gold hair is usually pretty memorable, Calla.

I don't have time to worry about how memorable I might be, though, because the elevator door melts away and I join the rest of the guests in the home of designer Lucien de la Mer. It's a feast of sights and sounds and smells. Small glass orbs with tiny lights inside them float near the ceiling, while the polished floor glows faintly beneath our feet. I see winged figures skating in formation across a pond of ice, a band of musicians raised on a stage of smoking coals, faeries dressed in every color imaginable, wigs of clouds and feathers and ribbons, and faces painted with exotic patterns.

"Guys?" I say. "I feel a little underdressed."

"No," Perry says. "*That* is underdressed." I follow his gaze to a silver-haired girl laughing at something her reptiscillan companion just said. Threads of shimmering spider silk are draped over her body, covering her important bits and pretty much nothing else.

"Oh my," Gemma says. "That looks ... cold."

I laugh at Gemma's description before we turn and walk the other way. As we move further into the crowd, we pass floating trays of food and drink: chocolate bonbons of varying shapes, apples carved into miniature versions of Estellyn Tower, tall glasses of glowing blue liquid, and various other tasty treats I'm longing to try.

"Do you think he's here?" Gemma asks once we've all acquired a drink and have positioned ourselves near tall glass windows that cycle through displays of various exotic locations around the world. "Lucien, I mean. Or do you think he's hiding somewhere in one of his other rooms, relaxing in a bathrobe while all these people party it up at his expense."

"Well, I have no idea what he looks like," I say as I raise my glass to my lips. "So I won't know if I see him." I take a sip of my layered drink. The colors—pink, purple and orange—mix together the moment I tilt the liquid into my mouth. When I lower the glass, the layers immediately separate. "Mm. Tastes like sunrise," I say.

"Sunrises don't have a taste, silly," Gemma tells me as she eyes the floating jelly spheres in her colorless drink.

"But if they did, they'd taste like this."

"Mine tastes like medicine," Perry says. A tray floats past us, and he places his half finished drink on it.

"Perry, you can't put it back!" Gemma says, sounding as horrified as she did when he fist-pumped the air in front of the whole lobby.

"I just did. Come on, dance with me," he says to Gemma as the music changes to something with a lively beat.

"Oh. Um ... but what about—"

"I'll be fine," I assure her as she looks hesitantly my way. "You guys dance. I'll find you just now." They disappear into the crowd of dancers, Perry doing some kind of wiggle that's no doubt meant to embarrass Gemma. I think they'd be cute together—except that Gemma has a crush on someone else. I wonder if Perry knows about that.

I walk around the edge of the room, sampling food and looking at the framed designer styluses displayed on the walls. A solid gold one, a diamond-encrusted one, a wooden one with intricate embossed patterns. In a glass display case, I see one with dozens of butterfly wings wrapped around it. I wonder if any of them actually work, or if they're for display only.

"Hey, pretty lady," an elf with spiked white hair and various facial piercings says to me. His eyes rake over me before he adds, "Can I get you a drink?"

"Uh, no thanks." *Creepazoid.*

After receiving several more offers—not all of them as tame as the first one—I keep moving without meeting anyone's gaze. I wander around carved pillars and between groups of fae before I find a section of the vast room where the light is dimmer and several spheroid chairs, each open on one side, hang from the ceiling. I settle into one made from woven branches, grateful for the privacy is provides around me. I lean back against the cushion and sway gently in the seat. I wonder if Gemma and Perry are still dancing, or if they're looking for me. Since these hanging chairs are as private as it gets in this room, I should probably take the opportunity to pull up the bottom of my dress and find my amber. I lean forward.

And that's when I hear his voice.

Chase.

CHAPTER TWENTY-FIVE

I FREEZE, LISTENING INTENTLY, BUT IT'S DEFINITELY CHASE. His voice has that deep, self-assured tone I've quickly become familiar with. A thrill races through me—*he's here!*—which I attempt to stamp down immediately. I peer between the woven branches, swinging my seat slowly around until I find him. He's standing with a woman beside one of the floor-to-ceiling windows, a clear one that provides an excellent view of stars glittering against a dark sky. He looks delicious in his well-tailored but understated suit—no feathers, sparkles or ribbons for him—and the woman looks equally elegant.

Did you seriously just use the word 'delicious'?

Shut up.

I push aside my internal argument and notice that the woman is the same one I saw when I traveled back to the scene from Chase's past. Her hair is shorter now, sleek, dark waves resting on her shoulders, but it's the same person. Confident posture and alluring smile. She looks fabulous in a form-fitting red dress and black lace gloves that are prettier than mine.

I don't like her.

"Are you sure he's coming?" she asks before taking a sip from her drink and surveying the room over the rim of her glass.

"Yes. He went to great lengths over the past two days to secure himself an invitation."

"Are you going to tell me how you know this?"

"No." Chase pushes his hands into his pockets. "You don't want to be part of my team, so you don't get to know my sources."

She pouts. "You know I don't play well with others."

"And yet you always agree to help me when I ask."

She looks away, and I can barely hear her when she says, "You know why."

You're eavesdropping, I tell myself. *You're definitely eavesdropping.* But I got here first, and it isn't my fault they're speaking loudly enough for me to hear. I shouldn't have to move, should I?

"Do you really think he'll tell me what he's after?" the woman asks.

Chase turns and looks out the window. "You've convinced many men to tell you many things. I have no doubt you can make him talk."

A sly half-smile stretches her red lips. "You're right. I do have an exceptionally high success rate."

Chase chuckles. "Thank goodness for that. There doesn't seem to be any other way of finding out what Saber's after."

Saber? Oh shoot. I do *not* want to run into that man again. I might not have his bangle anymore, but he's probably still furious with anyone involved in stealing and destroying it. I'm sure he'd be happy to take revenge if the opportunity presented itself.

"And if he won't tell me?" the woman says to Chase. "Then what? Perhaps you should move on to something else. This particular project has consumed far too much of your time."

"You know who he's working for," Chase says, crossing his arms and turning away from the window. He casts a glance across the room. "Undoubtedly the most dangerous man we know. I can't *move on* if I know he's planning something."

The most dangerous man? My thoughts turn immediately to Draven. He's definitely the worst threat our world has faced. But he's gone. I know Olive has her doubts, and there was that enchanted storm everyone was worried about, but Vi and Tilly—the two people who were actually there for the moment all the history books gloss over: the moment Draven was stabbed with a special weapon—seem to think he's gone. And didn't someone say the storm was caused by two faeries dueling each other?

"What about the Guild girl?" the woman asks. "You said she might be able to help you."

Guild girl? That's me!

"Yes, but working with someone from the Guild probably wouldn't end well for you and me."

"Just you," she says. "I'm not on your team, remember?"

"You're connected to me. If the Guild girl chooses to turn me in, it won't be long before they come looking for you."

"Then use her without giving her enough information to be able to do that," the woman continues. "Leave out details, or give her false ones. If she doesn't know enough, she can't do anything."

Okay, I can't sit by and listen while they talk about me like this. Here I was having ridiculous heart palpitations about the hot vigilante tattoo artist, and all he wants is to use my Griffin Ability. I swing my chair around and push myself up and out of it.

"That won't work," Chase says. "She knows too much already."

"I see," the woman says as I start walking toward them. She laughs, and the sound is enchanting. "How very interesting. You've managed to keep your secrets for years, and now one girl comes along and—"

"It isn't like that."

"Oh really?"

My feet come to a halt because I suddenly feel like this might be a conversation I want to hear more of. But I'm too close to them already and my sudden stop has caught their attention. Chase's eyes widen in surprise. "Calla?"

I close the distance between us with confident strides, crossing my arms over my chest. "What a surprise to see you here," I say.

"Indeed," he says. "You look ..."

"I look?"

"Older."

"How lovely. Because every girl wants to hear that she looks old."

He gives me a small smile. "I think you know that's not what I meant."

I turn my gaze to the woman, Chase's flawless companion, who appears to be examining me with shock. She looks at Chase, then back at me. "Woman in gold," she whispers.

"Excuse me?" I ask, although I'm pleased to hear her referring to me as a woman and not a girl. It makes me feel as though we're on more of an even footing.

"Uh, nothing," she says, then smiles, appearing to regain her composure. "I was just thinking of something Chase told me years ago. You're the Guild girl, I assume?"

"Yes. And you are?" I'm aware I'm being rude, but I can't help it. There's nothing about this woman that makes me want to be polite to her.

"I'm Chase's hair stylist," she says, leaning over to run her gloved fingers through his hair.

Hair stylist. Right. And I'm a purple fire-spitting bunny.

Chase reaches up and calmly removes the woman's hands. "Elizabeth," he says. "Don't you have somewhere to be now?"

She sighs. "Why do you always insist on calling me nasty names?"

"It's *your name*," he says. "It isn't nasty. Now you need to find Saber and get him to talk."

"Fine. If I must." She smoothes her hands down over her thighs. "You two enjoy each other's company," she adds with a knowing smile. She sashays away while I try to figure out if I'm brave enough to ask Chase why I'm the only girl to discover any of his secrets.

"So, I'm here because of Saber," Chase says before I can find my courage. "Why are you here?"

"Uh … didn't I tell you?" My mind races to come up with a clever quip. "I live here. In Estellyn Tower."

Chase's expression doesn't change. Probably because that was the furthest thing from clever and he can't be bothered to reply until I give him a real answer.

With a sigh, I say, "My friend followed a clue and found an invitation. I figured hanging out with celebrity fae was a good way to end a bad day."

"A bad day?"

"Just my mentor reminding me that nothing I do is good enough. Hey, did you also have to solve a clue and go hunting for an invitation?" Somehow, I can't imagine Chase doing that.

"No. I have ways of getting myself invited to events without having to *hunt* for anything."

"Of course. You hunt criminals, not party invitations."

An amused smile touches his lips, but he says nothing.

"I know, I know. You won't admit to anything. If you did, I'd be able to use it when I turn you in, right?"

"Calla—"

"You *know* I'm not going to do that."

"And you *know* I'm not going to just use you for your ability, so what are you upset about?"

"I'm—" What am I upset about? Elizabeth, probably. Trying to convince him to use me, putting her hands all over him, remarking about a comment from years ago to make me fully aware they have some kind of history together.

"You should go home, Calla. If Saber sees you here, things could get messy."

"And if he sees you?"

"He won't. My charming companion is going to keep him busy."

"Then he won't be paying any attention to me, will he?"

"Calla, you—"

"Please." I hold my hand up. "Don't do that overprotective thing. I get enough of it from my parents and my brother. I've been kidnapped and locked up, I've been ridiculed and teased, I've faced dozens of opponents during unofficial assignments, and I've survived it all. I think I can take care of myself."

Chase frowns. "You were kidnapped?"

"Yes. It isn't something I—"

"Callaaa! There you are!" Gemma runs over, flings her arms around me, and squeezes me tight. Perry follows close behind, looking concerned.

"Hey, we've been looking for you for a while," he says, "I think—"

"Oh my *gosh*," Gemma says, hanging onto my arm and staring wide-eyed at Chase. "You're the hot tattoo guy. And you're standing *right here*. Know what? I've always wanted to get a tattoo on—" she giggles, then whispers "—*my butt*. Do you do butt tattoos? Please say yes. You're the *best* tattoo artist in the whole world."

"Um …" I cast a questioning look over Gemma's head at Perry.

"I think she ate something weird," he says. "She's been like this for the past ten minutes."

"Some of the chocolate bonbons have alcohol inside them," Chase says, not looking the slightest bit disturbed by Gemma's outburst. "Human alcohol, not faerie alcohol. It acts quickly on our systems."

"That's probably it," Perry says. "She ate a whole load of different bonbons."

"They were AH-mazing," Gemma says loudly.

"I'm sure they were." I pat her arm. "Perry, maybe you should—" I duck as a group of sprites flying in formation swoop over our heads before continuing around the room where they receive applause from most of the fae they fly over.

"This Lucien de la Mer guy provides the strangest entertainment," Chase comments.

"Um, I don't feel so good," Gemma says.

"Chase?" Elizabeth hurries toward us. She frowns at Gemma, currently bending over and breathing deeply while Perry rubs her arm. Elizabeth steps closer to Chase and lowers her voice to say, "Something's gone wrong. I didn't get to Saber in time. I saw him grab Lucien's wife and pull her into another room through the door behind the ice pond. No one else seemed to notice."

"Damn. What does he want with her?"

"I don't know, but I'm not sticking around to find out." She touches Chase's arm, then backs away. "I'm leaving. I can't afford to get caught here if things go south and security locks this place down."

Chase gives her a quick nod and says, "I understand."

"Coward," I mutter under my breath.

"Calla, we should really get Gemma home," Perry says.

"Yes. Can you take her? I need to help Chase with something here."

Perry frowns. "Uh, okay. I'll message Gemma's sister. She helped her sneak out, so hopefully she's still around to distract the parents while I sneak her back in." He drapes Gemma's arm over his shoulders and helps her across the room toward the elevator. He'll have to get her down to the lawn before he'll be able to open a doorway to the paths.

"You should go too," Chase says, looking around for the ice pond. He spots the skaters and starts heading for them.

I hurry after him. "I can help you."

"I know, but I don't think your help is necessary tonight. I just need to get in there, stun Saber, and get him out of here before he hurts anyone or accomplishes whatever it is he's here for."

"And you don't think you could possibly use an illusion master to make your little rescue mission go more smoothly?"

Chase hesitates a moment, appearing to weigh up the options as he stares at the door on the other side of the frozen pond. "Okay. But you need to do whatever I say."

"I think I can probably manage that."

We move through the crowd of laughing, drinking, dancing guests as quickly as we can without looking conspicuous. When we reach the other side of the ice pond, near the door Saber took Lucien's wife through, I get to work. I picture the door with no one standing in front of it and project the image as far as I can. At least, I think that's what I'm doing. I've never really thought about distance or how many people my projections could influence at one time. I don't know if everyone in this room will automatically see what I want them to see, or if I have to imagine forcing the image further and further out. It seems strange that I don't know the limits of my own ability. Why have I never tested this before?

"Are you doing it?" Chase asks. I nod, and he moves in front of the door. He's gathered enough power to stun someone—which took him all of about four seconds—in case Saber attacks him the moment he opens the door. He tries the handle, but it's locked. "Just give me a minute to get this open." He kneels down and does some kind of spell on the keyhole with his stylus.

"Sure. I'll just be over here, imagining a blank door."

"Great. This shouldn't take too—Ah, there we go. Just a simple locking spell, as I suspected." He returns his stylus to an inside jacket pocket, stands, and takes hold of the handle. "Get ready to be creative if necessary."

I nod. He opens the door and steps quickly inside, both hands raised and ready to release magic. When nothing exciting happens, I peer past him and see an empty corridor with the same polished floor as the vast living area the party is happening in. I follow him and close the door behind me, finally letting go of the blank door image. We advance along the corridor. No doors lead off it, but not too far ahead, I can see it turns to the left.

A dull thud. The sound of running feet. My heart quickens, and I raise my hands to place a shield of protective magic in front of me. A second later, Saber comes sprinting around the corner. Chase sends his stunner spell shooting through the air. Saber ducks, skids to the side across the polished floor, and throws his hands out toward us. Sparks fly from his fingertips, morphing into a flurry of leaves that attack my shield and swirl around Chase's head before I extend the shield in front of him.

"Drop the shield," he tells me, so I do. He sweeps his hand out, and the leaves fall away. With the air clear now, I see Saber down on one knee, tossing a metallic ball across the floor toward us.

"What is—"

I don't have time to finish my question before Chase throws himself against me and pins me to the wall. An explosion deafens me, shuddering the ground and walls and filling the corridor with billows of thick grey smoke. Above the ringing in my ears I hear Saber shouting, "I've already got what I came for."

Chase pushes away from me and disappears into the smoke. My eyes sting and I can't stop coughing, so I form a bubble of protection around me while the smoke dissipates. After about a minute, it's gone. Chase comes running back into the corridor, shaking his head and looking grim. "I couldn't find him. He's gone."

"Lucien's wife?" I say. I turn and run in the other direction down the corridor. We find her in a sitting room around the corner, lying on the floor. She sits up as we reach her, rubbing her head and looking confused. "Are you okay?" I ask, helping her up onto a chair. Her arms are barely more than skin and bone, and her short hair is so thin, I can see her scalp though it. I remember bits of what I've read in the news about this woman's strange illness that her body's magic can't heal and no one can cure.

Still looking rather dazed, she says, "I think so."

"The man who brought you in here," Chase prompts. "What did he want?"

Her eyes are wide with bewilderment. "What man? What happened? I don't remember coming in here."

I notice a small glass vial on the floor. "He made her forget," I say quietly to Chase. "She doesn't know anything."

Running footsteps sound in the corridor. "Security," Chase says. "Can you make them think we're not here?"

I nod, already picturing the room without us in it. Just the polished floor, the square furniture, the overly fluffy rug, and the recovering woman. When several guards run into the room, they hurry straight past us. We walk slowly, quietly back to the corridor, then pick up our pace. Two more guards are stationed at the doorway, holding back the questioning crowd. I have to hold an image of the empty corridor in my mind as we walk toward everyone. It's scary, knowing I might lose focus at any moment and allow the two of us to become visible. Halfway down the corridor, I grab onto Chase's arm and close my eyes so I can focus on the illusion I'm projecting. "Don't let me walk into anyone," I whisper.

We make it out safely, quickly moving through the crowd after I accidentally brush against one of the guards. "I have to admit," Chase says once we're a safe distance from the corridor and the barrier is back up around my mind, "your ability was rather useful in getting us in and out of there."

I shrug. "You're welcome."

"I just wish I knew what Saber came here for." Chase clenches his fist and presses it against the pillar we're standing beside. "He's several steps ahead of me, and I don't like it. The fact that I know who he's working for makes it even worse."

Undoubtedly the most dangerous man we know. That's what Chase said earlier.

"Who? What makes this person so dangerous? It's not ..." I feel so stupid saying the name Draven. It can't be him.

Chase shakes his head. "I don't want to involve you."

"Right, like I'm not involved already." When he shows no sign of answering me, I say, "Does the Guild know anything about this ... situation? Guardians are the ones who should be dealing with this."

"The Guild is aware of some of this."

I raise my eyebrows. "And? You're going to make them aware of the rest of it?"

"And ... I think this is the end of our conversation."

I groan loudly and grab a skewer of strawberries from a passing tray. "You're infuriating. This is why we aren't going to be working together."

"Yes. This is one of the reasons."

"But, you know, we can still be friends. I'll help you pick out designs for your tattoo clients, and you can teach me the best way to stab an enemy without killing him."

Chase allows himself a smile. "Sounds like the basis for a lifelong friendship."

I nod and finish chewing my strawberries. I drop the skewer onto another passing tray and say, "Well, good night. I guess

I'll see you around."

"For a stabbing lesson."

"Right."

I turn to leave, but he grabs my arm. "Calla?" His gaze drops to the ground in a moment of hesitation. "When I said 'older—'" his eyes, beautiful and intense, rise to meet mine "—I didn't mean 'old.'"

I press my lips together as I try to hold my smile in. "I know."

CHAPTER TWENTY-SIX

I WAKE THE NEXT MORNING AND ALLOW MYSELF A FEW minutes to lie there smiling before getting up. I might have a mother in hospital and a mentor who hates me, but I'm finally doing what I've always wanted to do, I have actual, real friends who are doing the same thing, and I get to occasionally hang out with a cool Underground tattoo artist who thinks I look good in evening wear.

I get to the Guild dining hall in time for breakfast, but the only other person sitting at our usual table is Ned. Gemma is apparently 'not feeling well,' and then Ned receives a message from Perry saying he overslept and only just woke up.

"Must have been quite a party, huh?" Ned mumbles.

"It was. I think it's safe to say Gemma won't be eating any chocolate bonbons for a while."

Ned nods. He then shovels food into his mouth with alarming speed before excusing himself to go finish some homework. I'm pretty sure we had no homework yesterday, which means Ned is simply making an escape. I suppose he's still too shy around me to consider sticking around for a conversation without the safety net of his other two friends.

Since classes aren't due to begin for another twenty-five minutes, and—fortunately—I have no meeting with Olive this morning, I decide to go to the healing wing and visit Mom. The woman behind the desk in the waiting area makes a comment about me not observing visiting hours, but, with a conspiratorial smile, she lets me through anyway.

I sit on the stool that appears beside Mom's bed and watch her for a while. I try to find the anger I felt when I learned her secret, but it's mostly gone. I'm relieved. Hanging onto that anger would have been exhausting. When I look at her now, I just feel ... sad. I feel as though I don't know nearly enough about her, and, to be honest, she doesn't know me that well either. "We haven't had the healthiest mother-daughter relationship, have we?" I say as I place my hand over Mom's. "We smile at each other and skim the surface of our lives with pleasantries, but neither of us ever trusted the other enough to go deeper than that. There are things, so many things I could have shared with you. The nasty comments that left me in tears, my fear that I'd waste my life as an artist and never help anyone, the thrill I felt the first time I did a back flip, my crush on Zed, the truth about what really happened to ... that boy who committed suicide." I squeeze Mom's hand, wondering if she'll remember any of this when she wakes up. "Neither of us had to be so alone, Mom, but we chose to keep our secrets to ourselves. I guess we'll see if we can change that when you wake up."

I stand, then turn back as I remember something. "Ryn and Vi are finally having a proper wedding. Union ceremony, I mean." If Mom were awake, I know she'd correct me. "It's happening next weekend. I know that's barely any time to organize anything, but a friend of theirs has some time off so she offered to plan the whole thing. So, you know, if there's a wake-up date you're aiming for, any time before next Saturday would be—"

From the corner of my eye, I see the curtain sway. I look up as two male healers walk in. They're surprised to see me here, but not as surprised as I am to see them. Because despite the uniforms these two men are wearing, I know they're not healers. One is the scarred man who fought me and attacked my parents, and the other is Saber.

* * *

They stunned me.

I'm lost in a groggy no man's land of semi-consciousness when I become aware of this. I remember flinging sparks at them and grasping the air for a throwing star. I threw one— and that must have been the moment I was stunned because I don't remember anything after that.

I feel a rocking motion, but I can't tell if it's real or if it's part of my confused half-dreaming state. I swim in slow motion through water thick like syrup. My arms are weak. So weak I can barely pull myself through the thick water. I try to kick against it with my legs, but they're even more sluggish than my arms.

A cold breeze. It drifts across my face, smelling like salt. The rocking motion continues, and a sloshing sounds joins it. I drag one eyelid open for a moment and see dark clouds moving above me before darkness descends over my vision once more.

Mom. What did they do with Mom?

Over the next few minutes, I catch glimpses of the turbulent sky above, someone moving next to me, and then a dark shape blotting out the sky. By that point, I'm conscious enough to know I'm in a boat and that my wrists and ankles are bound. With a great effort, I manage to keep my eyes open longer than a second or two, and that's when I realize what the dark shape is: a floating island.

"Where ... are ..."

A face appears above mine. A face I recognize. "This one's waking up," Saber says.

"Well, we're here now," a male voice replies. "Probably a good thing she's awake."

"Are we in the right spot?" Saber asks.

"Yes, I just got the signal."

A moment later, the rocking and sloshing disappears. I manage to raise my head enough to figure out what's going on: The boat is rising through the air toward the underside of the floating island. I see dark earth, hanging vines, rope ladders, and falling streams of water. Then I see a distinct circular shape. As we sail smoothly upward toward the circle, I realize it's a hole. We rise through it, fly sideways, and, with a sudden lurch, the rocking and sloshing returns. We must be floating on water once more.

I'm fully awake now, although my limbs are still sleepy from the stunner spell. I look around and see metal gates and stone walls and flames dancing in torches. Saber leans over me once more. "Welcome to Velazar Prison," he says with a sneer.

Velazar Prison? "What?" I manage to croak out. "Why?"

Saber vanishes from my line of sight. Using my elbow, I manage to push myself into a sitting position. We're floating on an underground canal alongside several other small boats, and lying beside me, his arms and legs also bound, is Gaius.

"What's going on?" I ask Saber. "What did you take us for, and why are we at a prison?"

Saber laughs. "Did you hear that, Marlin?" he says to his scarred companion who's just finished securing the boat to a post on one side of the canal. "Thinks she can interrogate us."

"You know each other," I say, looking from Saber to the scarred man and back again. "You're working together?"

"Come on, Gold." Saber snaps his fingers several times. "Figure it out. It's not that hard to put the pieces together."

Marlin shouts something to a man on the other side of a locked gate. "He came after my mother," I say, nodding my head to Marlin, "because he wants to know about the vision she Saw all those years ago. And you ..." I think back to what Chase told me "... you wanted to travel back in time to find out something." The connection snaps into place. "The same thing Marlin wants to know. You were going to go back to the time my mother had that vision and find out whatever you could about it."

Saber snaps his fingers again. "Congratulations. Aren't you clever."

"But why? What's so important about this vision she had?"

He shoves his face in front of mine. "Now why would I tell you that? You're the girl who assisted in destroying an ability that was *mine*. I will never get that back, and after the boss is done with you, I'm going to make sure you *pay for it*."

I shrink away from his snarling words. Blinking against the last wisps of grogginess floating through my mind, I try to focus on projecting an—

"Everyone, put these on." The man who was behind the gate—a guard, I presume, judging by his uniform—walks to the edge of the canal and tosses four metal rings to Marlin. "You know the drill. You won't be able to step outside of your boat unless you're wearing them, and you won't be able to take them off until you're back in your boat at the end of your visit."

Marlin leans over and pushes a ring onto one of my fingers. "No more illusion tricks from you," he says.

So that's what this is. I thought I recognized the metal. I saw it in Zell's dungeon, wrapped around the wrists and ankles of most of the other prisoners. I was supposed to have a band made from this metal to stop me projecting illusions while I was locked up there, but Zell's men hadn't yet made one small enough for me by the time Ryn came to get me out.

"And leave any weapons in the boat," the guard adds. "You won't be able to get them past the first gate. Right, then, let's go." A flick of his hand produces a set of stairs leading down from the side of the canal to the edge of our boat. Clearly he still has access to his magic.

Saber cuts the cord around my ankles with a knife and pulls me to my feet. Then he shakes Gaius and slaps him a few times until the poor man wakes up.

Blinking, he stutters, "Wh—what is—"

"Just get up," Saber says, cutting the cord that binds Gaius's ankles and yanking him to his feet. He tosses his knife and several other weapons onto a cushion beneath one of the bench seats.

"I don't understand. Calla? What are we—"

"Shut up," Marlin says. He grabs my arm and pushes me ahead of him up the steps.

The four of us follow the guard through the gate—which is locked behind us by another guard who pats us down to check for weapons—along a cold stone passageway with water leaking down the walls, and into what looks like a waiting room within a cell. Two rows of slightly battered wooden chairs are lined up behind bars, and in front of the bars is a desk. The guard walks to the desk where a pile of forms sits, waiting to be filled in. "I presume you're here to see the same person you always see?" he asks.

"Yes," Saber says, and the guard fills in several of the blank spaces on the form.

"Right." He straightens. "I don't know what you've got going on here with people tied up, but you know I can only let one of you in at a time. The rest of you have to wait in there." He gestures to the chairs behind the bars.

"We need to see him together," Marlin says.

"That isn't going to happen. One at a time. That's the way

it works around here."

Marlin removes a folded envelope from one of his pockets and hands it to the guard. "Make it happen."

The guard opens the envelope and removes a page from inside. The dull, flickering light makes it hard to tell, but I think his skin loses some of its color as he examines the page. His jaw clenches. He returns the page to the envelope and hands it back to Marlin. "Even if I wanted to take you all through at the same time, I can't. There are twelve guards between here and the visitation rooms. Are you planning to blackmail all of them?"

"Take the ring off the girl," Saber says, "and she can get us there without anyone knowing."

The guard's jaw tenses again. "I can't do that."

"Unless you want your wife and children to know what's in this envelope, you'll do it."

The guard draws a slow, deep breath, watching Marlin as he considers this threat. Then he pulls me to the side of the room and lifts my hand. "Is it going to hurt?" I ask, unable to keep the fear from my voice. This is the same metal that scarred Ryn when it was removed from his arm. Vi went through the same thing. She told me she blacked out from the pain.

"Not when done properly," the guard says. "And I'm one of the few who knows how to do it properly." He rubs his finger back and forth over the ring, muttering words under his breath. Then he slips the ring off as easily as if it were any ordinary ring.

"Good," Marlin says. "I'm surprised you didn't demonstrate your ability the day I broke into your house," he adds as he pulls me away from the guard. "If I'd known what you can do, I might have asked for a little show."

"Why should I perform for you now?" I demand.

"Because I'll hurt you if you don't. Or I'll hurt this man over here." He gestures to Gaius. "Cut off a finger, perhaps. Or—" he taps his chin thoughtfully "—I'll simply remind you that I have your mother. That would probably be the most effective threat, don't you think?"

So he does have Mom. Despair threatens to overwhelm me as my fears are confirmed, but I do my best to stand my ground. "You won't do anything to her. You need her."

"I need her alive, yes. It doesn't matter to me if she's injured in any way."

I grit my teeth. "Fine. What do you want me to do?"

"It's simple. Whenever we pass a guard, he or she must see only Saber and this man." He points to the guard who's clearly being blackmailed into all of this. "If that doesn't happen, we're all in trouble—including your mother."

"Okay. I can do that."

Saber walks with the guard, and Marlin, Gaius and I follow quietly behind them. We journey past various guards through a confusing maze of stairways, corridors, and ancient, rickety elevators, all as dark and damp as the first passageway we walked through. Even if I wasn't focusing intently on projecting images of empty space, I doubt I'd be able to remember my way out of here. Before passing through another locked gate, the guard has to produce the form he filled in for approval from another guard. After receiving a stamp on the form, we're allowed through.

Finally, we walk onto a bridge stretching from one side of an enormous cavern to the other. And that's when I almost ruin everything, because I'm so stunned by what I see that, for a second, I lose focus. I quickly grasp hold of it, though, sending most of my energy into projecting the illusion that Marlin, Gaius and I aren't here, while allowing a tiny part of my brain to marvel at what I'm seeing.

Hundreds and hundreds of individual prison cells float in the air, filling the cavern and slowly moving in different directions so that no two cells are next to each other for more than about half a minute. The guard who's been leading us presents his stamped form to the man waiting at the gate halfway across the bridge. "Okay," the man says with a nod after checking the form. "I'll send him to Visitation Room 2."

As we walk through the gate, I see a cell high up near the ceiling pick up speed and move toward the far side of the cavern. I assume it contains the man we're here to see. We cross the bridge to the other side of the cavern and walk down another corridor before stopping outside a closed door with a number 2 on it.

"I hope you don't expect me to wait outside," the guard says. "There are other guards who patrol this corridor, and they'll want to know why I'm not in there with you."

"Oh, please do come inside," Marlin says. "We'll be needing you."

The visitation room is split in half by bars made of the same metal as the rings. We wait on one side, and a door on the other side opens. A man in dirty prison overalls and straggly two-toned hair walks in. There isn't anything remarkable about his appearance, nothing that would make him stand out in a crowd. His demeanor is anything but commanding, but I sense a change in the two men who brought us here. Out there they were in charge, but in here they answer to him.

"Oh dear," Gaius mutters. "Not good, not good."

"Good evening," the prisoner says, a pleasant smile on his face. "Thank you, Mr. Saber and Mr. Marlin for bringing these two here so promptly. Are the bonds really necessary, though? They make this whole business rather disagreeable. Our guests can't use magic, nor do they have anywhere to go. Mr. Saber?" Saber steps up to me and works at the knots around my wrists until the ropes come loose and fall to the ground. Then he moves to Gaius while the prisoner beckons to me. "Miss Larkenwood. Why don't you come a little closer so I can see you properly." Instead of moving closer, I take a step backward. "Oh, I can't hurt you, if that's what you're worried about," he says, holding his wrists up to show a metal band around each one. "You've probably figured out by now that this substance blocks magic. It's a rare metal, used in most prisons but difficult to find elsewhere. Prince Marzell managed to acquire some, which is how I initially got to see it in action."

I frown at him. "Who are you?"

"My name is Amon. I was a spy within the Creepy Hollow Guild for many years. First I worked for Prince Marzell, and then I worked for Lord Draven. Now—" he steeples his fingertips "—I work for no one but myself."

This must be the man Chase was talking about. *The most dangerous man we know.*

"So ... Draven really is dead? That enchanted storm that

showed up last week had nothing to do with him?"

The hint of a smile appears on Amon's lips, but other than that, his expression remains unreadable. "How would I know anything about that? I'm locked inside a prison." He lowers his hands and clasps them behind his back. "You're probably wondering why you're here," he continues. "It wasn't part of the plan. I didn't even know about you. The plan was to take your mother, but you happened to be in the room at the time, so you were taken as well. When Saber visited earlier today, I told him to simply get rid of you. But then he told me you can produce illusions of some sort, and I had to see that for myself."

"Well then," I say, because I see no other way out of this. "What would you like to see?"

"Hmm." Amon tilts his head to the side. "Show me a unicorn. I've never seen one in real life."

I resist the urge to tell him he still won't have seen one in real life when this is done. Instead, I relax the control on my imaginary wall and picture a unicorn inside the cell with Amon. He jumps back, startled, then laughs.

"Remarkable," he says, reaching forward to touch it. His hand passes through the unicorn, of course, because it isn't really there. It vanishes as I lock my mind back up again.

"Anything else I can do to entertain you?" I ask, unable to keep the sarcasm from my voice.

"No, no, that's all for now." He looks over my shoulder to where Gaius is standing. "And this is the man who took your power from you, Mr. Saber?"

"Yes, sir."

"Impressive. That's a skill that can definitely be useful to me. First, though, I'd like to see a demonstration."

"A—a demonstration?" Gaius stutters.

"On her." He points at me.

"What?" I back away, but there's nowhere to go.

"I want what she can do," Amon says simply. "And you, Gaius, are going to be the man who stores all the abilities I want to collect until I can get out of here and make use of them. Now take it. And don't stop there." He grasps the cell bars and peers intently at me. "Take all of it. Every drop of magic she possesses."

"*What?*" I gasp.

"I—I can't do that," Gaius says. "I can take Griffin Abilities, but I can't take core magic."

"Can't? Really? How do you know that?"

"Well, I've never done it. I don't know if—"

"Now's your chance to try. Treat this as an experiment. But please don't pretend you can't do it in a weak attempt to save her. That won't work out well for either of you."

Gaius continues to shake his head as he backs away from me.

Amon sighs, as if this little drama is keeping him from something more important. "You'll be saving her life by doing this. I promised Saber he would have his revenge, and the way we're doing that is by removing all her magic. So if you can't do that, I'm afraid we'll have to kill her."

Gaius grows still, but his wide eyes never leave me. I see his resignation, and I know what decision he's come to. "Don't do this, don't do this," I beg. "Please don't do this." I don't want to die, but I don't want to wind up magic-less either. There *must* be another way out of this.

"I—I have to," Gaius says, tugging uselessly at the ring on his finger. "I can't let them kill you."

"You. Guard," Marlin says. "Come over here and remove this man's ring."

The guard hesitates, then puffs out his chest and places his hands on his hips. "No. I can't let you do this. It's all gone too far now."

"Oh, don't be ridiculous," Marlin says. "This is not your moment to be a hero. Do you really want to watch your own life—your family's life—go up in flames because you tried to save someone you don't even know? Do you really think that's worth it?"

The man looks tortured, but in the end, with a cry of anger, he crosses the room and removes Gaius's ring. Then, before I can think to fight back with magic, he grabs my hand and pushes the ring onto it.

"No!" I shriek. I run for the door, but Saber and Marlin catch me before I'm halfway there. I kick and scratch and hit, but they pin me to the floor. Gaius advances on me, guilt and fear written across his face.

"Please forgive me," he says. "I'm only trying to save you." He catches my flailing hand and hangs onto it. He closes his eyes, and I make one last desperate attempt to get away. I scream and kick and thrash, but Gaius never lets go of my hand.

I don't know the moment when I finally lose my Griffin Ability, but I feel it when he begins to draw my core magic out of me. It's my essence, my energy, the thing that distinguishes me from other magical beings and beings with no magic at all. I slowly grow weaker. Weaker and colder. My vision dims, and I wonder if this will kill me anyway. Is magic what keeps me alive, or can I survive without it?

Weaker ... colder ... darker ...

Blackness clouds the edges of my vision as the last of my magic is sucked from me.

CHAPTER TWENTY-SEVEN

I HAVE NOTHING. NO ILLUSIONS, NO GUARDIAN WEAPONS, no magic at all. But I'm not dead. I lie on the cold stone floor feeling weak and sick and ... different. As if a hum I was never aware of is gone. Like a background noise you don't notice until it's no longer there.

You have no magic.

I don't know how long I've been lying here, the tears drying on my face and the chill creeping through my clothes. I'm vaguely aware of the others in the room: the guard pacing in the corner, dealing with his own personal demons; Saber and Marlin conversing with Amon; Gaius hovering near me, almost protectively.

You have no magic.

I blink a few times and see the ring back on Gaius's hand. Is he extra powerful now that he has both his magic and mine? What would he be capable of if he wasn't constrained by that ring? I want to hate him for taking what should always have been mine, but I can't muster the strength. Besides, I know none of this was his fault. He was only trying to save me. If only he knew that life as an empty shell isn't a life worth saving.

You have no magic.

The realization hits me again, reminding me of all the things I'll never do or have. I want to crumple in on myself and cry until there are no tears left inside me. What am I supposed to do now? Who am I without magic? Where can I go? Where will I ever belong?

I've never felt such despair before. I expect it to consume me, to finish me off, but I'm still lying here, very much alive. If anything, I feel more awake than I did just now. Perhaps I'm slowly recovering from the shock of losing everything. At first that makes no sense to me, but then I remember that beings without magic are also capable of healing. Humans get sick and wounded, and their bodies manage to fix themselves.

"Keep him somewhere secure," Amon says, nodding toward Gaius. "Somewhere he can't harm himself or hope to escape. Collecting Griffin Abilities certainly isn't our focus, but since the opportunity has presented itself, we can make use of it."

"Yes, sir," Marlin says. "We've got the Seers at the mulberry house. It's never been compromised, so—"

"No. Not there. Keep him at one of the other locations. I don't want all my assets in one place."

"Of course, sir."

"Take the first two Seers somewhere else as well. They don't all need to be together."

I'm distracted from my own misery as I listen to Amon's instructions. He's going to use Gaius to steal Griffin Abilities. No more army of special soldiers, like Draven used. He won't have to keep hundreds of Gifted people under control. Now he can store the abilities in jewelry or other objects until he decides to make use of them. And it doesn't matter that he's locked behind bars. Not when he has followers so clearly willing to do his bidding.

For a moment, I'm reminded of why I've always wanted so badly to be a guardian: to protect others. To stop the kind of evil that locked me and hundreds of others in cages and then proceeded to lay waste to our world. The kind of evil that sees the unique magic in others and wants to steal it away. I want to stop that. And now I never can.

You know you can do all that without being a guardian, right? The memory of Chase's voice brings color to the dismal grey painted across my mind. *You don't need guardian weapons. You don't even need magic.*

Don't need magic? What an unimaginable concept.

"That will be all for now," Amon says. "Let me know when the Seer wakes up. It could be a long time still, but I'm a patient man."

Through my half-open eyelids, I see Marlin nod and take hold of Gaius. "Get ready to start using your new ability. You'll be getting us out of here with an illusion."

"But … I've never used it before. I don't know how to make illusions." As Gaius says this, images of guards dragging us away flicker across the walls. "What? How did I ..."

What Gaius doesn't know is that creating illusions won't be his problem. Figuring out how to keep them to himself will be.

"You've got about half a minute," Marlin says, "so you'd better figure it out. And don't even think about revealing us all so the guards can catch us. We know about your grandmother."

Gaius's fear-filled eyes grow even wider.

"What must we do with the girl?" Saber asks, walking to my side and nudging my arm with his shoe. Anger burns inside me, sparking life in my limbs. I almost feel strong enough to kick him.

"Throw her into the ocean," Amon says.

My anger freezes as fear takes its place.

"You can't do that," Gaius protests. "You said you wouldn't kill her if I took her magic."

"I know, but I was lying," Amon explains. "Come now, be reasonable. She knows too much. I can't let her go back home and tell everyone what happened. Besides, what kind of life can she have without magic? It will be kinder to throw her into the ocean."

Kinder? Kinder, my ass! A few minutes ago, sinking into hopelessness, I would have agreed with Amon. And I still can't begin to fathom how I might live without magic, but the only thing I know now is that *I don't want to die.*

"I look forward to pushing her out the boat," Saber says, grasping my arm and pulling me up. "Preferably from a great height."

I waver on my feet as dizziness spins my head, but I manage

to stay upright. I'm still far weaker than normal, and I have no idea how I'm going to fight my way out of this, only that I must. First, we need to get past as many guards as possible. "Gaius." I wave my hand feebly toward him. Even my voice is unsteady. I hate the sound of it, but the weaker everyone thinks I am, the better. "Picture what you want them to see," I say, keeping my voice at a croaky whisper. "Hold that image in your mind. Focus. That's all it takes."

The guard and Saber head out, Gaius follows them, and Marlin pulls me along at the back of the procession. "All this trickery getting in and out of here just so he could see two Gifted," Saber mutters. "They're not even part of the main plan. If we get caught doing this—"

"Then we'll face the consequences," Marlin says. "Or doesn't your loyalty extend that far?"

"Of course it does," Saber grumbles.

None of the guards stop us, so I assume Gaius is managing to maintain the illusion. Nevertheless, I tell myself to be prepared to run at any stage. I don't know how fast I can go in my current state, but the element of surprise could help me. I wiggle my right leg around a bit to see if I can feel Dad's knife in the sheath inside my boot, but I can't tell if it's there. Would Saber and Marlin have thought to check there for a weapon?

We eventually arrive back at the first corridor. We pass the waiting room, and I see another guard sitting at the desk there. He must have come in after we left to take the first guard's place. With the waiting room behind us, Gaius sighs in relief, and I know he's let go of the illusion. We don't need it anymore. Only one more gate to get through, and the guard there knows that four of us came in together. On the other side of the gate, the blackmailed guard escorts us back to our boat.

My move is coming soon.

Adrenaline pumps through my system, readying me for what's to come. The stairs appear, Saber goes down first, and I'm pushed after him. I make sure to wobble more than necessary as I step into the boat. I collapse onto a pile of blankets and let my eyelids flutter half-closed. I hate the pathetic act, but it's necessary if I don't want them watching my every move.

The men remove their rings. The stairs vanish, and the boat starts moving with the current. The guard watches us with folded arms and a grim expression. We're heading toward a kind of whirlpool, which I assume will pull us down and drop us out the underside of the floating island. The boat moves faster. My breath quickens. My fingers wrap around the edge of the boat and tighten.

We hit the whirlpool. The water draws away from us, and the boat drops down. With spray spinning around us, the underside of the island comes into view.

And this is where my brilliant plan kicks into action.

I leap up and launch myself out of the boat, aiming for one of the many hanging vines. I snatch hold of it as I begin to fall. It tears into my palms, burning my skin as I slip down it. The vine swings forward with my momentum, and I let go and grab hold of another one. My stinging palms scream out at me, but I *will not let go*. I'm only one more vine away from my target: a rope ladder. I leap again—and this is the vine that breaks.

I fall, scrabbling at the air, my momentum carrying me just

close enough to grab onto one side of the ladder. The rope burns more skin from my hands, but I hang onto it tighter than I've ever held onto anything. I hear an angry shout somewhere behind me, but I don't look back. As the swinging of the rope ladder slows, I find a foothold on a lower rung and begin climbing. "Ignore the pain," I tell myself through gritted teeth. "Ignore the pain, ignore the pain."

I'm climbing toward a narrow, vertical hole in the ground. Through it, I see dull, grey light. I'm almost at the base of the hole when the rope ladder jerks abruptly below me. I look down and see Saber at the bottom. A trail of swinging vines tells me he took the same route I did. "Dammit. Climb faster," I instruct myself. "Climb faster, climb faster."

I reach the bottom of the hole—and it's narrower than anything I've ever climbed through. Panic chokes me. Saber is below, catching up quickly, and ahead is the one thing I never want to face.

I freeze.

Saber will kill you! I scream at myself. *MOVE!* I take a great gulp of air and continue climbing. The earthy walls of the vertical tunnel are so close to me, I can almost feel the sand brushing against my back. I shrink away from it, a scream building in my throat. I climb faster. "Keep going, keep going, keep going," I chant through my sobs. I can see the clouds above me, and I can feel the tunnel pressing closer, feel the phantom grasp of Saber's hand around my ankle, and I climb and climb and climb—and then I'm through! I dig my fingers into the grass, pull myself out of the hole, and climb onto shaking legs. The prison rises up on my left, a dark, imposing fortress of stone. On my right, a wall encircles the edge of the floating island.

I run.

I don't know where I'm going or how this is supposed to help me get home, but I know I can't let Saber catch me. I leap over a stream of water that flows out from the base of the prison. Sparks shoot over my shoulder, and I duck to the side in fright. I stumble as I avoid a hole like the one I climbed up, but manage to steady myself before I fall. Another spark shoots past me. It morphs into a leafy vine and snakes back toward me. It wraps around my ankle and tugs me to the ground.

With no chance to land properly, I feel the left side of my body slamming into the ground. I cry out in pain, but there's no time to wait for it to subside. I slide my hand into my right boot and feel for the sheath—and Dad's knife is there! I pull it out, slash at the vine, and roll away from it. I push myself up and see Saber jumping across the stream.

I turn and run. I run and run and run, and I'm *so* tired, but I have to keep going. I can see the end of this side of the prison, and I know I'll turn the corner soon. Maybe there'll be somewhere I can hide. Some place I can duck into before Saber sees where I've gone. Another hole, or a ladder, or stairs. *Something.*

I turn the corner—and see a solid stone wall ahead of me. *Dammit!* I keep running, but I veer to the right. The wall encircling the edge of the island is lower than the one ahead of me, and the crumbling stones would provide footholds here and there. If I can get onto that wall, then I can walk along it and—

A laugh behind me tells me it's too late. I swing around, holding up my knife. It's the only protection I've got. I'm not even wearing my protective vest under my clothing. Right now, the one time I *really* need that vest, it's sitting inside my training bag at the Guild. But it's useless to think of it now when all I have to rely on is the knife. *You can do this*, I tell myself as I tighten my shaking grip on the carved handle. *You don't need guardian weapons. You don't need magic. You can do this.*

"One knife," Saber says, "and nothing else." He laughs again. "This should be easy."

We'll see about that.

I swap the knife to my left hand. I lower myself to a crouch, grab a flat stone with sharp, broken edges, and throw it at him the way I would a throwing star. It catches the edge of his shoulder as he jerks away. I reach for a small, round one and hurl it at his head. It strikes the left side of his brow, leaving a gash. With a cry of anger, he flings magic at me. His sparks shoot through the air and form flames by the time they've reached me. I dive out of the way, fall into a shoulder roll, and let the momentum carry me back onto my feet.

Then, since I can't run away from him, I hurtle straight toward him. I see him tense and bend his knees slightly, getting ready to flip me over his shoulder. *Not gonna happen.* At the last second, I force all my energy into a jump, bring both knees up to my chest as I sail toward him, and kick as hard as I can. He hits the ground, and I land on the other side of him. He groans and coughs and climbs to his feet, but I'm ready with a side kick that sends him stumbling backward. I advance on him, slashing with my knife when he tries to jump at me.

With a grunt of anger, he pushes hard at the air between us. A pulse of magic slams into me, sending me flying backward through the air. All breath is knocked from my lungs as I hit the ground. Struggling to suck in air, I push myself up onto shaky legs. My spurt of adrenaline-infused energy is fading fast.

"Come on, I can do this all day," Saber calls, taunting me.

I can't, and he knows that. But I have a knife. A knife I know exactly how to throw thanks to the hours of torturous practice Olive put me through yesterday. Even my dreams were filled with knife-throwing last night.

Another spark shoots toward me, and I duck down to avoid it. "Do you want to keep dancing for a while longer?" Saber shouts. "Or shall we end this now?"

Let's end this now. I pinch the knife handle between my thumb and forefinger. I raise my hand, then bring it down fast. The knife spins—and hits its target. Deep in Saber's chest, right where his heart is. He lets out a gasp of shock. He clutches at his chest, then falls onto his knees. He wraps his hand around the knife and tugs it from his body before slumping onto the ground.

He isn't dead. I know that much. Stab wounds don't kill faeries unless they're so bad the body's magic can't heal them before the magic runs out. If I leave Saber, he'll recover. What I should probably do—what Olive would tell me to do—is run over there and finish the job while he's down. A few well-aimed stabs to the head. That would certainly kill him.

The thought makes me sick.

I don't ever want to end another life again.

All I want is to get away from here, and now that Saber's down, I can do just that. I turn and run back the way I came as fast as my exhausted limbs will carry me. My magic-free body is fading fast, but I'm not ready to give up yet. I need to find a way back into this prison so I can get help. The guards will help me, won't they? I'm not a criminal. Even if they decide to lock me up while they contact the Guild, at least I'll be far from Saber. Unless he recovers quickly and comes into the prison looking for me.

"Hey!"

The shout comes from behind me. I spin around. Saber is running toward me with difficulty, as if every step is a great effort. He slows to a halt. He raises my knife. And he throws it at me.

A cry escapes my lips as the knife pierces my abdomen. I stumble backward a step or two. I look down in horror, barely able to believe that this weapon—*my* weapon—is protruding from my body. I watch a dark wetness seep into my clothing around the knife hilt.

I am going to die.

I raise my eyes and see Saber lurching toward me. He lifts his hand. Fiery sparks shoot from his fingers, and this time I have no hope of dodging them. They strike my chest, just below my right shoulder, and knock me backward onto the ground. My head hits something hard, and the sharp throbbing pain mixes with the searing ache from my chest until everything is just pain and dizziness and nausea.

A shadow passes over me, blocking out the spinning grey sky for a moment. But then Saber steps into my line of vision and I realize the shadow must have been him. He looks down at me. "You should have finished me off when you had the chance," he says. Then he bends and picks me up. He walks toward the wall—

"No," I whisper.

—and he throws me over.

I let out a wordless cry as I fall. The air sizzles and flashes around me as I pass through a layer of something invisible. I tumble and spin, grasping at the air as if I could catch onto it. Clawing, snatching, clutching—and then I see a spark leaving my fingertips.

Magic?

But whatever it is, it's too late, because swooping shadows are darkening the edges of my vision and waves are rushing toward me and—

Something grabs me before I hit the water, shocking the breath out of me once more. My toes skim the waves before I'm suddenly rising instead of falling. There's an arm around my waist, just above the knife, and a grey, leathery wing flapping beside me.

Jarvis?

"Hang on!" shouts a familiar voice.

This is a dream. It must be. I've hit the water and I'm dying and my final thoughts are of Chase and his gargoyle appearing at the exact moment I need them most. Darkness and dizziness fight to claim me. The jerky flying sensation starts to feel as though it's happening in slow motion.

Everything speeds up again as we come to a sudden halt. Arms cradle me, and my face is pressed against Chase's neck, and he's whispering something I can't hear properly. Something desperate, something pleading.

Then I'm lying on a hard surface. A hard surface that rocks gently from side to side. "Get us out of here," Chase shouts to someone. His face appears above me, anxiety twisting his features. "Calla? Can you hear me?"

With the pain and the dizziness and the darkness that wants to pull me under, I find it takes great effort to force words out of my mouth. "How did you ... know I was ..."

"I didn't," Chase says. His eyes dart across my chest. I feel his hand on my shoulder. "But I knew Gaius was here. Tracking device inside his watch. The signal disappeared once he was inside the prison, but I knew where he was by then." He tugs my sleeve back and wraps both hands around my arm.

"Did you ... find him?"

"Don't worry about him. You're going to be fine, okay? You can easily heal from this. I'm boosting your body's magic right now."

"But I have ... none ... to boost. He took it all."

"What?" Chase's anxious expression turns to alarm.

"Gaius ... took it." He took it all. But I saw a spark, didn't I? Or did I imagine that?

"That doesn't matter," Chase says, but I can see the fear in his eyes. "I'm giving you magic now. You're going to be fine." He lifts my arm and kisses my hand, and his lips are as warm as the magic I can feel flowing into me. "You have to be. You're supposed to be around for a long time still. It is *not* your time to leave the world."

I nod and let my eyelids slide shut. The pain is easing,

giving way to a deep weariness. Sleep beckons, and I'm happy to let it take me. Then I can forget everything that's happened since—

Mom.

"Mom," I say out loud, managing to rouse myself enough to open my eyes. "They have her … in … the mulberry house."

"Okay," Chase says, removing one hand from my arm and cupping my cheek. "I'll find her. I'll get her back."

With that weight lifted from me, I let myself sink back into the darkness.

CHAPTER TWENTY-EIGHT

I CAN TELL FROM THE SMELL THAT I'M LYING IN A HEALING institute. Memories of my encounter with Amon and my fight with Saber flash across the back of my eyelids, scenes painted with desolation and pain and thoughts of death that tear into my mind's canvas. I wait a while, allowing myself time to wipe the images away with an imaginary cloth.

My canvas is clean. Whole.

I am alive.

I lift my eyelids and find myself in a bed exactly like the one Mom was in. After blinking a few times, I turn my head to the side and see the elf girl from Wickedly Inked sitting on the stool beside the bed. Before I can say anything, she leans closer to me and tells me the story she's apparently told everyone else: She was on her way to Velazar Prison to visit someone and passed a boat that had just left. I was in the boat, and I was fighting two men. Using an oar, she surprised them and knocked them out of the boat, then rescued me. She sailed as quickly as possible to where the faerie paths could be accessed, and brought me straight to the healing wing at the Creepy Hollow Guild.

I push myself up in the bed, feeling a hundred times better than the last time I was awake. "So you want me to lie?"

"For that part of the story, yes. You can tell the truth about everything else." She stands up. "Well, goodbye."

"Wait. Where's Chase? Was he here?"

"No. If he were able to be here, there would be no need for you to lie about the last part of your story."

"Has he found my mother?"

"I don't know. I'm going now. Your family will be back soon." Without another word, she slips away between the curtains.

I immediately push back the blanket and climb out of bed. Peeking beneath the stiff patient gown at my abdomen, I find that the knife wound is perfectly healed. Chase must have given me a lot of magic. I cross the enclosed area and stick my head out between the curtains. I don't see anyone I recognize in the corridor.

"Miss Larkenwood!" Startled, I look the other way and see a woman healer hurrying toward me. "Please get back into bed," she says.

"But I'm fine. Is my brother around?"

"Why don't you get back into bed, and I'll have a look in the waiting area for you."

"But I don't need to be in bed anymore. I'm fine. I'm just taking up space you could be using for another patient."

"Miss Larkenwood." She ushers me back through the curtains. "You arrived here yesterday evening with severely low levels of magic. You might feel fine, but I highly doubt your magic has fully replenished itself yet. In order for that to happen, you need to rest." She points at the bed. I roll my eyes and walk back to it.

"Cal, you're awake."

I turn around before reaching the bed and see Ryn pushing the curtain aside. I run back past the healer and into his arms. "Is Dad here?" I ask as he hugs me tightly. "Do you know anything about Mom?"

Ryn steps back. "Dad's having a shouting match with the manager of the healing wing, and I've heard nothing about your mom yet. What happened? Dad was gone, so I was the one who got the notification yesterday about your mother going missing. Then no one could find you either. Not even Vi." He hesitates for a second, his eyes flicking to the healer, but he hasn't said enough to give away Violet's Griffin Ability. "Then an elf arrived here last night with you and a story about Velazar Prison. What's—"

"Mr. Larkenwood, please let your sister lie down," the healer interrupts. "She needs her—"

"—rest, I know," I finish for her, climbing back into the bed. "Can I talk while I'm sitting down, or is that not restful enough?"

The healer makes an irritated noise at the back of her throat and leaves in a huff. Since she didn't answer my question, I assume I'm allowed to talk. I tell Ryn about the two men who showed up while I was visiting Mom yesterday morning, about waking up on the way to Velazar Prison, and about being forced in front of a prisoner who was a spy for Prince Zell and Lord Draven. I tell him everything, leaving out any reference to the time traveling ability Saber had, and then end with the elf's version of the story. It doesn't matter too much that it isn't the version that actually happened; the end result is still the same. I was rescued, Saber and Marlin got away, and they took Gaius with them.

"So it was just bad luck that you happened to be here at the same time they came to take your mother," Ryn says.

"Yes. They were going to get rid of me, but when Amon heard about my Griffin Ability, he told them to—" I freeze. Like a heavy stone sinking to the pit of my stomach, a realization weighs itself down on me. "It's gone. My Griffin Ability. I don't ... I don't have it anymore. I thought Gaius had taken all my magic, and I was so relieved to discover I still had some left that I didn't realize I no longer had *that* magic." Tears spring up in my eyelids. My Griffin Ability is the one thing that's made my life more difficult than anything else, but right now it's the one thing I want most. It's *mine*. It's part of me, and I've never wanted to be rid of it, no matter how much easier my life would have been without it.

"Hey, it's not that bad." Ryn leans closer and takes my hand. "This man, Gaius. Do you know if he can give Griffin Abilities back once he's taken them?"

I nod and sniff as I whisper, "Yes."

"Then it isn't gone for good. We'll find him, and you'll get your ability back."

I continue nodding. Ryn is right. Even if no one at the Guild comes close to finding Gaius, Chase will. I have no doubt of that.

I hear hurried footsteps outside my curtain, and then Vi walks in. "You're awake!" She rushes to my side. "I have good news. I just heard that the guards who patrol the forest outside the Guild have found your mother. She was lying near the Guild entrance, still asleep. No one saw who left her there."

Chase, a voice inside my head says immediately. I'm sure it was him.

"Wow, that's ... suspicious," Ryn says. "Who would bring her back? Where is she now?"

"They're bringing her into the healing wing as we speak."

"Oh thank goodness," I lean back against my pillows in relief. "Will there be someone to guard her in case Saber and Marlin come back for her?"

"Yes, there will be more than one guard," Ryn says. "And those men hopefully won't be able to get back into the healing wing, at least not the same way they did yesterday."

"How did they get in yesterday?" I was wondering about that. It's supposed to be impossible to get into the Guild if you're not authorized to be here.

"Remember that party you were at the other night?" Ryn says. "Lucien de la Mer? Well, since he and his wife spend so much time at various healing institutes because of her illness, they each have access pendants to all of them. And guess what he reported missing this morning."

"His access pendants," I say slowly. So that's what Saber was doing at Lucien's party. "But access pendants have names written on them. Whoever scanned those pendants should have seen that the names didn't match up to the people wearing them."

"That's what should have happened," Vi says. "But the entrance for healing wing employees isn't as carefully guarded as the main entrance to the Guild, and if a guard isn't paying attention, he can miss details like that."

"That's what Dad is currently yelling at the manager about," Ryn says. "Incompetent guards."

"Perhaps someone should tell him that Mom is back."

"Probably," Ryn says. "And you should—"

"—rest. I know. I've heard that one already."

After several more hugs and hand squeezes, Vi and Ryn leave. I open the drawers of the bedside cabinet and find my belongings in a neat pile inside one of them. I search through my clothes until I find my amber and stylus. Then I write two words to Chase: *Thank you.*

* * *

After a few hours of boring rest, Gemma arrives unexpectedly. "I don't think I'm supposed to know you're here," she says. "I mean, none of us were told anything. We just know that people were looking for you yesterday. Saskia told everyone you probably decided to skip a day or two because you're soft and can't handle the way your mentor pushes you. Anyway, my mom overheard that you were here, so she told me."

She asks what happened. After hesitating for too long, trying to figure out what's safe to tell and what isn't, I end up saying, "It was to do with my mother. Some men came for her, and I happened to be visiting at the time, so they took me as well. That's all I'm allowed to say."

Gemma stays for a while, filling me in on the lessons I missed yesterday and today and telling me all about Perry's triumphant defeat of Blaze in the Fish Bowl yesterday afternoon. The setting was a circus tent, and Perry used stilts and a spinning metal hoop to bring down his opponent.

Not long after Gemma leaves, I hear a "Well, well," coming from the gap in the curtain. I look up in surprise to see Olive standing there. "So," she says. "You couldn't wait until after your graduation before getting involved with the big league criminals. Oh no. Once again, you had to skip ahead of everyone else." She crosses her arms. "Velazar Prison. You don't mess around, do you?"

Fabulous. My friendly mentor has obviously spoken to Ryn, otherwise she wouldn't know any of this yet. "I didn't *choose* to get involved with a dangerous man who spied on the Guild for both Prince Zell and Lord Draven," I say. "But since I did wind up having an involuntary audience with him, we now know what information he's after, and we know he doesn't have it yet. That's a *good* thing, right? And the Guild also knows they should be going after Marlin and Saber, the two guys who are still out there doing Amon's dirty work."

Olive shakes her head slowly. "You think it's as simple as that."

"Yes, I do. Why shouldn't it be? Someone points out the bad guys, and guardians go out and get them."

"There are processes, procedures, laws. There are time constraints. There are many problems the Guild is dealing with, in both this realm and the human one, and this case doesn't require immediate, urgent attention just because one trainee thinks it should."

"But this is important!"

"That's what everyone says about their cases. And a case where the 'bad guy—'" she mockingly repeats my words along with air quotes "—is already locked up for life isn't high on anyone's priority list."

"But ... you guys are supposed to fix stuff like this. That's what the Guild is for."

"What's there to fix? You're alive, and your mother's been found. Yes, the two men who captured you are still out there, but as long as no one is in immediate danger, and as long as the Guild asks to be alerted as soon as they attempt to visit the prisoner again, there isn't too much else to be done at this point. The investigation will remain open, but any guardian working on it will dedicate his or her time to more important cases first."

I try to reel in my frustration, but it's difficult. "I expected more from the Guild."

Olive throws her head back and laughs. "I'm sorry to disappoint you, but that's the way things work around here and at every other Guild. If you were hoping for something different, you are more than welcome to leave."

She'd love that, but there's no way I'll give her the

satisfaction. Besides, the Guild is still where I want to be, even if the whole system doesn't work as perfectly as I thought it would. I stare defiantly back at Olive, and she leaves after letting out a sigh of disappointment.

After she's gone, Dad shows up and convinces the healers to let me rest at home instead of here. As far as I'm concerned, I've had enough rest to last me a full year of training. And speaking of training, I've missed out on almost two full days of it and I'm anxious to get back to work. Dad won't listen to my protests, though. He sends me straight to bed when we get home. I spend the remainder of Wednesday afternoon sitting in bed sketching pictures of stormy skies and turbulent seas and trying not to look at my amber every two seconds to see if Chase has replied.

The next day, I meet with the guardians working on Mom's case so I can repeat my story to them, leaving out the part where I had a Griffin Ability stolen from me and adding in the alternate ending. I have to pay attention so I don't lose track of exactly what I'm allowed to tell who. Chase will get the whole story, Ryn and Vi get most of the story, and anyone else at the Guild gets whatever they need to know about the bad guys and not much else.

After that, I go back to classes. I endure spiteful looks from Saskia and questions from other trainees. I spend the afternoon in the training center.

And then I get a message from Chase.

Old Guild ruins? 5 pm?

CHAPTER TWENTY-NINE

I SMILE FOR THE REMAINING FOURTEEN MINUTES OF MY final training session. When I get to the old Guild ruins, it's raining there. I was hot from an hour of arm strengthening exercises, but the air out here has a chill to it. I remove a hoodie from my training bag and pull it on over my head. A wide moss-covered archway stands not too far away. It's crumbling in places but still intact enough to provide shelter from the rain, so I wait beneath it, leaning against one side.

Chase arrives through a faerie paths doorway. He looks around, then walks toward me with his hands pushed into his coat pockets. He reaches the archway and leans against the opposite side. Droplets of rain cling to his hair, and his eyes appear brighter than usual in the strange light brought on by the rainy weather.

"You look like you're back to normal, Miss Goldilocks," he says. "Didn't I tell you you'd be fine?"

"You saved me," I say simply. "That's why I'm fine."

He looks away for a moment, an indefinable expression on his face.

"You found my mother."

"I did," he says, returning his gaze to me.

"How?"

"I'm aware of some of the locations that Amon, the prisoner I assume you were there to see, has been using. One is a house on an estate behind Thistle Orchard in Eilemor. It's secluded and surrounded by mulberry bushes. That's where I went first, and, sure enough, there she was. It's protected, of course, so it took me some time to get in."

Based on only the words 'mulberry house,' it would have been almost impossible for the Guild to find Mom. Chase did it in under a day. "I don't know how to thank you. Without you, I'd be dead and my mother would still be missing. My family would be broken."

Chase smiles. "I would say it was luck or chance that I arrived in time to catch you, and that I know the location Amon refers to as the 'mulberry house,' but I don't entirely believe in either luck or chance."

I'm starting to think I don't either. No one's that lucky, are they? "You were there looking for Gaius," I say.

"Yes. He was taken from Wickedly Inked where he was waiting for me. I keep my day job separate from my night job, so the tattoo shop used to be a safe spot until Saber discovered I work there."

"And you could track Gaius because of his watch?" I was a little overwhelmed by pain and dizziness by the time Chase started transferring healing magic into me, but I think I remember him saying that.

"Yes. I knew he was at Velazar Prison before the tracking signal disappeared. It reappeared as I got closer to the island, so I knew he must have left. I began circling the area with Jarvis, hoping to see him somewhere on the water or on the island outside the prison, but then the signal disappeared. That's when I saw you with Saber. I couldn't get to you because of the protective layer around the island that keeps magic in and out. So, if you think about it, the best thing that could have happened to you was Saber throwing you over the wall."

"And the reason I fell through the protective layer," I say as I remember the flash in the air around me, "is because I had no magic."

"Well, you had very little magic. Probably too little to be detected."

"How, though? Amon told Gaius to take everything."

Chase shakes his head. "Gaius can't have taken everything. If he had, you wouldn't be here. Taking magic from someone … most people can't do it, and most people have never seen it done, so they don't know what it looks like. Most people don't even know it's possible. Gaius can do it because that's his Griffin Ability. The only other way is to use dark magic. Dark spells. If it's done properly—if every bit of your magic is drained from you—it kills you."

I feel my eyebrows jump up. A tendril of nausea twists around my stomach. "It *kills* you?"

"Magic is part of who we are, Calla. We can't survive without it. Amon obviously doesn't know that, or he would have known that Gaius didn't do the job properly."

"It sure felt like he did the job properly," I murmur, remembering the sick, hollow feeling as I lay on the prison floor. "Have you found him?"

"No. He wasn't at the mulberry house. I've sent people to check the other locations I know of, but so far no one has found him."

"I'm sorry." I feel partly responsible. If Chase hadn't come to my aid, would he have been able to find Gaius in that time?

"There's no need to be sorry. I will find him." He pushes a hand through his hair. "Now that you're no longer at death's doorstep, can you tell me what happened yesterday? Amon is the dangerous man I was telling you about, the prisoner Saber has been reporting to. He's planning something, but I haven't been able to figure out what."

"I think I can help you out there," I say, remembering the moment I realized Saber and Marlin were after the same thing. "As strange as it sounds, whatever Amon is planning, it has to do with a vision my mother had decades ago. The vision she was so traumatized by that she fled the Guild."

"I see." Chase rubs his chin. "Thank goodness she didn't wake up before I found her."

"Yeah." I tell Chase everything else I remember, in case there's any information that might mean something to him. He listens intently, his face betraying no emotion except when I tell him about being pinned down so Gaius could take my magic. He seems disturbed, so I move on quickly, glossing over the horror of that ordeal.

"I'm sorry you had to go through that," he says when I'm finished.

I shrug. "You know what they say about things that don't kill you, right?"

"They leave you lying semi-conscious in a boat with a knife in your stomach?" he says, a teasing gleam appearing in his eye.

"Yes. I believe that's exactly what they say."

A grin curls one side of his mouth up, but then he looks down. "Sorry. I probably shouldn't joke about something as serious as being stabbed. Or about losing your magic— *especially* not that."

"It's okay," I tell him, trying to sound nonchalant. "I'm fine now, so you can make light of it as much as you want. It's better to laugh than get sucked down by despair, right?"

After considering my words for a moment, he says, "Yes. It is. I didn't look at things that way for a long time, but I think you're probably right."

Teasingly, I say, "I've been known to be right on occasion."

The smile he gives me does strange things to my knees. It's stupid. It's *so* stupid. Isn't this what happened with Zed? I let myself get carried away with ridiculous *feelings* and the next thing—*wham!* I found rejection slammed in my face after a spontaneous, one-sided, most-awkward-of-all-time kiss. Would the same thing happen now? Would Chase tell me I'm too young? Would he say he doesn't think of me like that? With the way he's currently looking at me …

No. Don't be silly. Gaius is still missing, your mother is still in an enchanted sleep, and you've still got an enormous amount of work to do before your nasty mentor will even think about letting you graduate. This is not the time for romance.

I clear my throat and force my gaze away from his. "Um, there's something I'm curious about. I know I was fading in and out of consciousness after you caught me, but I definitely remember you saying something strange."

"What's that?"

"You told me that I'm supposed to be around for a long time still. That it wasn't my time to leave the world. You sounded pretty certain. How did you know that?"

"Oh, you know." He looks away. "It's just one of those things you tell people when you want to reassure them."

"Really? That's all it was?" I thought it sounded like more.

"And …" He removes one hand from a pocket and rubs the back of his neck. "I know things."

"You *know* things?"

"Yes."

I pull my head back slightly and narrow my eyes. "Does this cryptic, mysterious act work for all the girls?"

With a grin that makes him look younger, almost boyish, he says, "Seems to be working for you."

Flames ignite my cheeks as I attempt a look of indignation. I'd like to stammer out a denial, but I'm pretty certain my blush is already giving me away. I look to the side, shaking my head and trying hard not to laugh.

"I also wanted to tell you something," he says.

I look back at him as my silly heart begins to soar.

"I'm going away for a week or two. Some business I need to attend to."

My heart crashes back to the forest floor. "Oh. Are you going to be searching for Gaius?"

"No, I've got other people doing that. This is something that was planned a while ago. Something I can't put off."

"Oh. Okay. That's unfortunate." I twist my hands together. "I was going to ask you to come to—well—it doesn't matter now."

"Come to what?"

"My brother's wedding—union ceremony—whatever you want to call it. He's actually been married for over seven years now, but he and his wife never got to have the big celebration, so they're finally doing that. I was going to ask you if, you know, you wanted to go with me. As my date. Not like a *date* date, but just … to accompany me. But you won't be here, so don't worry—"

"I'll try to be back for it."

I hesitate, wondering if he's being serious. "Really?"

"Yes. I'd very much like to go with you. As your date."

"Oh. Great. Well maybe I'll see you there."

"Hopefully." He smiles again.

I say goodbye, he says goodbye, and then I disappear into the faerie paths with a bounce in my step.

CHAPTER THIRTY

THE WEATHER COULDN'T BE MORE PERFECT. A WARM afternoon sun hangs in a clear sky, illuminating the forest floor with shafts of golden light. The trees are dressed in an autumn palette of reds, oranges, golds and yellows more beautiful than anything I could ever paint. Leaves drift to the ground like confetti. Glass jars of glow-bugs hang from branches. At the center of the scene is a simple pavilion with slim branches woven into a domed canopy. Vines with tiny cream flowers twist around the structure, and petals of the same color are sprinkled over the ground. On one side of the pavilion, family and friends are seated on rows of simple wooden benches.

This wedding was pulled together in record time, and the organizers—Tilly and Raven—did a spectacular job. The scene isn't *quite* as perfect as it could be, though. Mom isn't awake yet, so she isn't here, and Chase hasn't returned from his 'business' so he isn't around either. But Mom is safe, and Chase is still alive, and this glorious celebration is everything I've always wanted for my brother and Violet, so I'm brimming with happiness despite the two empty seats.

A hush falls over the gathering as Vi and Ryn's friend Natesa rises from her chair and stands to one side. She begins singing, and her enchanting voice is the cue for the ceremony to begin. As per tradition, Vi and Ryn enter from opposite sides, with Vi appearing on the left of the gathering, and Ryn on the right. They walk slowly toward each other, their gazes locked, as if they exist in their own world oblivious to the rest of us.

Vi's ivory lace dress is simple but elegant with a V-neckline, a strip of lace over each shoulder, and a lace train that isn't too long. I can't see her feet, but I know she's barefoot. Raven presented at least twenty different shoe ideas, and Vi said she wasn't interested in any of them. Her hair is loose with tiny flowers pinned into it, and she carries a simple bouquet of three roses.

Ryn meets her in front of the pavilion. They share a look filled with meaning. Realized dreams, old fears, shared hopes, and a lifetime of memories. They clasp hands and step beneath the canopy together where the Seelie Court officiant is standing. He talks about the bond of the union, the strong magical connection created when two people pledge their lives to one another. And even though this has all technically happened before when Vi and Ryn signed the union scroll at the Guild, it didn't feel nearly as special or real then as it does now.

A tear slides down my cheek, and Filigree—mouse-shaped, standing on my shoulder and clutching my earlobe—attempts to wipe it away. I pat him affectionately as I watch the officiant produce the two rings that Vi and Ryn usually wear over their ring markings. If this union were being created for the first time, this would be the point in the ceremony where the two of them receive the gold tattoo-like markings encircling their ring fingers. But those markings are already there, so they simply place the rings on each other's fingers. The officiant holds their hands together and speaks the final bonding charm.

The ceremony ends with a kiss and plenty of applause. Everyone stands and crowds around the couple. Laughter and good wishes and congratulations on the coming baby fill the clearing. The happy gathering of people slowly moves from the pavilion through the trees to where tables have been set up in a U shape. As the afternoon sun slides closer to the horizon, we take our places around the table. We eat and drink and share stories, and all the worries of recent days—Gaius missing, my Griffin Ability gone, Saber and Marlin on the loose—fade into the background.

* * *

After the first course is finished, I leave the table for a while and wander back to the pavilion. It's so pretty there. I want to see it in the soft light of sunset as the glow-bugs in the jars become brighter. I lean against one of the legs holding the structure up and lift my gaze to the tree tops. Red-orange light filters through leaves of the same color, making the scene look warmer than it feels. As a shiver runs along my bare arms, I try to enjoy this last moment of peace before the hard work really begins.

Apparently I'm not trying hard enough, though. I can't help picturing the pile of extra studying waiting at home and the extra training sessions scheduled for this coming week. Olive obviously decided that if a combination of disinterest and verbal abuse wouldn't drive me out, perhaps overwork would. Her plan will fail, though. I've spent the past week pushing myself in every training session to be faster, stronger, more skilled. I'm determined to prove to Olive that I *am* cut out for this life and that I'm not going anywhere. She can shred me apart with her words and pile as much work on top of me as she wants, but she will not break me.

Gemma, Perry and Ned help me out wherever they can, pointing out useful textbooks in the library and volunteering for extra Fish Bowl time if I'm in need of an opponent. It was difficult at first to accept their help when I still don't really believe we'll be friends for long. But as each day passes, and they continue to laugh at whatever story Saskia digs up from my past, I wonder if perhaps these are the friends who will stick around.

"You look a bit cold, Miss Goldilocks."

My stomach flips over at the sound of his voice, and I'm already smiling by the time I turn around. "You came," I say.

"I'm sorry I'm late." He walks toward me and shrugs his

coat off as he steps beneath the flower-laden pavilion. It's the coat he always wears, the black one that reaches just below the tops of his legs. The one he always looks so darn sexy in. Warmth rises to my cheeks as he places the coat over my shoulders. I look up. His face is close enough to kiss, if I stood on tiptoe and leaned closer. Then I notice the fading bruise on his cheekbone. "Did that happen while you were taking care of your 'business'?" I ask, raising my hand and touching my fingertips to his skin.

"It did," he says. A faint pink flush appears in his cheeks, and it makes me feel ridiculously warm inside knowing it's my touch that's causing that.

I lower my hand and ask, "Is it finished? Whatever it was you had to do?"

He nods and catches my hand before it reaches my side. His fingers slide between mine, and I suddenly find it harder to breathe. I look down at our intertwined fingers and can't remember what it was we were talking about or what I was planning to say next. Holding hands isn't supposed to be this big a deal, is it? It isn't supposed to quicken my breath and speed up my heart and set my skin on fire.

Is it?

A spark of bright light appears above us, and then another and another. I look up and see the tiny flowers twisted around the domed canopy igniting, each one bursting alight with a tiny flame before fizzling out.

"Is that supposed to happen?" Chase asks.

"Uh, I don't think so." Fortunately, the small spontaneous fires stop moments after they began. I meet Chase's gaze once more with a frown. "Strange."

His grin tells me he knows something I don't. "Strange, indeed," he says. His eyes remain locked on mine as his expression turns serious. He looks down, then back up. "Is your heart still set on working for the Guild?"

He sounds almost hopeful, and I hate that my answer will smother that. "Yes. It isn't quite what I thought it was, but I still want to work there. It's still my dream to be a guardian."

He nods slowly, but says nothing. I know what he's thinking, though, because I'm thinking it too. How will anything ever work out between us if one of us is upholding the law and the other is continually breaking it?

"Tell me what you do," I say. I think I've guessed correctly, but I want to hear it from him.

"I ... help people."

"But you work outside the law in order to do that."

After a pause, he says, "Yes."

"Why? If what you're doing is good, then why don't you work for the Guild?"

The smile he gives me is sad. "They wouldn't have me."

"Why not?"

He looks away. "If they knew my history ..."

"If they knew my history they wouldn't take me either."

"I keep secrets from enough people already," he says. "I don't want to add anyone else to that list."

That list. His words wake something inside me, jolting me from warm dreams to cold reality. I'm silly to think I'm different or special, or that this could possibly work out. Not when I'm on that list like everyone else Chase keeps secrets from. I pull my hand out of his and step back. "We don't just have the problem of me working for the law and you working outside it," I say. "There's the problem of all the secrets you're keeping from me."

After a long moment, he says, "Yes. But that isn't going to be a problem after I tell you everything."

Everything? After all the mystery surrounding this guy, I didn't expect to hear those words. "Do you mean that?"

He takes in a breath that sounds a little shaky. "Yes. If you want to hear the truth."

The truth. Do I really want to know Chase's truth? Perhaps not knowing is better. It will be easier to face the Guild every day if I don't know all the details of his illegal activity. But not knowing means there can't be anything ... *more* between us. Because a relationship can't work when there are secrets.

"Calla? Cal, are you out here?" Violet's voice pulls me from my thoughts.

"Who's that?" Chase asks, a frown creasing his brow.

I look over his shoulder to the trees where the voice came from and see a figure in white moving between them. "My brother's wife."

"Cal, come back," she calls, waving as she sees me. "Tilly wants us to do that silly dance and I'm *so* not doing it without you."

"Come on," I say to Chase, deciding I can make my choice to hear his truth or not later. "You can meet my family and make fun of me while I pretend I can dance." I tug at his hand, but he doesn't move. His face is frozen into an odd expression.

"No," he murmurs, staring unseeingly at the ground.

"What?"

"I *do* know you."

"What do you—"

He looks up, his gaze suddenly intense. "The moment I first saw you, I knew I recognized you. I *knew* it."

"Chase—"

"I'm sorry, Calla." He takes a step back, and over his shoulder I see Violet coming toward us.

"Chase, what's going on?"

"I've never lied to you, I swear. This is who I am."

"What are you …"

My voice trails off as Vi stops just outside the pavilion, her mouth open to say something before she freezes, her expression turning slowly to one of horror. Several things happen at once then, and I see them all as if in slow motion: Vi's arms rising into position and grasping a bow and arrow, Chase's hand sweeping through the air as he backs away from both of us, and snowflakes—snowflakes?—falling everywhere.

Then everything speeds up. The snow is a blizzard, and the wind whips my hair around my face, and all I can see is white as I raise my hands to protect my face.

The wind dies down. The snow drifts away. A hush falls over the area.

Chase is gone.

I'm utterly confused. I look back at Violet, at the stunned expression on her face. "It can't be," she whispers. And then the greatest secret of all comes crashing from her lips:

"Draven."

LOOK OUT FOR THE
NEXT BOOK IN THE
CREEPY HOLLOW SERIES!

FIND MORE CREEPY HOLLOW
CONTENT ONLINE
www.creepyhollowbooks.com

ACKNOWLEDGEMENTS

Several years ago, when I was writing *The Faerie Guardian*, I planned for the possibility of continuing the Creepy Hollow series with Calla as a main character. When I reached the end of *The Faerie War*, I was exhausted. I needed a break—which came in the form of the Trouble series—but I knew in the back of my mind that this series wasn't over yet. I loved the world and the characters too much to say goodbye after only three books. I didn't make any promises. I didn't set any specific dates. But observant Creepy Hollow fans reached the end of *The Faerie War* and noticed I'd left a few loose ends untied. And since they love this world and its characters as much as I do, they asked for more.

Well, this is the first part of the 'more,' and I hope you've enjoyed it. There is a lot *more* to come!

My first thanks, as always, goes to God. I'm grateful every day for all He's given me, including a career that came out of my love for crafting stories. My second thanks goes to everyone who has played a part in bringing the beginning of Calla's story to the page: Creepy Hollow fans begging for more, my writer friends' support and teaching, my early readers' enthusiasm, and my review team's dedication. And my last thanks (also as always) goes to Kyle. For everything. (Which I would list, but I might run out of paper …)

© Gavin van Haght

Rachel Morgan is a South African author who spent a large portion of her childhood living in a fantasy land of her own making. After completing a degree in genetics, she decided science wasn't for her—after all, they didn't approve of made-up facts. These days she spends much of her time immersed in fantasy land once more, writing fiction for young adults and those young at heart.

www.rachel-morgan.com